SEARCH FOR TRUTH

The seeker begins...

Bryan Radzin

SEARCH FOR TRUTH

The seeker begins...

UNRELENTING POSITIVITY

AUTHOR: BRYAN RADZIN

COVER ART: SANDY FACTOR

ISBN# 978-0-578-14570-9

I DEDICATE THIS TO THE POWERLESS WHO FEEL THEY CAN'T FIGHT THE POWERFUL BECAUSE THEY HAVE NO CHANCE. YOU DO HAVE A CHANCE. WILL YOU BE OPEN AND READY TO RECEIVE WHEN THE OPPORTUNITY ARISES?

ACKNOWLEDGEMENTS

Thank you Mom for all the positive reinforcement, kind words that I can achieve my goals, for instilling in me the passion and consciousness to spread peace and love and for the ability to see beauty all around me wherever I go; when I help the human race take its next evolutionary step, it will certainly be because of you. Thank you Dad for always helping me realize what's in front of me, and if I really want something out of life I should just go out and get it; your words of wisdom are something I will always cherish.

To Grandma Laurine for always being a pillar of strength and for showing that love of family and knowing what's really important, is what's important; I will remember you always. To Grandpa Melvin for being the best Grandpa a kid could have, not only will I always remember warm sodas in your van when we would go fishing, but the connection I felt whenever I was with you. To Grandpa Herman for opening a door into our families' history, it gives me a greater understanding of who I am and what kind of person I want to be. To Grandma Yona for instilling in me a culture that is my culture, our people's culture, thank you for proving I can be proud of it and can share it with others. To Uncle Eugene for always caring about me enough to pick up the phone and ask how I'm doing, I always enjoy our conversations. To Uncle Gary for showing me that fun and enjoying yourself is what makes life worth living.

To Aunt Lisa, even though I haven't seen you in a while, you'll always be part of who I am; thank you for all the encouraging words with my writing. To Cousin Shawna, I haven't seen you since you were very young and now you're a woman looking to build a life of your own, I wish you the best of luck; as long as you pay attention to what's in front of you and stay present in the moment, you can achieve anything.

To Rainbow, there I said it ☺ Thank you for all the good conversations exploring the depths of who we are as humans, you have helped lift my energy to give me motivation more times than I can count; I can't put my gratitude fully into words, just thank you thank you thank you ☺ To Zeb for being a great example of what can be accomplished when one sees what's important and what's not, and the confidence to know the difference. To Chris for always being there with a smile, a laugh and a good story; some of my best times have been when you're around. To Jerry for being a perfect mixture of determination, light heartedness and a strong work ethic; thank you for always asking how I'm doing and actually caring about the answer.

Thank you Sean for being my buddy through many different stages in my life, and for proving that a person can build a happy family if they really want to. To Ryan, thank you for all the good times and all the classic toasts, Saturday night beers and Sunday morning coffee surely isn't the same without you man. To Jen for not only being one of the best neighbors I've ever had, but also for being one of the most genuinely warm people I know; thank you for providing me uplift to take the next step.

To Jeff for the safety meetings and conscious conversation that always followed; I wish you all the best. To Amber for always having my back in my search for the woman that makes my soul sing. To Tim for being my oldest friend and a constant happy reminder of my past, also a great example of what happens when somebody goes after what makes them happy; and brother, when I become as accomplished as I hope to be, you will be one of the first people I thank. Thank you Laurie for providing me positive energy even if we haven't hung out in a while or talked, you have been such a positive influence for me and I am eternally grateful; I only hope that I can make you proud and not squander all the great lessons you've taught me.

To Lisa for being the greatest boss anybody could ask for, but you're so much more than that; thank you for always putting a smile on my face just being around you, you have helped in all aspects of my life more than you know. To Kayleen for being the sister I've always wished I had, and a constant reminder of what happens when you mix strength, with fun and happiness; you're more than a coworker, you're a true friend. To Doug for always telling me I am good enough, and that I can achieve anything I want, I just have to go out and make it happen. To Marshall for always putting up with my stupid jokes because you know my heart is in the right place.

Thank you to all the ladies at the bank for making me feel welcome, and for proving that just because somebody works for a giant corporation, doesn't mean that they aren't a warm hearted nice person that genuinely cares. Thank you to all the checkers at the COOP, you have started my day off with a smile and a conscious thought countless times; you provide the community with something it so desperately needs, authentic humanity.

Thank you to College Cove and all the beaches along Scenic Drive, you have filled my cup numerous times and provide the most beautiful beaches anywhere. Thank you to the Marsh for being my refuge, my Walden Pond, the place I can go no matter what mood I'm in, and reminding me to stay conscious to the beauty that's all around even when I've tricked myself into not seeing it; no matter where I'm at or what I'm doing, I can picture your peacefulness and it always fills me up.

Thank you to my soul for getting brighter each time I take a step forward in my evolutionary journey. The things I want to accomplish won't be easy, but become easier the more truthful I am with myself, and the more facets of my soul I discover. We can rise as a people because we truly see each other, or we can fall as a people because we refuse to look outside of ourselves and see how everything is interconnected.

We can make the world and humanity better by building it up, or we can make it worse by tearing it down. Or is it a combination of both? We have a choice. It's up to us and only us.

FORWARD

There is a passion that burns within me for positive, social and political change. The solutions to fix most of the world's problems are simple, but difficult at the same time. Ever felt like you were running around in circles? What if you suddenly weren't interested in eternally chasing your tail anymore, and were ready to not only seek out and live your true potential, but to heal and then improve the world for all its inhabitants? My reason for writing this book is to encourage movement towards conscious evolution.

It's time we slowed down and took time to smell the roses. I'm not always talking about leaning down to smell flowers that are important to some gardener but not you. That's the thing though, sometimes it's literally stooping down to smell pretty flowers on the side of the road. Sometimes it's taking a walk on a sunny day, going to see a movie, or getting ice cream with friends.

This is only the first step, it helps us relax and realize that to grow and bring in the things we need to bring in, we need to let go. We need to let go of the things that don't mean anything to us, because if we don't, how do we expect to allow in what's important? It's like we only have so much storage space and need to prioritize the important aspects of our lives. What are we going to fill it with, something good or something bad?

Everything we need to know we learned in kindergarten, humans need to get back to nature, we all need to get back to basics, however it's vocalized, it all describes the same idea. We need to get back to what makes us human.

We need to remember our humanity for each other. We build from there, it's where we start.

If we could start our day remembering to treat others how we'd like to be treated, to share, to not destroy land where we live so it's healthy for us and everybody that comes after us, that we all want to be loved, that nobody is better than anybody else, to see each other in ourselves, to see our common humanity, to courageously and vigilantly hold those in power accountable for their transgressions, and to remind the string pullers of their responsibility to the people that vastly outnumber them. If we could do all that, we wouldn't be worried about the huge obstacle in front of us.

We simply need to remember why we took the first step. It's because of us that we move forward, nobody else. We raise our consciousness, precisely so we can raise everyone else's consciousness.

PROLOGUE

Jason and Christina are average twenty somethings with long term goals and a fiery passion for making the world a better place.

Jason was walking through Stewart Park one day trying to get some air, process where he's at in life, where he's been and where he'd like to go. He rested his 5'4" frame on a bench beneath a huge, beautiful Japanese maple tree that caught his eye. He knew he needed rest, but there was another reason he sat down; like some other force wanted to see if he was ready to let go of what didn't serve him, and grab onto what did. Feeling his life was in limbo, he decided to not hold onto the beauty of the world, but allow it to flow through him.

This was the moment Christina sauntered by and parked her equally short stature on the same bench. On a normal day, Jason would have questioned why she sat next to him. There were many empty benches and many beautiful trees to sit under, why did she choose this one and this bench? But he didn't endlessly question, he just decided to let it happen, whatever will be, will be and what is meant to come will. Was it the tree, Christina and her long flowing brown hair, or some other cosmic force trying to show him the path he should be taking?

After talking for a while, Jason and Christina realized they had much in common. They both had a strong passion for helping the world evolve and become more conscious. The more they talked, the more they knew their passions were aligned.

Jason was raised by his dad after his parents got divorced when he was three. Jason's dad always questioned things, but didn't take it the next step once he found the answer. He never really knew what to do or where to go with information even though he listened to the news, the radio, read and took in as much information as he could.

New people would come in and out of Jason's life teaching him lessons he needed to learn, and helping him grow in the direction he needed to grow. It was his love of information and truth finding behind the scenes that led Jason to his degree in journalism and creative writing, and an extremely long beard he didn't cut until after he graduated. He wanted to move forward, which was the first step in searching for truth. Light was illuminating the first section of path Jason was supposed to take.

Christina's story is much the same, but a little more focused. She was raised by activist parents who always told her something bigger and better was out there, but she'd have to find it herself. They could help guide her when she needed help, but the majority of choices would have to be made by her blazing her own path. That is what led Christina to school and her search for truth, which came in the form of an anthropology degree. Her path included tracking down forensic evidence to discover why things happened.

Why are some things covered up while some aren't? Why is there a block in front of humanities evolution?

Jason and Christina have a strong sense of responsibility to question why things are the way they are. Is society waiting for people to be conscious enough to know all that the world needs, is for them to realize that humanism and accountability are the solutions to the deeply ingrained and generational problems that have been fought over and over and over again? Jason and Christina's deep love for positive change is what brought them together, and what guides them together. They both know that it's not about bringing the revolution so change can begin. It's about the next revolution that will push humans forward, because they know how many revolutions society has been through to get to this evolutionary point in its existence.

Jason and Christina feel a strong injustice is keeping people from coming together, distractions that keep them from agreeing on what they already know they agree on. If they can bring working class people together, they would have the support of the majority of the world's people. Elites don't give up their power without a fight because they've been building it up for long periods of time. This illusion of power crumbles however when the elites realize they can never overcome the peoples numbers no matter what weapons they have at their disposal. This is when the top dogs figure if they can't beat the people, they might as well join them.

This is a concept Jason and Christina always knew was possible, but never knew what the first step was to making it happen. Now that they've met each other on a beautiful day under an amazing Japanese maple, they know. They know they were pulled together for a reason bigger than themselves that is only beginning to reveal itself. Like life, it becomes clearer over time.

Jason and Christina hung out a lot after that first chance meeting. The more time they spent getting to know each other, the more they discovered they were alike in what they were looking for, what they wanted, what they needed and what they wanted to do for the world. Each day was a new expedition, a new hill to climb, a new issue to decipher, and a new reason to love the world and humanity. The love they have for each other proved they were waiting their whole lives for someone like the other.

Adventure starts anew every day, and always finds a way to teach something. Whenever they wake up together, Jason and Christina look into each other's equally brown eyes and know a better world is out there. If they could help each other find what they're looking for, maybe they could help the world find what it's looking for.

Jason and Christina help the world build up its positive energy, by building up their own positive energy; they have to take time to fill their own cup. They must move forward with consciousness, openness, love for all things, but most importantly, gratitude for just being alive. They know that being thankful for what they have, instead of being upset over what they don't have, is what will truly move them and the world forward.

CHAPTER ONE

"Do I take the job I've always wanted, or stay with the only woman I've ever truly loved? I don't know what to do. Is there a way to do both? Why do I have to make a decision? I've always been shy with the ladies, ever since I was very young. I used to pass notes to girls because I was too nervous to speak with them face to face. I always wanted to feel their touch. You know, feel their warm embrace like the old cliché goes. Seriously, until I met Christina, I hadn't kissed many girls, let alone made love to many. Even though I wasn't very experienced, she said I had quite the loving ways.

I love that she knows what I'm thinking, when I'm truthful, and when I'm happy. Sure, I dated before, but none of them were truly interested in me. Christina is tuned into me, gives a shit about what happens to me, and always wants me to strive for more in life. I had always seen an angel in my dreams, until that fateful day when the angel decided to sit next to me on a bench under a big Japanese maple. Little did I know that angel would be my love, my woman, my completeness, my world, my life.

Well I guess that's not entirely true, maybe just 90%. I've always wanted to be a journalist. I remember playing baseball when I was seven with the other kids in school, always wanting to be an announcer. My other spare time was spent reading and writing short stories. All through my school days and even now I love writing, I feel it's a very honest way to express one's inner thoughts. I published poems, football articles and other small and short feature pieces.

Now I have a job offer and I don't know what to do. Should I take the job that's a springboard into the business? It would give me a higher salary than anybody I've personally known. When I go to write a book it would be a lot easier to sell, because people would know who I am. Or do I stay with the only woman I've ever truly loved, the only woman that's ever truly loved me (except my mom of course which is something totally different). Christina is my soul mate, if there could ever be one.

How can I as a person be made to choose between my love and my future life? I mean if I take the position I'll love my life. I'll have the perfect job, and will be fulfilling a lifelong dream to spread consciousness to the world; raising collective thinking so people can see outside their bubble. I'll also miss out on the woman I love, maybe once I make a name for myself I can move back, or at least find where she is so I can see her regularly. I'd be able to write from wherever because I could send anything to anybody; my name would prove my reliability.

If I stay with Christina I'll be with my love every day. I'd wake up next to her, make love to her, make breakfast for her, have romantic dinners with her, stare into her eyes and know I'm not alone in life. I love her so much I'm thinking about kissing her right now. Even though she wasn't the first person I ever kissed, she tasted so sweet. She has a very special aura about her. If I stay with my love, I'll always have this undercurrent of what if? I'll always wonder what could have happened.

Sure there are magazines in California, and I might be able to get my name out with them and then work for whomever, but it wouldn't be the same. It's not a question of whether I would have made it, but a question of luck, and how long it took. Should I take advantage of instant stardom and money, or stay with my love?

I still hold onto the position that no human being should have to choose between their dreams and love. Why can't people have both? Why should someone have to choose between love and money? We need both to survive in society, but is one more important than the other? If a person chooses to take a job in their field for less pay because of love or location, they can have love and a job that can be built into what they might have turned down in the first place.

Society runs into trouble when we try to decide between love and money. Both are necessities of being human, at least in the western world. The Beatles said "all you need is love." Well you can have all the love in the world, but if you don't have any money you will be homeless just like that crack-head you passed on your way to school who was talking to himself. So if society dictates that we need money to survive, what importance does love hold? It's one of those things that you can't define so I'm not going to try. It's something so primal, something passed down through the ages.

I'll say one thing, if the world was more concerned with love than money, we wouldn't have as many wars, ethnic struggles or any killing in the name of religion. People would actually be accepting of others, instead of hurting them for being different. If everybody had love, it would magnify to such a great extent that it would spread across the universe like wildfire.

The need for money would no longer be there, anything anybody needed as far as food, clothing, or whatever else would be provided by friends or neighbors. Materialism would melt away and corporations would fall, as would many governments. The people that were left would reinvent the world so anybody on earth could go anywhere and would be welcomed with open arms.

If it still comes down to love and money, can one bring the other? Can a change be made from within or without? I need to remember that love and good feelings are extremely contagious, and can cause money to come in, or eliminate the need for it all together. Money can bring the power to change the system and inject the love the world so desperately needs, also eliminating money.

Love or money, love and money, the chicken or the egg, it doesn't matter which one came first, it just matters how each ends up. What the finished product ends up being, no matter what anybody says, thinks, acts, or writes, it's me who decides."

Christina and Jason were sitting at the breakfast table when Christina observed Jason staring off into space. He was either deep in thought or, waiting for his coffee to kick in.

"What are you thinking about sweetheart, I can see the hamster running on its wheel inside that noggin of yours," Christina expressed as she sipped her coffee, trying to charge her batteries for the day ahead.

"Yeah, I just feel so lucky to be with you. We both have the want and need to bring truth. I sometimes ask why I've been blessed like this?" replied Jason as he looked adoringly into Christina's eyes.

"We just have a connection that can't be ignored. I might come from the path of science and you might come from the path of the media, but we meet up at the same enlightenment apex that we're both striving towards. It's just from our own unique paths. Kind of how the world's major religions are basically the same at their root, all striving towards the same basic place of light and love," Christina continued as her thoughts started flowing easily.

"That right there, is one of the reasons I love you. You took the words right out of my mouth. Not only do you and I have a lot in common, obviously, but so does the world. I would bet that most people could agree more than not, they just have to get out of their own way."

"Yeah, kind of like everybody has to figure out what kind of human being they want to be."

Christina got up from the table to pour another cup of coffee, and look out from their second floor apartment. The windows were big, which made them easy to look through considering Christina and Jason were both 5'4''.

Outside it was cloudy and damp, but inside was filled with love, and the delicious smell of Christina's famous pancakes and eggs, and Jason's famous hash browns. He always got them just right.

"How do you get the hash browns so crispy without burning them? Whenever I try making them I always mess them up somehow, either not cook them enough and they're soggy, or too much and it's like chewing on pure carbon," inferred Christina, looking to Jason for guidance on the subject.

"I just focus in. It's all about how it looks. Not flipping it too early, being patient, and paying attention the whole time is the key," Jason retorted with a smirk on his face, waiting for a smart ass comeback.

"I guess it would be easier if I took three hours to make breakfast too, but sometimes I get a little hungry before 12 o'clock."

"Yeah my food might take a while to prepare, but it always tastes good. It's like a fine wine. It takes a while till it's at its most delicious."

"Well seeing as how I'd like to eat breakfast before tomorrow, I thought I would do it."

Jason got up and moved over toward the stove where Christina was standing, he grabbed her yoga pants covered hips and pulled her close to him, rubbing up against her.

"That's not how we do it faster," blurted Christina, realizing that she threw Jason a softball he wouldn't be able to resist.

"I can do it faster or slower, however you want. As far as the hash browns, you just stick them in and move them around until it feels right. Then you work with the potatoes." Jason lovingly looked into Christina's eyes with as mischievous a smile as any American man would have who had a beautiful woman in his arms.

"Okay, we can have plenty of fun after breakfast, but I'd like to get some food and coffee in me so I have energy for you, as well as for me."

They both smiled knowing they were being turned on in the same ways, sexually, intellectually and spiritually by the person that was meant for them.

Their apartment was an average after college residence, two bedrooms and a kitchen to cook a nice meal in with plenty of room, or entertain friends with their newest cooking creation. Jason and Christina loved to cook. They both believed that through the stomach was the way to the other one's heart.

It was cloudy, and the wind was picking up a bit, but no threat of rain. Nothing like ten years ago when the rain didn't stop pounding and the rivers were full. Now there was a drought and they were wondering like CCR did, had they ever seen the rain?

"It looks crappy outside, I don't know what we should do today," Christina deduced as she sat down to breakfast with no help from Jason who had been lovingly grinding against her the whole time.

"It does, but I'm sure we could find something to do," Jason sniped with a wink and a smile.

"That's always great when it's nasty and cold outside, but I want more. I feel something extraordinary is right around the corner."

"It probably is. Something always happens when you get those feelings," Jason exclaimed as he sat down and took a bite of the delicious pancakes, causing syrup to drip everywhere. "There does seem to be electricity in the air. Like something is on the precipice of happening."

"Yeah, it's like we're on the path we're supposed to be on."

"Wasn't without it's pitfalls though, and it's challenges. This is starting to feel like the water park."

They both immediately swan dived into their thoughts, like an automated flashback switch had been pulled.

"That was a crazy time, and a crazy story," Jason remembered as he guzzled his coffee, needing the caffeine to circulate through his veins so he could fully articulate his feelings on the subject. "Who knew all those things would happen because I felt like going on the big water slide. It was a hot day, I just wanted to cool off."

CHAPTER TWO

The Fun Rapids water park was like any other refuge for an overheated community to cool off. They had the basic array of water slides, and a wave pool for people too scared to go in the actual ocean. There were many spots to relax, enjoy a snack and a cool drink before you went on a plethora of water adventures. There were twisty ones, short ones, long ones, and as any water park worth their salt would have, the big colossal thrill slide that either a person would go on because they conquered it before, or because they were dared to by a friend or family member who was too scared to go on it themselves.

Jason decided to go to this particular water park because it was the only place in town where he wouldn't feel like the weirdo that possessed his soul when the temperature crested 100. He went without Christina because she was working, and he happened to have the day off with nothing to do. Instead of hiding in their air conditioned apartment all day with the blinds drawn, Jason decided to venture out and cool off somewhere fun.

When he entered the main drag of the park, massive crowds were corralled like cattle around the most popular rides and slides. The bumper boats were always Jason's favorite, but since Christina wasn't there, they wouldn't be as entertaining without trying to bump her into the water. They had an amazing bond, but they both saw nothing wrong with keeping each other on their toes. If they could make themselves laugh without offending and upsetting the other person too much, they would do it. They lived to test each other's limits.

Jason walked up to the snack bar, grabbed a soda and sat down at the nearest table to figure out which slide he wanted to go on first. Lots of women in bikinis were displaying themselves while men were checking them out like a T-bone steak in a butcher shop. They knew the other was playing games, but they didn't care because each move the other made was a boost to their own ego.

Jason decided to walk around and check which line was the shortest. He walked up to the Twisty Goat because it was a medium sized water slide, and an easy way to work into the day he needed to be fun.

Jason bought the all-day pass, which allowed him access to the fast moving express line. Some people bought per ride tickets which were cheaper, but the lines were ten times longer. The all-dayer was surely the better deal, but with the economy the way it was, people saved a buck whenever and wherever they could.

The only catch was, when the person ran out of tickets it caused arguments between the person wanting to ride, and the person working the ride. The verbatim response went something like, "Come on man, let me on. What would it hurt you? Like it would be so much work for you to just wave your hand and let me by." This would usually be followed by, "I'm sorry but you have to go buy more tickets to ride, or get an all-day pass."

Sometimes the people were courteous, and would head over to the ticket booth to purchase more tickets. Sometimes though, the person wouldn't take the advice. Sometimes they would get downright angry. "What do you mean you won't let me ride? You have something against me? Do you not like the cut of my jib or where I come from? Maybe I slept with your girlfriend in high school, and now you can finally pay me back because you feel you have power over me."

It was this exchange that Jason was used to, just part of the whole water park experience. He knew some people try to get away with whatever they can, constantly testing their limits. It was in this context that he entered a crowd gathered around the big slide, changing the trajectory of his life forever.

The Big Lizard slide was known for making wusses out of big egos, and heroes out of nerdy weaklings. Jason rode it once before, and knew it was no joke. Not only had it scared the crap out of him, but his shorts almost flew off about halfway into his run.

Since the slide was so big and tall, many people stood on the sides and watched people ride down. Sometimes young boys watched and hoped for a girl's bikini top to fly off, or foreign tourists being entertained by the latest crazy American. Sometimes, it was just bored people waiting for something new to happen.

Jason walked up and got in the express line. After fifteen minutes and a ton of stairs, he was at the front and ready to go. The guy working the slide told him to wait till the person in front of him was clear. Of course this particular delay was because the guy working the slide was staring down the bikini top of a particular busty rider. After a bit of a chuckle, he let her go down.

The slide guy placed Jason in position to be next, when somebody came up behind him and started yelling. "Hey man, let me on."

"No man, you have to wait in line."

"Like last night, when I made your wife wait until she couldn't wait anymore. I gave her more pleasure than you could ever dream of."

"You have no idea what you're talking about. My girl would never go for someone like you when she has someone like me at home."

"Is that why she said I was so much bigger than her small dicked husband that never amounted to anything."

"You shouldn't say stuff like that, you never know what people are capable of."

"That's right, you never do."

In response the crazy guy walked away and back down the staircase of the slide, disappearing into the crowd like it was a cornfield. After a very heated exchange, Jason wondered if this particular slide operator was okay because his eyes were twitching. "You alright man?"

"It's none of your business. Besides, some people think they can get away with anything because nobody ever told them they aren't the center of the universe. He needs somebody to teach him a lesson."

It was at this point that Jason just wanted to go down the slide and get away from this emotionally unstable and volatile situation. The guy sat him down in position with his legs crossed, and his arms crossed over his chest. When Jason was ready, he was told to go. Whoosh, he went so fast down the slide, he could already feel his shorts slipping off. Not wanting them to fly off when he hit the middle of the slide, (just the point when pieces of clothing that were bound to come off did) he held onto his shorts with one hand as he made his way down the remainder of the slide.

This precise maneuver kept Jason's shorts on, but flipped him around in the process. He went down the bottom third of the slide backwards, hitting the splash down pool without knowing which way was up. The crowd was cheering him on as Jason struggled to catch his breath, and figure out what happened. As he blearily looked around at everybody laughing and applauding the crazy ride he just made, the guy at the top of the slide gave him an evil glare; the type reserved for the most hated people in society, like Jason had stolen his soul or raped his mother. Although he thought it was a bit odd and wondered if it had to do with the comment he made, Jason decided to let him be the little man he was, not wanting it to spoil what was turning out to be just what he needed.

After getting pelted with water and the intense sun light simultaneously, Jason bought one of the parks famous homemade ice creams and sat down in the shade. After he finished, Jason went over to the locker he put his bag in, and grabbed out his cell phone to call Christina.

"Hey baby, how are you? I'm down at the water park enjoying this beautiful no clouds in the sky day, but mainly trying to cool off. The water feels so good I wish you could enjoy it with me. You're probably busy right now, so I'll let you go, but give me a ring when you leave work. I'll make us a good dinner tonight. What the hell is that?"

Not the best way to end a voice mail to the love of your life, but when Jason turned his glance from the way too hot for their own good nineteen year olds in string bikinis back to the slide he just rode down, something wasn't right. The water cascading down had a dark red tint. Everybody started screaming as a badly mangled, and blood spurting body plopped into the splashdown pool.

Having abruptly ended his message to Christina, Jason walked up to take a look. Being a news reporter he knew he had to prepare for anything, because anything was possible when searching for truth.

Jason looked into the eyes of the victim. It was the crazy guy who heckled the slide operator.

CHAPTER THREE

Michael was normal as far as society thought, but, if you looked under the covers, you'd know his was not the life of a nobody. He was a 6'2", bald headed track star in school, married his high school sweetheart, started his own construction company, and had two beautiful, intelligent and very driven kids. They were the stereotypical happy family, so why did he end up dead going down the area's most popular water slide?

"It looks like his throat was cut, and then pushed down the slide," observed the young and clean security guard hungry for action like he was auditioning for the elite force of the army. "That's a good possibility considering the marks on his throat, but the real question is why? Why kill this guy with everybody and their brother watching? He must have wanted to make an example," the senior security officer shot back who had actually been in an elite unit, but was thrown out for shooting up heroin.

Jason strolled closer to the scene that was being cordoned off with yellow crime scene tape. A crowd of very curious onlookers were gawking. "Looks like that dude lost his head," a guy whispered to his girlfriend, trying to make her laugh." "You shouldn't joke about your boss like that. He might have been a jerk, but he didn't deserve this, nobody does."

Jason moseyed over to the young couple who were both no older than twenty two. "My name is Jason and I'm a reporter for the Times. I overheard you saying this guy was your boss?" Jason spoke with care and thoughtfulness, but a straight to the point directness that was about to make him a star at his small town paper. He held the job for some time, writing human interest stories, features, reviews, obituaries, basically everything nobody else wanted to write.

Jason knew that stuff had to be written, and would lead to bigger and better things. He had to pay his dues, and pick through the crap to find the one golden nugget that will lead him forward. Jason knew this might be one of those nuggets.

"So how long did you work for this guy?" Jason queried with a concerned but intense look because he knew he was onto something.

"Three years, he hired me a year after high school," the man answered while clearing his throat because he was sincerely heartbroken. "He didn't deserve to go out like this." The dead guy had been his boss for a few years, what he didn't add was the guy took him in after his parents threw him out.

He got into trouble with the law, had no direction and fell into drugs pretty heavily. When he forged a check from his mom's purse to buy a twenty sack, his parents booted him out, leaving him to wander the streets. He looked like he'd be lost forever until a nice man with a construction company took a chance.

"You obviously have an emotional connection to the guy, do you know anybody that would want to harm him?" questioned Jason as the afternoon sun was shining right in his face, causing multiple beads of sweat to tumble down his forehead. "Any enemies that hated him enough to display his mangled body for the world to see?"

"I don't know. He was the nicest, most hard working guy and treated everyone with respect. Nobody ever spoke ill of him. That is until we did some work on a high end development downtown. We were under a tight deadline because the corporation sub-contracting his company were assholes, and demanded everything be done yesterday."

"I rode that slide right before his body came down. I witnessed him and some guy at the top screaming at each other. At first he was giving the guy crap, and the guy was giving him crap back. Then the heckler started talking about how he slept with the other guy's wife, and how he could never satisfy her like he could, basically fighting words. The verbal onslaught started when he saw who was giving the okay for people to slide," added Jason, feeling like this wasn't a chance meeting.

"Sometimes the person funding the job would cruise by to check things out, and ask how much longer it was going to take. The big boss would always have a pissed off look on his face, accompanied by his trophy wife who wore way too much makeup to be anywhere near a construction site. I mean who wears high heels to walk through mud?"

"You think your guy was sleeping with her?"

"They always gave each other the eyes whenever she walked by, you know the ones that undress the other?"

"I know the look. It's the same one my girlfriend and I exchange every morning. Anything else you can tell me?"

"Well he did just...." The guy was cutoff by his girlfriend pulling his arm with a let's get out of here, very bored look.

"Aren't you done yakking? I'm hungry and it's like a million degrees out here," the girl bellowed with a very annoyed, but happy look on her face. "I'm going to the snack bar for something to drink, then under that palm tree for some shade. Just don't make it to long alright we have to be at my friends by five."

"No problem honey, I'll be just a few more minutes," the young guy conveyed to his girlfriend as he watched her ass all the way to the snack bar.

"You have some other stuff to tell me, what is it?" Jason quizzed with a very eager look on his face.

"I just didn't want to say anything with her around because she'd kill me," chuckled the guy with a smirk on his face.

"Kill you figuratively not literally, right?"

"Yeah of course"

Jason and the guy had a good laugh as they moved to a nearby picnic table for the rest of their conversation.

"Remember that lady I thought was having an affair with my boss who came down the slide. She was sleeping with most of the work crew, guess the old man really couldn't satisfy her," blurted the young guy with a devious smile.

"So she slept with everybody? Including you?" Jason insinuated, even more interested than before because he felt some truth coming on.

"Yes, that's why I didn't say anything around my girl. The old man's wife usually slept around very indiscriminately, but sometimes was just a tease. She knew you were checking her out, and liked it. Instead of following it up by pulling you into the bathroom, she was sent in to smooth over problems."

"What do you mean smooth over problems?"

"She would talk to the workers when they had a complaint. Whether it was a problem with the company itself, coworkers, their rate of pay, or working conditions, the boss would always send his lady in to take care of it. I corroborated this by talking to other people that went through it."

"So whenever there was a complaint, they would send her in huh?"

"She would meet them in the boss's office when he wasn't there, almost like they both planned it and got off on it. Anyway, I made a suggestion for a small cost of living adjustment. You know how it is when you work hard every day and never seem to get ahead. I told the big boss that if he couldn't give me that raise, I would look elsewhere for work. Not wanting to lose me he sent his girlfriend or wife or whatever in to talk to me. When he left his office, she walked in. She said a raise wasn't in the cards, but she could raise something else."

"You think that's what happened here?"

"Michael was a family man and carried himself like he was satisfied by his wife every night. I don't know why he would want that sleazy trash. I mean its crazy right, a boss sending his wife to fuck his employees when they had a complaint. I mean he was probably jerking off in the corner when it went down."

"Any idea what Michael's complaint was?"

"I don't know exactly, but he did express concern about some illegals the big boss hired. He was feeling pushed out by somebody that would work harder and for less money. Kind of the problem I had too, but the difference is I didn't end up dead."

"Thanks, you've been very helpful. The only thing I'm curious about is when I was at the top of the slide, Michael yelled at the guy working the slide that he slept with his wife?"

"Yeah sorry, the guy I currently work for and the guy that Michael used to work for also owns this water park. For some unknown reason he works the big slide on the weekends. I swear it's only to look down the cleavage of hot ladies."

"Well thank you again for your time. You should get back to your girlfriend. She's giving the death look, like aren't you done yet, jeez," Jason cajoled as they both cracked up, completely relating to each other and the situation.

"No problem man, if more reporters were as down to earth and human as you, people would pay more attention to the information they need."

Jason and the guy parted ways, walking off in opposite directions. It was at this point Jason immediately pulled out his cell phone to call Christina because his voicemail ended so abruptly.

"Hey babe how you doing, sorry about that earlier," Jason attempted to say lovingly.

"What the hell happened? Are you okay?" Christina queried with contempt in her voice, tinged with worry.

"I was watching people come down the big slide as I was talking to you, when a dead body rolled down."

Christina hurriedly turned on the news to see if they said anything about what happened. "The news is saying some guy was killed at the top of the slide, and shoved down for everybody to see. They don't have a suspect yet, but are talking to a bunch of witnesses."

"Right before I came down, I heard this guy Michael having an argument with the guy operating the slide. I didn't think anything of it other than this guy has issues, so I rode down. Next thing I know, I'm leaving you a message and Michael comes down the slide with his throat cut," explained Jason with his voice breaking because he was still freaked out.

"When the cops figure that out, they'll want to talk to you."

"They probably will, but being the diligent reporter I am, I questioned people who might know something. Some very interesting incidents happened between Michael and the other guy, who happened to be his boss," stated Jason with authority.

"Really, the major TV networks aren't even talking about that, you must have gotten a scoop they weren't able to get," revealed Christina in a very sweet tone.

"I think I have enough for a story here, I'm going to come home so I can write it up as soon as possible. The Times could put it on the front page."

"That would be awesome," exclaimed Christina as she hung up the phone. Knowing Jason would want to talk about his water park adventure when he got home, Christina prepared for an onslaught of truth seeking. After all, it drove both of them. What would a perfect couple be without helping the other grow and become a better person?

After settling down, her phone rang again. Thinking it was Jason asking if he should pick up anything at the store like he asked every night, she answered it and abruptly said, "We don't need anything."

"Sorry, what? Christina it's me, Mellissa, your sister. I need to talk to you about what happened at the water park."

"I know there was a murder there, crazy stuff."

"That's true, but I saw something that will burn in my memory forever."

CHAPTER FOUR

"What did you see?" Christina nervously inquired with terror in her voice.

"I saw the murder happen. I saw that man get his throat sliced before being pushed down the slide like trash down a garbage chute," Mellissa stated numbly and still in shock.

"Do you want to talk about it?" Christina poured herself a cocktail and sat down in her most comfortable chair.

"I had never been on a really big slide before and wanted to try it out. I've always been scared of heights, but I wanted to conquer it. If I'm to move forward in my life and go after what I truly want, I have to confront my fears and overcome them. Little did I know that what happened would make me never want to go on a water slide again."

"It's good you confronted what you're scared of. You couldn't have known what was going to happen," Christina compassionately replied as she took a big sip of her bourbon and ginger ale.

"That's true, but still. Anyway, so I start making my way towards the slide. There was a long line and it was really hot, it seemed awful to have to wait an eternity for a ride that lasts less than a minute. Then I realized that by the time I got to the top, I'd be so eager to cool off, I would just go down the slide, no problem."

"Then what happened?"

"The line moved like a snail slithering along. After what seemed like hours, but was probably less than one, I was near the top. I saw Jason and was waving at him to say hello, but he couldn't see me. It looked like he was talking to the guy operating the slide. Then some other guy comes up and starts screaming. That lasted for a few minutes before the guy moved back towards the stairs to leave."

"Yeah Jason told me about the two guys arguing, but then he said they stopped and he went down the slide. He doesn't know what happened after."

"Well I hope I can give you a more information so Jason can write up a big story, and nail this guy's ass to the wall."

"I'll definitely let him know when he gets back," Christina supportively expressed, so transfixed by what her sister was saying that a bomb could have exploded next to her and she wouldn't have noticed.

"The guy walked away, but must have been so pissed off, that he walked back up and started yelling even louder this time. The funny part was that the loads of people in line didn't seem to notice what was going on. They were too busy talking or just zoning out, but not me. I saw each and every thing that happened.

The guy jumps on the slide like he was going to ride down. Of course since he was just arguing with the guy that would give the okay, I knew there would be a fight. It all happened so fast, but if I wasn't tuned in, just knowing in the depths of my soul that something crazy was about to happen, I wouldn't have seen it. The slide operator pulled what looked a knife from his pocket.

The other guy was in the ready position, so he didn't see the slide operator take a quick slice across his neck and then push him down all in one motion. The operator waited a minute, sent one more person down the slide and then nodded to his coworker that he was going on a break. They must have an employee's only way of getting up and down because I didn't see him after that.

Needless to say, I scurried out of line and flew down the stairs. I didn't want to stay in that water park one more second, so I left and got in my car. That's when I decided I needed to tell somebody and called you."

By this time Christina had finished her drink awash in disbelief. Was her sister telling her the truth, did she just witness a murder? How was she the only one to see it when there were hundreds of people around?

"Do you want to come over? Want me to keep you company or anything?" Christina offered with much sisterly concern.

"That would be good. I need to do a few things first, and then I'll swing by," Mellissa related with ease in her voice that somebody had her back.

Christina leaned back in her chair, eagerly awaiting Jason's return so she could tell him what she discovered; it was a sign. The irony was not lost that her boyfriend called to say he saw a dead body come down a water slide minutes after he went down. Followed by her sister calling to say that she saw it happen, synchronicities reveal many layers of truth.

Christina decided to pour herself another beverage when the phone rang again. "Who the hell could it be this time, maybe the murderer is calling me to confess," she flippantly ruminated to herself, not thinking it possible, but not sure about anything at this point.

"Hey babe, I'm on my way home, do you need anything from the store while I'm out?" Jason questioned excitedly as he knew he would see his love soon.

"Oh good it's you"

"Of course it's me, are you okay? What's wrong?"

"I can't really explain over the phone. I need to tell you in person. It would be great if you could just pick up some burritos, I don't feel like cooking."

"No problem. Is everything all right, you're not hurt are you? You haven't been cheating on me?" Jason bantered half-jokingly.

"Of course not, just an interesting call from my sister."

"About what, care to give me a clue so I'm not guessing all the way home, the suspense will kill me."

"She witnessed a murder."

CHAPTER FIVE

Reminiscing about the past, Christina inquired, "Don't you remember it was your article that brought the guy to justice? It was because of the details in your story that the cops investigated, and then arrested him right in front of all his workers.

They took him to jail where he stayed until his trial. It should have ended with the death penalty, because it was definitely premeditated. Instead they gave him life in prison without the possibility of parole. The justice system knew he would get the respect that a slave driving, employer who takes advantage of hard working illegal immigrants deserves." Christina's face was beet red with rage.

"It's coming back to me now. They put him in a prison that was 80% Mexican. Once they heard who the new fish was, they showed him a real good time," smirked Jason very darkly.

"If you call being repeatedly raped and beaten every day a good time, then he had a blast."

"More like, they blasted something inside of him."

"You're gross."

"You know you like it. Anyway, after a while they put him in solitary for the rest of his term where his only human contact was his lawyer once a week, and the prison guards who were antsy to see him experience all the pain he dispensed."

Christina couldn't handle the gory details anymore and got up from the table. "I'm going to grab a whiskey, you want one?"

"It's eleven in the morning. Although it is Friday, and you know what they say, it's five o'clock somewhere," chided Jason with a laugh.

"Yeah after that conversation, I need a drink."

She filled two glasses with two fingers each, and then sat back down at the table. Once they took a sip, they both knew this was the good stuff.

"You didn't open my bottle of fifteen year did you?" Jason inquired.

"No, it's the twelve year," Christina fired back, eager for liquid refreshment.

"The water park can't be coming up now for an inexplicable reason. I mean, why did we randomly start talking about it two years later?" Jason theorized, second guessing his own thoughts.

"Maybe it's a sign," Christina added reassuringly.

"For some reason Mellissa was the only person to witness the murder, and then called to tell you all about it. If it wasn't for her, nobody would ever know what really happened."

They settled in to eat what was left of their breakfast, which was now cold because of the trip into the dark recesses of their minds. Without saying anything, they just ate the room temperature, boring food. It tasted good sure, but it didn't have the same pop as when freshly made.

With both of their plates empty, rinsed off and in the sink, the two lovebirds sat on their couch to relax and smoke a joint.

Christina was always the best at rolling, even though Jason tried really hard. His were functional and would smoke, but were always pregnant in the middle.

"Aren't you done rolling that thing yet," Jason needled, eager to get high and explore why the water park story flowed back into their consciousness.

"Hold on, hold on, don't get your panties in a bunch, I'm almost done. Mine take just a few seconds longer than yours because they're beautiful, just like me," Christina teased back with a devilish grin.

"Well you are beautiful, and I would love to wrap my lips around you, just like that joint."

"Let's smoke this thing and then maybe I'll let you."

They settled in, easily finding the well-worn spots that seemed designed just for them. They pulled the coffee table up close, made sure the ashtray was within reach and then sparked up.

"This tastes good, what strain is this?" Christina wondered after taking a long, deep hit.

"I think its good green bud number five which is better than that stuff I had last week. What was it called, oh yeah, good green bud number six," Jason joked as she handed him the joint so he could take a rip. "The whole water park thing feels like it was yesterday.

I remember the whole series of events, me going down the slide, me seeing the body and then calling you about it. Me coming home with burritos, and you telling me your sister saw the slide operator slash that guy's throat before escaping down the staircase. Me writing up the story, and having it printed on the front page because I had the exclusive interview with what appeared to be the only witness. Goes to show that a construction magnate who owns a water park, shouldn't be working a water slide if murder is anywhere on his mind, the whole thing was crazy."

"It was crazy, but don't forget it wasn't just about the murder, it's the why that was the craziest thing," Christina recollected, trying to settle the uneasy mess sitting next to her.

"You're right, it didn't just happen out of the blue. An influential man with lots of money thought he could get away with smuggling illegal immigrants for construction work at slave wages, while cramming them in little shacks after a sixteen hour workday.

If anybody complained, he'd report them to ICE, which only happened a few times. Everybody was frightened because they knew they could disappear at any moment.

He kept them fed with crappy food, living in crappy houses, wearing crappy clothes, and held all their IDs and personal papers for what he said was their own security. Well if it was for their own security, then how come he kept them in a big safe in a special room at his house that always had two armed guards outside of it?"

"He knew how to keep them in line. He knew that if they couldn't run to the police, couldn't run to another employer, and they couldn't escape home, he could make them do whatever he wanted," fumed Christina.

"Yep, another example of the powerful taking advantage of the powerless for personal gains."

Jason took a big drag off the joint, so much that it started a big run.

"Do you have any oars, because its looks like you want to go canoeing? Oh wait you already have." Christina laughed heartily while she grabbed a lighter to fix the joint.

"I was going to ask you earlier how much you got paid an hour?"

"How much do I get paid an hour?"

"How much do you get paid to babysit that joint?" teased Jason like he told a joke that just wasn't funny.

"Yeah, it doesn't really work when you make a comeback five minutes later. That must mean you're stoned. What do you expect though with good green bud number five, or is it, number nine?"

They both laughed so hard that their bellies rumbled just like Santa's would if somebody told him a joke. The joint was almost gone, so Christina decided to twist up another. It was Friday and they didn't have anything to do, except get high, chill, go out and do something, or just stay in and love on each other. Of course if they went out they would probably love on each other anyway, they did love adventure and were both turned on by the possibility of getting caught.

"What the hell, it sounds like something is ringing," Jason remarked with a surprised look on his face that showed how truly stoned he was.

"Relax, I think it's the phone. How high are you?"

"I'm fine, I can still speak straight words right?"

"Sounds like it."

"Good."

Christina comically reached over Jason to answer the portable phone. It was sitting on the coffee table, so they didn't have to get up when they were hanging out.

"Jason, it's for you, and I hope you're ready."

CHAPTER SIX

Jason grabbed the phone out of Christina's hands like it was the last doughnut. "What are you talking about? Am I ready? Who is on the phone?"

With a huge smile Christina very happily replied, "Life works in very mysterious ways. Sometimes all we have to do is talk about something, and it becomes real. We were reminiscing about the water park and all the crazy crap that happened. How you discovered details of the story that nobody else did, and why we were thinking of it out of the blue. This phone call is the universe listening."

Jason thought of all the possibilities, but it made his mind spin like a dreidel on the eighth night of Hanukkah. When the whole thing snowballed, he knew whomever was on the other end of the phone was sure to take him the next step. The conversation/flashback he and Christina had was a step forward in their consciousness, this phone call, was yet one more step.

"Aren't you going to answer it," Christina pushed with excitement protruding from the deepest part of her soul.

"Of course, I'm sorry. I feel like an avalanche just hit me and I had to quickly assess what was happening, what the possibilities of this phone call could be, and what could happen with it." Jason took a deep breath and looked at Christina. They stared at each other for a minute, as if Christina was trying to tell Jason through her eyes and heart like only two people who were bound to each other could, that it was okay, and she loved him, whatever ended up happening.

"Hello, this is Jason."

"Hi, this is Marty from Democratic Republic magazine. How are you doing today?"

"I just finished up some coffee and breakfast with my girlfriend, and now we're relaxing before we decide what to do today. Wait, you said you were from Democratic Republic, just like that big time magazine in New York?"

"Yep, just like that big time magazine in New York. I must say that was one of the more interesting responses I've gotten when I've called somebody without warning. I'm definitely going to pass that around the newsroom later. Anyway, the reason I called, remember the article you wrote about the waterpark murder? How you helped uncover a conspiracy dealing with construction sites run by human smuggling rings to keep them supplied with extremely cheap labor?"

"Yeah I remember that, in fact my girlfriend and I were just talking about how crazy the whole sequence of events was," Jason remarked. He thought it was weird some guy was calling about a story he wrote two years ago, a story nobody had asked about since. Plenty of people inquired after it happened because he had the exclusive statement from Christina's sister. Nobody knew that the big boss had his wife sleep with his "legal" employees who had complaints, and would retaliate hard against those who refused the gesture. A whole operation was uncovered because of what Jason was told and what he heard.

"Some colleagues and I have been talking about that whole series of events too. How were you able to get what nobody else could? Everybody was asking about the murder, how could anybody do it? Where was the security? Where were the safety precautions that would have prevented it in the first place? Basically, the big networks picked up the story and talked about all its sensational elements, but not the details.

As more media outlets picked up the story, it became hyped more and more. When they made the murder sound more scripted than real life, I knew a TV movie was around the corner. Half the time, they report what they portray as a story, the other half they report on each other reporting. Not you though, you were actually talking to somebody who saw it. It was as if everybody was concerned with the what, when, how and where, instead of the why," Marty pointed out to Jason, because his cynical mind had been thinking about it all day.

"All I know is that doing my job as a reporter, drives me to find hard facts. Why something happened is the most important part of the process. That's what they taught me in journalism school," Jason orated with a confidence he only expressed when he was passionate about what he knew in his heart was the right thing.

"I have to know, how did you get a statement from that woman? How could she be the only witness? I mean there were hundreds of people there and half of them were in line for that slide, how could anybody else not have seen it?"

"Obviously, I can't tell you how I interviewed her. I have to protect my source. All I can say is that I was in the right place at the right time and things just came together."

"That sounds like fundamentals, or a big coincidence. What else can you tell me?"

"I was really glad to help end that smuggling operation. Nobody deserves that when they're trying to make a better life for themselves and their families. I believe in what this country is supposed to be about, freedom for everybody, not just for the few at the top with money and influence.

They think they can get away with anything because of who they are and what they do. They feel above the law and think they write the law, which in some cases they actually do. So you asked what else I can tell you, I'm very passionate about making the world a better place one event at a time.

I struggled to find my voice for a while, not knowing where to go or how to move forward. Everybody in my life seemed to be doing so many more important things than me. When I saw a body come down a big water slide in front of me, I knew it was a life changing opportunity.

I was given a chance to make a difference in a real way. Like somebody was looking right at me and asked what I was going to do, how was I, Jason, personally, going to fix this problem and make everything better? That's when I started talking to people. The network execs must not have liked the truth I printed, because they eventually dropped the story."

"It's interesting that you felt this story was your opportunity to make a real difference in the world. When we talked about the story in the newsroom, we discussed all its ins and outs and how it came together. We started thinking about why it came together, and how somebody was able to put it together. We realized we were being struck by an opportunity of our own," Marty identified with an authenticity that exuded beauty from his soul.

It was at this point Jason knew something was about to happen. He knew that when an improbable but not impossible series of events begins to commence, you have to go along for the ride. It started with a joint with his beautiful girlfriend after breakfast on a lazy Friday. Then the conversation, then their thoughts of the people and the exact series of events, everything began flowing and they had no control over it.

When a guy called to say he was chatting with his colleagues about his story at one of the country's leading authorities on investigative journalism, Jason had to go along for the ride

After the challenges he's had, he was nervous about what was out there and what was to become of it, making it hard for Jason to take the proverbial next step. It felt like a bunch of waiting and loneliness. Once he met Christina however, she helped put things in perspective; which is why they work so well together, and have the ability to help each other grow.

Christina made Jason remember to never take life too seriously, to always have fun, and realize situations aren't always what they seem; and can have different inherent meanings if looked at in different ways.

This phone call to Jason seemed like it was meant to happen, like he was expecting but not waiting for it. He was bettering himself and his life while helping out as many people as he could along the way.

After an eternity of internal dialogue which was really only half a second, Jason spoke up, "What kind of opportunity did you realize you had? Was it like any I've had that I hoped would last longer, or at least until I left a positive mark on the world? I need to feel in my heart that the planet is a little better for me having lived in it."

"Well, seeing as we're all humans and have gone through much of the same stuff, I'm sure at some point there were similarities. This differs from all those events in the past because it will shape the future, and affect everyone. Our opportunity you asked, what is it? You are."

CHAPTER SEVEN

Jason didn't know what was going on or what to say, he was caught totally off-guard. Why on earth did this guy really call him? Why would an editor from one of the most well-known and respected media outlets call him? How on earth could somebody with as huge an apparatus as the Democratic Republic, miss something that a lowly, small town reporter didn't? How did he get the best of them?

"What do you mean I'm your opportunity?" Jason blurted out with much wonderment and intrigue. He was having a hard time sitting down and had been pacing around the kitchen in his slippers for the last five minutes while talking to Marty. Christina, who was watching from the couch, was enjoying the show like a kid about to get a Christmas present they always wanted.

"You're our opportunity because you come from a small town paper and aren't known outside media circles. We want you to work for us," Marty stated with as much confidence as he could muster.

"You want me to come work for you, little ole me? Well how could I turn that down? I have to know though, how did you not pick up the story angle I did? How did you not find the larger conspiracy or the wife sleeping with the employees or any of that?" Jason theorized with a certain edge, not ego per say, but validated confidence. He didn't know where this line of questioning was going, but he had to ask. He had to prove worthy of the position they were about to offer him.

"We hunted and searched for anything we could find, but all we located was the physical evidence of the murder, and some witnesses around the splashdown pool that saw the body slide down. I guess we didn't talk to the right people," Marty fired back with arrogance, as if he knew Jason was bettering him.

Marty knew the best reporters were always trying to prove themselves, trying to be one step ahead of the next guy so they could get the bigger scoop.

"I guess you didn't talk to the right people. Of course I didn't know who the right people were either until I talked to them. A former employee by the pool gave me all the inside information I needed to investigate, and then prove the sequence of events. It was as if I was the right person in the right place at the right time.

I'm very passionate about helping people and bettering their situations. Once I discovered that illegal immigrant laborers were forced to live in horrible conditions while making slave wages, I got fired up. I had to do something." Jason was speaking with a fiery passion that burned throughout his soul because this conversation brought up the exact reasons he was a truth seeker.

"That's exactly why we want you. You're passionate about what you report. You want and need to report the truth. Too many reporters get caught up in corporate network politics of what the higher ups want. If it's not the editors, it's the publishers, advertisers, the FCC or any number of government, military or spy agencies breathing down your neck to portray a story in a certain way.

I can tell you go after what you feel passionate about, and screw what other people think. Others get caught up in million dollar contracts and not losing the comfortable position they feel they've earned. They think the eventual next step for them is to be where they are. You don't care about the prestige, the position or the money, all you care about is truth. That's the reason you're our opportunity. We must have you on our team."

Marty didn't know how Jason would reply. He knew Jason was the most raw and talented reporter he'd seen in a long time. Would the newsroom be happy he hired somebody like that, because Jason was just like him when he was young? Marty remembered what it was like to have passion and go after what he believed in. He knows he used to have it. Had he become too comfortable, like the people he warned Jason about, the people too comfortable in their positions to rock the boat? Had Marty grown afraid to ask hard questions and cover the tough stories no matter what anybody or anything said, because it was the right thing to do.

"That is quite a compliment coming from you. Your magazine has published amazing investigative pieces over the years, from all corners of the globe," Jason respectfully noted. There was a loving energy surrounding him, controlling his thoughts and actions. "I love that I'm getting this opportunity, I'm getting the chance to really move forward."

Jason knew this was the chance of a life time. How on earth could he possibly turn it down? How could he lead the life he wanted if he didn't consider it? His life was heading in the positive direction he always dreamed of, but could never get to. That is until he let go of all the crap that stopped him from moving forward. He learned a lot of things in life are placed in our way to slow our progress and evolution. Jason came to realize most of these road blocks are placed by ourselves because we don't want to give up the unfulfilling, but very comfortable existence we've built for ourselves.

"Moving forward, it's interesting you use those words. I was just telling one of my reporters the other day that if we aren't moving forward we're moving backward. In the news game, if you aren't growing, you're dying. If you're dying, then the public won't be as informed as they should be, ignorance will spread. The country will then be taken over by conservative and religious zealots who only want to make a buck for themselves and their inner circle, while screwing over the rest of the world. Wait, that's already happened." Marty was extremely passionate when he spoke. He knew all his years of reporting in the trenches were leading to this point in time. "Sorry about that, when I get passionate about something, I let it fly."

"You and I are a lot alike in that way. When a problem seems impossible from every angle, sometimes I feel like there has to be a way," Jason shot back as a smile crept in because he sensed what was happening.

"I respect that about you, it's one of the reasons I called. You have a passion that burns deep, constantly yearning to be put to good use, and to help human-kind take the next step in its positive and collective evolution. I'd like to offer you a job. Would you like to work for us?"

"Wow, that's a big opportunity. Would I work there or from anywhere I wanted because I'd be reporting from all over?

"While it's true you'd be reporting from all over making major travel a must, your home base would be here in New York."

"I'm guessing I'd have to move there?"

"You would."

Jason wasn't sure what to say. He knew Christina couldn't leave because she was plugged into Shane Corp. who did forensic work for major federal agencies and task forces. When a really crazy case sprung up that the government couldn't solve, they'd give it to Christina's company.

True she was the low person on the totem pole and would have to work her way up to the fun stuff, but she was working towards her passion. That is one of the reasons she and Jason got together in the first place, they both had a deep burning passion for truth which they had to go out and find, and then, they found each other.

"Did I mention the pay," Marty teased, hoping he could sweeten the deal because he knew how important Jason would be to his magazine and the world because he was such a passionate truth seeker.

"Sorry, I was in a daze for a minute, what did you say?" Jason hesitantly replied, a little scared but excited thinking about possibilities. He wasn't feeling a buzz off the joint he and Christina smoked what seemed like an eternity ago, but he had the deep thoughts that usually accompanied it. This conversation had sobered him up.

"The pay, I got so caught up in talking about our passions for seeking truth that I forgot. The pay is $200,000 a year to start, with stock options, full retirement and health benefits. Basically, we'll provide whatever you need to stay healthy so we can get as much truth out of you as we can.

You'll have a corner office with a view. A personal secretary will take care of appointments and interview scheduling, as well be your advisor if you ever need a second opinion. You will have complete creative control in how you report and what stories you choose to cover. We want to give you as many resources as you need, then turn you loose and see what you come up with."

"What can I say?" Jason spouted nervously because this is what he always dreamed of.

"That's easy, just say yes," Marty quipped, very eagerly wanting Jason to join the DR team, and willing to do anything to get him.

"It sounds like everything I've been looking for. I just need some time to think about it. I have to discuss this with my girlfriend to see what she thinks about the whole idea."

"That's completely fine, and I would do the same thing. The only thing is we need a decision by tomorrow morning. Today is Friday, and we want to go with somebody new on Monday so we can start the week off fresh. Take tonight and think about it, it's a major decision and a major move.

If you can't decide or don't call back in the morning, I won't respect you any less and neither will my team. We will just have to go with somebody else on the list even though you were our number one choice by far. My number is 212-555-7685 I very much hope to hear from you tomorrow."

"I'll sleep on it and let you know. Thanks again for the opportunity," expressed Jason, feeling gratitude like he never felt before.

"No problem man, good bye."

"Goodbye."

Jason hung up the phone after what seemed like forever. Christina was staring at him with baited breath, wondering who was on the phone, and what they had to say.

"So, who was that? When I answered the phone all he said was this is Marty, can I talk to Jason. So I'm dying to know, who was he and what did he want?" Christina inquired with a lot of excitement in her voice. She hoisted herself from the couch where she was watching the whole phone call transpire, to being 5 inches from Jason's face. "What happened?"

"When you handed me the phone, you asked if I was ready. Well, I think I am. I've been waiting for something like this for a long time. But I think the question really is, are we ready for it? Can we handle it?"

CHAPTER EIGHT

If there ever was a time for Jason and Christina to have a deep conversation about the foundation of their relationship, it was now.

"Do you think I deserve the chance to advance my dreams and bring into reality all the things I know are possible," Jason pondered with an edge in his voice.

"Well, of course, I can't believe you'd even ask me that; like you're asking if I want you to succeed. You want to know if I think you deserve it, of course you do. Jason, I love you. No matter what, I'm always here for you," Christina countered in a very supportive and loving voice. "So, are you going to tell me who Marty is and what he wanted?"

"He works with Democratic Republic magazine in New York, and wanted to offer me a job," Jason told Christina very anxiously.

"That's great, and definitely something to go after, but why did he call now? We didn't have any warning something like this was coming, no clue."

"Marty called because he and some colleagues had been talking about the water park story, and wanted to speak with the no name reporter who broke the story. He said because I got exclusive eyewitness testimony and uncovered a vast conspiracy complete with payoffs and illegal workers, he wanted me to work for them. Apparently nobody was able to get the quality information that I did. Little old me, working for a cheap nothing paper, got a bigger scoop than the big wigs with all their fancy equipment, foreign bureaus, extensive research and assumed best education money could buy. Jason out scooped the big boys. Then they dropped the story because their corporate overlords wouldn't let them spell out the truth."

Jason and Christina sauntered over to sit at the kitchen table. Both of them were pretty long winded when they were passionate about something.

"What do you want to do?" Christina queried Jason, genuinely wanting to know the answer.

"I want to take it of course. This is the opportunity of a lifetime. They offered me lots of money, a corner office, creative and editorial autonomy, basically everything a reporter dreams of, and I can do any stories I want," Jason exclaimed excitedly. "The only thing is they want me to move to New York and work out of the main office."

Christina had a hard time finding words to accurately portray what she wanted to say. "New York huh, that's a long way from here. You know I'm locked into working for Shane Corp. right? You might say I'm working my way up in the field that is my passion. If I want to be a forensic scientist, I have to pay my dues, and the company I work for is the way to do that."

"I know you can't leave, in fact you shouldn't for the reasons you just stated. That's what makes this decision so difficult. On one hand I could take a job that is a sure fire gateway into the halls of power, I'll be able to uncover truths that hold us as a society back.

On the other hand, I could stay with the only woman I've ever truly loved, and continue to work for a small paper. Discovering truth in whatever way I could," Jason explained as if he just unloaded something that weighed on his mind for years. In actuality, it had really only been for the couple minutes since he hung up the phone.

Christina sat in her chair and leaned back. She then got up for a glass of water, as she became extremely parched all of a sudden. "I think you have to go after your dream, I'd never forgive myself if you stayed." Christina conveyed honestly as tears welled up in her big hazel eyes. She filled a glass with water from the sink and took a big gulp before she spoke again. "You're also the only man I've ever truly loved. You've taught me so much in the short time we've been together.

You supported me through all my trials and tribulations, and the fact that you were completely and utterly behind me when I took the Shane Corp lab job, showed you honestly care what happens to me and my life." Christina took another gulp of water before setting her cup by the sink and sitting back down. The sun was now pouring in the window, which was one of the things she and Jason always loved about their place; especially now, they could use all the warming energy they could get.

"I love you Christina. I love the fact you're a truth seeker just like me but from a different angle. I love that you go after what's swept under the rug because you genuinely care, and truly want to make the world a better place for all its present and future inhabitants." Jason spoke with a glow in his eyes because of the beautiful woman sitting in front of him.

"I know you do, which is why you have to take this job. Let me prove the love that has kept us together. We both care about what happens to the planet. Our love for each other is designed and built on the idea that we help each other grow and achieve much more in the furtherance of collective evolution, than we ever could by ourselves."

"That's true I've felt that ever since we met. You're the only woman for me, I couldn't imagine my life without you," Jason expressed with fright creeping into his voice.

"Our lives can still exist without each other, but only if we continue moving forward. Don't get me wrong, there is nothing I want more in the world than to wake up next to you every day.

However, if I held you back from achieving something that would help you truly be who you're supposed to be, not only would I never forgive myself, but I'd be a detriment to your personal evolution. If I cared more about myself and the hurt you caused me by leaving, instead of thinking about your hopes, dreams and what you want, it wouldn't be a healthy relationship, lamented Christina."

Tears were seconds from falling on Jason's face, but stopped just short. "I love you so much. I spent so many lonely years thinking there would never be a woman out there for me. I went on dates, I just never found that special connection. Sometimes out of loneliness I'd go after what I thought I wanted, which only made me happy for the moment. Then, you came along."

"They say great things come when you least expect them, and from what it sounds like, you definitely weren't expecting this. I've always loved your honesty and ability to open up," Christina asserted from the bottom of her soul.

"I'm only really able to open up because of you, and everything you mean to me. I can't open up to just anybody, lord knows, I've tried. I just feel so at ease whenever I'm around you, like I can get through anything."

"I feel the same about you. You are the man of my dreams."

Jason and Christina stared into each other's eyes thinking about all their time together, and the adventures that helped them experience life on more than just a cerebral level. Christina reached for the jar of weed that was usually kept in a kitchen cabinet so she and Jason could smoke whenever they felt the need. Christina definitely was feeling the need, and from the quickness Jason got up to open the cabinet door for her, he was feeling the need too.

"I don't know about you, but I could definitely use a treat," Christina relayed eagerly as she put some buds in the grinder that would eventually become their smoke-able peace of mind, if only for the moment.

"That sounds good to me, I could use a little help in getting my head straight, or at least a little buzz so I can relax and make this decision." Jason was trying not to sink too deep into thought to quickly about the decision he had to make.

Christina finished rolling the joint, always making them perfectly straight, something Jason couldn't pull off if his life depended on it. "How do you always roll those so straight, I've never been able to do that no matter how hard I try," Jason bantered with a smirk.

"Practice, practice, and more practice," Christina retorted with an even bigger smirk as she reached into Jason's pocket for a lighter.

"Hey, that's not a lighter,"

"Are you saying that I can't grab it, hit a button, and make it hot?" Christina volleyed with a devious smile on her face.

"Of course you can, I just know it's hard to light a joint that way. Can't say I've ever tried it myself, but I would like to use this thing again one day for its intended purpose."

Jason and Christina both had a huge laugh, and then exchanged a hug and kiss that intertwined their souls. Christina grabbed the real lighter and brought the flame to the doobie, exhaling out a gargantuan cloud of smoke. "Ahhhh, that's better," Christina exclaimed as she handed Jason the joint.

"Thank you, another winner in my book," Jason suggested as he took a long deep hit, and exhaled a smoke cloud equally big as Christina's.

"So this huge decision, I can help you weigh the pros and cons, the advantages and disadvantages of staying here or going there, but ultimately, it's up to you. You and only you can make this decision, but whatever you decide, I'll back you. How long do you have, when do you have to let them know?"

"I have to call them back in the morning. Marty said if I take the job, I need to be on a flight there Monday, they want to start off fresh for the week."

Christina expected to have more time to help Jason decide, or at least more time to get her own bearings straight if he decided to go. "That's really quick, they aren't messing around. Really, that quick huh? This is a major decision, they can't expect you to leave your whole life behind at the drop of a hat just because they throw a bunch of money in your face," Christina reacted defensively.

"I thought you said it was the best thing for me, that I needed to explore all my options because this might be the opportunity I've been looking for," Jason added with concern in his eyes.

"I know I said that, but I didn't think it was going to happen so fast. I mean we woke up this morning, made a great breakfast, chilled and contemplated the problems of the planet like we always do. We were going to have a great day just holding and loving each other."

"I know that's how it started, and I agree this is very sudden. Haven't you always said though, that great things happen all at once? That sometimes opportunities show up whether you're ready for them or not. Sometimes they're only around for a second, and then they're gone. It's like a window or door only opening for a short period of time, waiting on us to do something or know something."

"I just didn't think I was going to have it shoved in my face so abruptly."

"Trust me, I would never shove anything in your face that you didn't ask me for." Jason slyly winked which made

Christina smile. "I just have to seriously consider this, or else I'll regret it."

Christina and Jason moved over to the couch where they held each other tightly. They kissed like they had never kissed before, like they were exploring each other for the first time. They took a breath to look into each other's eyes and the same thought popped into their heads. What did I do to deserve such unconditional love?

"Why, or should I say how did I end up with such a special angel as you?" Jason inquired as he looked straight into Christina's soul.

"I was going to ask you the same question. We really are on the same page aren't we?" Christina was amazed every time she was in Jason's presence. "I love you so much, I feel like I can't take it sometimes."

"I feel the same way sweetheart." They hugged and kissed for a bit longer, remaining on the couch in each other's arms. They looked out their oversized living room window, wondering what life was going to bring them.

"Life is funny sometimes, you think it's going one way, and then it throws you a curveball, sending you in a completely opposite direction," realized Christina whose mind was wandering.

"I feel the same. I think I'm a broken record," Jason quipped laughingly.

"This is great, this moment, right here now. So what do you think? Are you going to take it?"

CHAPTER NINE

Jason's head was beating like a drum played by the energizer bunny. Christina tried to help him make up his mind, but was having a hard time because her own feelings kept creeping back into the equation. Nobody's perfect and nobody has it easy, except for maybe politicians and trust fund babies. Since Jason and Christina were neither of those, they knew they would have to fight and claw for everything.

"What's the time, how much longer do we have? When does this impatient asshole Marty want us to call him back? I mean who asks somebody to make a life altering decision on a whim? Does he think that will make a good reporter?" Christina was trying to view the situation rationally, but her better logic was floating away. All that remained was raw emotion, what she knows she loves, and her job.

"I think we have some time, I'm not sure." Jason was trying to comfort Christina, which didn't seem to be working. "Why would you get upset at Marty, he's only trying to give me a chance at the big time?"

"I feel like he's trying to break us up. I know he's just looking out for the best interest of his publication but still, what right does he have to break up a perfectly happy couple that has been waiting their entire lives for somebody like the other?" Christina blurted out from the entirety of her being.

"I feel the same way baby. All those lonely nights I wondered if I'd ever be graced with a love that would not only help me grow and evolve, but also help motivate me so I actually want to move forward. An incredible force was out there waiting to show me the world wasn't so bad, and everybody has the right to be loved.

I had been through bad breakups and girls cheating on me. Heck, I even had multiple one night stands pulled on me when I didn't want them to. Which usually happens to the girl, but it happened to me. I guess I was just a nice guy looking for a nice girl he could evolve with."

Christina and Jason stared at each other for an eternity. They both would go to the end of the earth to make the other person happy, whatever it took so they never felt alone. They knew this was a futile task, not only because it's unhealthy to be with somebody 24 hours a day, but because it is impossible to always be next to somebody. Being attached at the hip they wouldn't be helping each other grow, they would be holding each other back. One person would seem like they're growing and evolving, but would actually be falling backwards with the false illusion of what might be or could be. Not to mention the other person would have to put all their hopes and dreams on hold until they practically forgot about them.

This is the opposite of what Jason and Christina's relationship was all about. They helped each other grow, and had a done pretty good job so far. All this was coming to the forefront of their minds because they're human. Love can do funny things to a person's reasoning skills.

Jason and Christina held each other, not saying a word. All of a sudden like a hurricane, (or maybe a tropical storm with a great chance of being upgraded) a thought struck them like they'd been manifesting it the whole time they were figuring out their collective quandary.

"We love each other, and want to help each other grow and become the best people we can be right?" Christina questioned Jason with the burning honesty that made him love her in the first place, he could feel her authenticity.

"Of course we do, what kind of question is that? I want to help you grow, and you want to help me grow, that's what makes us go together like peanut butter and jelly," answered Jason, agreeing with the thought that emanated from Christina.

"If we love each other, if we truly and honestly look at what's in front of us, if we see all the options and what they mean for me, you and our careers, we should be able to make this decision. There's nothing I wouldn't do for you, and would never hold you back from taking advantage of a once in a lifetime opportunity."

Jason leaned back on the couch and looked as if his eyes were rolling back in his head, but he was just trying to put the right thoughts together. "I know you want to help me, like when I helped you when you started at Shane Corp. You had just got your degree and were looking for work, when they had an opening for a bottom-runger willing to do all the grunt work because of promotion possibilities."

"I remember that like it was yesterday. I was so nervous about accepting, not only was it a huge step towards my ultimate dream of becoming a forensic scientist, but it was something that might also take me away from this amazing guy that only wanted to love me. Truth seeking is definitely something that attracted me to you," Christina reminisced as she flashed back to a time when their lives were in front of them (even though they still are, they're just further along in the same direction). You might say their lives were growing and evolving whether they wanted them to or not.

"I thought to myself, here is this sexy woman, beautiful brown hair, curves in all the right places, and a mind for uncovering what gets swept under the rug. I noticed that right away, almost like I could smell it on you," chuckled Jason.

"I could smell you too. You smelled like sausage and onion pizza. A free piece of advice, never eat a bunch of onions and sausage when you're about to meet, hang out and possibly kiss a girl. Chances are she'll be grossed out, unless she likes all that stuff too."

"You do, don't you remember us getting an extra-large, eating the whole thing then making out for like two hours afterwards? We were sharing our stinky breath love with each other." They both laughed heartily, the kind of laugh that makes your stomach and mouth hurt because you laughed so hard.

"I love making you laugh," asserted Jason as he gently ran his fingertips along Christina's face in a very gentle and romantic manner.

"I love making you laugh too, it's a pathway into your soul," declared Christina, feeling that she could do anything with this wonderful and amazing man by her side.

"We know we work well together right, we know we want to help each other grow right? Jason theorized with a slightly serious, but still loving tone.

"Of course, isn't that what we just spent time going over sweetie?" Christina countered while looking at Jason with a loving grin that made him melt.

"How we help each other grow, I mean really help each other grow is for me to take this job. Its times like these that always puts love to the test, and makes everything fall away so we can find the true answer."

"Are you trying to say that this is one of those times that tests if we really love each other? Do we believe enough in ourselves to make the other person know there is somebody looking out for them?"

"Yes. We'll always look out for each other. All the time we spent looking down the road at possibilities might have been leading to this. Heck, it must have been leading to this point, because here we are. We have to decide if we can handle it, I have to decide if I can handle it."

They held each other for another moment knowing the time of truth would arrive soon, and the decision would pop out like the break of day; they just needed to talk it out and it would appear.

"I think we can handle this, I mean we've made it this far right? Overcoming adversity has only made us stronger, and has led to the happy lives we now lead. Of course we can't live in one moment forever. We have to recognize it, acknowledge it and then let it go.

If we don't let it go and hang on forever to what we think is right, it'll block the next step. It will make our lives worse and less fulfilling. Life is all about getting out of our own way," exploded Christina like she had an epiphany.

"We can't let our own issues bog us down. We don't want to get stuck in the doldrums. We want to keep our minds moving so we keep moving," retorted Jason with a determined but thoughtful and honest look on his face.

"That is the exact reason I want you to take the job. I want you to grow and become the person you always dreamed you could be. I want you to know what success feels like. I want your passion for not only truth, but also humanism and accountability to bleed through your work. I want anybody coming in contact with it to feel its power and either join with it, or get out of the way. I want to get out of your way, I want to see you grow, blossom, and become a person destined for great things, because you are."

"Its reasons like that why I love you. You always know what to say, and genuinely care what happens to me, you are the love of my life Christina. I want to move forward, I want to accomplish so much. I want to show people there's a lot more they can agree on than they disagree on. If they look within themselves and see that when they hurt others they're really hurting themselves, it should keep people in power accountable.

I would love nothing more than to unseat corrupt officials that believe they'll never get caught, like I was a crime fighter. Hell, you could join me and we could be a crime fighting duo, fighting the powerful to give to the powerless so all of us know that we have power."

Christina looked into Jason's eyes and knew that her love for him was unending and once in a lifetime. She also knew that if she didn't let him pursue this, not only would she regret it, but their love wouldn't be as authentic as what she built up in her head; that when given a huge chance to be proven in real-time, it failed. She didn't want it to fail, she wanted it to succeed. "I love you with all my heart, but my job is the path towards my dream. I want to help with the path that's meant for you. Yeah we might part for a bit, but it will help you find, realize and then harness your true potential."

"I love you baby, I've been searching my whole life for somebody like you. I love the fact that you're behind me one hundred percent, just like I am for you. So I think you're right, it will be difficult, but I will take this job. It's my only option if I really want to grow," Jason reiterated with an undeniably reassuring tone. Just then the phone rang, as if it was waiting for Jason to finish his previous thought.

"Hello?" Jason wondered if the quickness of his decision corresponded to the speed of the phone ring. He thought to himself, is their irony in life?

"Yes Jason, this is Marty from New York. Just wondering if you made a decision yet? I need an answer so my partners will quit breathing down my neck."

"I accept."

CHAPTER TEN

Jason knew the next couple days would be the hardest of his life, but also the most exciting. He just accepted a job with a well-known and respected political magazine in New York, a great starting off point in his journey into the unknown. It was scary sure, but he knew he had to do it. Jason realized the unknown didn't need to be scary. It could be exciting as well.

"Well that's it then huh, you're now a big time New York journalist person huh?" Christina sniped with a twinge of jealousy, but also with a happiness that could only be felt when one truly loved another. When Jason and Christina experienced something great, the other felt it as well; maybe that's what happens when two people's souls are connected.

"I am, well, not until I get there and step foot into my office. Maybe it will be when I get my first big interview or maybe my first big story." The possibilities were streaming through Jason's mind like an unending montage.

"You'll have access to the most well-known people in the entire world. I'll bet the material given to you, not to mention the information whispered in your ear off the record would make any normal person's head spin."

"That's true, but I feel like I've been training for this moment my whole life; just like all the rejections and bad relationships with women led me to the big ball of amazing that you are. This is just the next step."

"It's ironic that something that drew you in is now pushing you away. Life is funny sometimes, like somebody is a big trickster up there," Christina speculated like she was one of the tricksters.

Jason thought very carefully about the next words that spilled from his lips. "I'm taking this job in New York, and I have to leave on Monday right?"

"Yeah, you said they booked a flight for you so you could hit the ground running in the new week."

"That's right, that's why they wanted me to make a decision so quickly. Since I'm taking this job, what will happen to us? Will we still be together, can our relationship survive 3000 miles and very busy schedules?" Jason conjectured with great concern on his face.

"I don't know if it can, but we will certainly try. We'll say we'll talk all the time, keep in touch for all the little, big, cool and exciting things that happen as we progress down our similar but different life paths, but I don't think it will happen. We will mean well, but slowly over time, calls will get less and less. Letters and emails and funny text messages will get less, until one day we wake up and are so wrapped up in our lives and careers it won't register to us as important enough to contact each other."

"I had a feeling you were going to say that, because I was thinking it too. We really are on the same wavelength, we think the same way which is probably why we get along so well," agreed Jason as he tried to collect his thoughts, but zoned out instead.

"Jason are you still with me, it looks like you wandered off?"

"Yeah I'm here, talking to the most beautiful woman in the world and how I'm going to move across the country and never see her again."

"We might see each other again, we just don't know when and we don't know where. What we do know however, is that if our lives really are intertwined as we both seem to think then we will meet up again one day."

"That sounds like when women broke up with me when I was younger, like another version of the "it's not you, it's me" speech."

"In some sense I guess it is. We're parting ways for a bit, we might find our way back together and we might not. One of those things I guess. If it was meant to be, it will work out and if it wasn't, it won't. At least we'll know we tried and didn't deny the other the pursuit of their dreams. This will prove beyond a shadow of a doubt that we really love each other, and not just how the other makes us feel."

Jason wasn't sure what to say because it seemed like everything had already been said. Everything that could possibly be thought of to analyze the situation had been thrown on the table, and now the mad dash was on to find workability.

"I think life is the ultimate joker. Just when you think you have it figured out, something comes along to knock you on your ass. If you pick yourself up you grow and live, and if you don't you wilt and die. I don't want to wilt and die, I want to grow and live. I also wouldn't mind taking down a few greedy Washingtonians in the process," Jason related, starting to gain his composure back.

"I wouldn't mind seeing you take down a few of those guys either. Of course when they hide a body, or try to get rid of it in a manner they think nobody will discover, I'll be there," Christina snapped back, feeding off the energy in the room and was compelled to beat her own drum a bit.

"I must do this, I must go there. I can make so many good things happen, I will have power and money at my disposal. I'll be able to pursue and get to the people I always dreamed of getting to."

"I just pray that you don't get corrupted. If you're around those kinds of people for a long period of time, they might try to make you one of them. You know, they might try to jump you into their gang."

They both laughed trying to picture the halls of politics as a gang to be jumped into, but it wasn't too far from the truth.

"Your scientific instruments will be your guns, and my pen and computer will be mine," echoed Jason with a huge smile.

"That's true, but what about our thoughts and our minds," quipped Christina in a smart-aleky but loving tone.

"Our minds and thoughts are like nuclear bombs. When we drop them, I mean really let go and drop them on something that allows them to flow freely, there is nothing more powerful on earth, not the toughest armies or biggest guns. If a pen is mightier than the sword, then the mind and thoughts are the ink that goes into the pen. And if we don't spend time to gather the best quality ink, we'll drop a dud when we try to help the world consciously evolve."

"You're so sexy when you wax philosophical, just makes me feel all tingly inside," Christina postulated as she gave Jason a long and passionate kiss, before grabbing his hand and leading him to the bedroom. "We have to take advantage of the time we have left."

"I couldn't agree more."

They went into the bedroom and loved each other like they were teenagers. Like they never would have sex again, which of course was ridiculous, but the mind can be a funny thing when it's open.

After what seemed like hours, they both lay next to each other and wondered what the next couple days were going to bring. "That was wonderful, but what is going to happen tomorrow, or Monday, or after?" questioned Christina. She was very satisfied from the hot loving, but nervous because she knew what was coming down the pike.

"Solutions to our problems will come. All I know is that when I get on that plane and fly to New York, you'll always be with me, if only in spirit. Not that you'll be dead obviously, but thoughts of you will always be with me, and your warm energy will tuck me in at night," Jason emphasized with a loving tone that always put Christina at ease.

They held each other tight, not wanting to let the other go. This was a good idea because of the scary, but exciting actions they had to take while delving into the darkness.

The next morning, they woke up refreshed, but with their energy zapped. Jason didn't know what he was supposed to do, and neither did Christina. They both just sat on the end of the bed and contemplated what their day was going to consist of.

Were they going to spend time rehashing the conversation they spent all day and night on, going point by point to see if any new solutions popped up? Or were they going to spend their last moments just enjoying each other's company?

Jason got off the flannel sheet covered bed, and went to the bathroom to relieve himself. Christina scooted back to her side of the bed, got back under the covers and grabbed the pad and paper she always had sitting on the nightstand and started writing.

"It's crazy that life has gotten to this point. The fact that the whole thing has been building up to this is crazy. This is yet another step in our journey and we have to take it. Yeah it's scary, it's downright terrifying. It's also the greatest feeling we can feel, the energy can be so strong and supportive if we allow it to be. We have to let this great experience help us, because it won't happen without our say so.

We will work out, this will work out and everything else will too just as it should. I love you baby, and I always will. When we meet up one day again, we will have found each other because of our dreams, not in spite of them. That is the true authenticity we both have always looked for.

Some call it the truth. I call it living the only way we know how. See you soon, I love you." Christina finished writing the note while Jason was still in the bathroom. She got up off the bed and walked over to his favorite jacket he'd be wearing on his flight, folded up the note and stuffed it in the pocket. Jason would see it as he flew out and would read it when he got to his new office as instructed by Christina on the front.

This was going to be crazy, but completely exciting at the same time. Jason and Christina knew the only thing they had to fear was the unknown, but they flipped the script, they were now excited to take the next step.

CHAPTER ELEVEN

Being ready to take the next step and actually taking it are totally different concepts. It's as if you prepare your whole life for something, then all of a sudden there's a chance to make it happen, and you don't know if it's real. You don't know if you should trust it. Jason fell into this category because he wanted to do good things for the world, he wanted to add a little consciousness, truth and spread as much love and peace as he could along the way. He just thought this opportunity might be too good to be true.

Christina is similar to Jason because she also prepared for her dream of bringing truth and consciousness to the world, and through that show how accountability and humanism can fix most things. The difference however is that Christina stepped into it gradually. Jason thought he was working towards his dream slowly, but then a great thing happened all at once. Who gets a call from a big magazine out of the blue without expecting it? Who has a great opportunity thrust upon them without a clue it was coming?

Jason was putting some magazines and other media in a beige carry-on bag, knowing he would be on a plane the next morning and away from his love.

"I love you Christina, it's going to be very hard to be away from you," Jason relayed like something within him deflated.

"I love you too Mr. Jason, it's not going to be easy for me either, but I'm pushing you to take this job because I love you. It's exactly for that reason that I have to support you and your dream. If I didn't I wouldn't actually be in love with you, I would just love the idea of being in love," Christina persisted trying to fight back tears.

"I know I know. The connection we have is real and will never fade. Even if we lose touch, we'll know the other helped set us on our path, and ingrained in us the confidence to achieve anything."

"You're right you're right. I love you, but I can't say that I'm not excited for you, I mean New York. I said it before, but I'll bet you'll uncover so much that's been swept under the rug. That's one thing I always loved about you, you never shy away from a puzzle. If there is something that doesn't make sense, doesn't seem quite right and is in no way shape or form anything close to the official story, you'll find the truth. You have that power Jason, I believe in you."

Jason used his best cramming skills to put clothes in a suitcase, while Christina was boxing up some of Jason's knick-knacks around the house. "Do you want me to ship the rest of your stuff out there?" questioned Christina with a smile in her eyes.

"Sure. They set me up with an apartment in Manhattan, so once I get there I will be like a New Yorker. It almost makes me sick just to think it, let alone say it," chuckled Jason.

"For sure, you always said you could never live there, which is one of the reasons you didn't go right after high school. What about shipping your stuff?"

"We can pack most of this stuff now, and then when we go to the airport, we can drop it off at the shipper on the way. That way once I get to New York, it will be there shortly after."

Jason and Christina robotically organized Jason's life, this goes in that box and that goes in this box, not much creativity, almost as if they knew what was coming, and wish it didn't have to be, but it did. They wanted to pack as much as they could, so they could chill and enjoy their last moments together.

"I can't wait till we finish, you never know how much crap you have until you move, it's the biggest pain in the ass there is," complained Jason trying to be funny, attempting to cover up his frustrated rage.

"That's so true I remember when I moved into my own place for the first time. I thought the pile of boxes would never get packed. Once the whole pile was packed however, it became how was I going to move it? Then came how are we going to fit all this stuff into the place, it's only an apartment. Once we got it all in, I had to unpack it all. Basically, life never fails to show that we always have more work to do," responded Christina with edge in her voice.

"That's true, life does provide many challenges, but it's a journey and not a destination. Sometimes it turns out like we planned, and sometimes life throws us a curveball that completely changes our way of thinking so we don't know which way is up, let alone right from wrong."

"That is the fun part, we never know what to expect. I mean we plan and plan and plan, and then something comes along and shows that we have to adjust if we want to move forward. The only constant in life, is change."

They both decided to take a break and have a joint, considering they were almost done. "I definitely need a safety meeting, I don't know if I'm feeling safe enough," Jason teased with a smile that would be burned into Christina's memory banks for years to come.

"I can agree with that, but can I roll it? I don't like your joints, they're ugly," retorted Christina with a smile that would be equally burned into Jason's memory.

"Whatever, I don't care. My joints might not be pretty, but they're always functional. Sometimes things don't go exactly as planned, but if we remember what's important and where we want to end up, our path will light up for us. The signs will come we just have to pay attention."

"We're still talking about the joint right?"

"Sure, the joint, that works. Even if it isn't the prettiest but is functional, isn't that what matters? Even if goals aren't achieved like originally planned, it's okay because we chose to move forward when we knew where we wanted to end up. Isn't that what matters?"

"Okay Socrates, sit down with me on this couch and let's smoke."

They chilled on their couch for what might be the last time. Tomorrow Jason would be on a plane to live in a place he said he would never live.

Christina would go to work like she did the day before, but this time without the man of her dreams to come home to. Trusting her thoughts and feelings were tough, especially when trying to make herself believe the old truth that when you love something let it go.

"This is going to be great, I mean not the being away from you part of course, but the part where I really have a chance to do something great. Something I can leave my mark on the world with," Jason exclaimed with refreshed energy. He knew this opportunity was inevitable for anybody who felt deep in their soul they must to do good for humanity.

"That's true, you do have that chance, and I hope you make the best of it. Make it worth going there, and most of all, make it worth leaving me," Christina admitted sadly as her eyes welled up, causing her to drop the joint on the coffee table just as she was going to lick it closed, making weed fly everywhere

"I'm not leaving you, I'm letting you go, and only for now. I have to do this, you know that. Heck, you pushed me to take this job. I wouldn't have this opportunity without your love and support. I'll always love you and will always be with you even when I'm not with you," replied Jason. He looked into Christina eyes before he gave her a long deep kiss that hugged her soul.

Jason picked the joint off the table and re-rolled it himself so they could get to smoking. He figured if they could relax a bit, then their last night would be easier. Of course he also knew that lying to yourself was a coping mechanism, which only makes you think life is easier.

"You sure you can finish that thing?" quipped Christina, wiping away the tears surrounding her smile.

"Yeah I'm going to finish it, mine always smoke. Plus, I don't really care about this joint I just want us to chill.

We'll have plenty of time to deal with the aftermath of being apart tomorrow.

Let tonight be just about and for us, for making us happy so we breed good thoughts and feelings about moving forward. Just think about all the amazing people and events ahead. I'm moving to Manhattan, and will work the media and free form angle of truth finding.

You take bones and other evidence to find truth scientifically. We're both searching for the same thing, just utilizing different mediums. That's another reason why I love you, because you're as passionate about finding truth and bringing it to light as I am."

"That's true. Shane Corp. is a major stepping stone for me. Each day and each case I get a few more responsibilities, they have to make sure I can handle anything."

They sat back and anointed the joint that would be one of their last together for a while. The night was coming fast and they knew they had to eat something.

"Want to go out for dinner for my last night in town, anywhere you want to go, my treat?" Jason inquired with a twinkle in his eyes.

"I think I want to stay in. Mind if we just have some pizzas and hot wings delivered so we can put our energy towards what's in front of us," Christina stated more confidently than at any other point in her life.

"No problem, I'd like that. Plus, what guy wouldn't love to have pizza and hot wings with a beautiful woman that might let him fool around with her."

"You better fool around with me, show me why I'm beautiful and I will show you why I think you're beautiful as well."

With that they ordered a large Hawaiian and a pepperoni and jalapenos with some hot wings, and were left spaced out on their couch wondering what the next day would bring.

After the pizza and wings came, Jason and Christina pretty much ate everything without saying a word. Just an occasional smile and wink to break up the shoveling, letting the other know the person they loved most in the world was sitting next to them. In the end that's all they needed, to love somebody and have that person love them back equally.

They wanted to feel present in each other's lives, which is something that was never questioned. They just needed to prove it on their last night together.

"I say we smoke our brains out, then hop in bed for one more romp. What do you say?" suggested Jason, knowing exactly how cheesy he sounded.

"Sure, that sounds good to me. Just don't give me a Dutch oven okay. I know that pizza had pepperoni and you think farts are so funny, but please don't," bantered Christina knowing the first thing Jason was going to do was fart under the blanket, and hold her under just because she told him not to.

"Don't worry baby, although I've always found farting extremely funny and always will, I'm just not in the mood for that tonight. I would rather just hold you. Honestly, I don't care if we do nothing else but look into each other's eyes all night."

Jason and Christina crawled into bed knowing tomorrow would be tough, but they would get through it. They made it through immense challenges just to get to this point in their lives, and could take on anything they set their minds to. They had been raised to be truth seekers, now they not only had to prove it to the world, but also to themselves. When Christina watches Jason fly away and out of her physical life, she'll know they'll always be connected in their love for each other. One day, it might even lead them back to one another.

The next day was going to be huge. Jason and Christina just had no idea how huge. The trip to New York would change both their lives, but they also knew the change you expect, isn't always the one that decides to show up.

"I love you Jason, sweet dreams."

"I love you too Christina. May your dreams bring you clarity, success, understanding, love and peace; all I want is for you to be happy."

"I'm happy now, and I'm sure I'll be happy at some point tomorrow. Once you're gone though, it's up to me."

Jason and Christina fell asleep easily, while visions of love, truth and airplanes danced in their heads.

CHAPTER TWELVE

If tomorrow leads to the future, what can be done today to ensure we never waste or kill time, but spend it in the most uplifting way possible? Jason knew today was the day that would prove if he could take an opportunity presented to him, and run toward his dream of changing the world.

Countless thoughts were pounding in Jason's head as he rolled out of bed. He looked over at Christina who was still asleep and thought, "how did I get so lucky to be lying next to a beautiful woman that truly loves me, and pushes me towards my dreams?"

As Jason got up and went to the bathroom, he knew it was going to be a long day. He looked in the mirror and stared through himself, asking his soul if he could handle all that was about to transpire. Could he handle the trip there? What about the change, influence and power that emanates from the words he writes?

"You're up early, how did you sleep?" wondered Christina as she blearily strolled in the bathroom, and found Jason staring at himself in the mirror.

"I didn't, too many thoughts were cascading in. I need to splash some water on my face." Jason was exasperated by the marathon his mind was putting him through.

"Don't worry. I have a really good feeling about all this," assured Christina, trying to zap the worry out of Jason's body while she lovingly put her arms around him. "You can do this. I believe in you, and the truths you're trying to bring that we all desperately need."

"Thank you baby, I'm so lucky to have you."

They enjoyed a long deep kiss that bonded their souls, transferring pure love energy back and forth between them. These two people were exactly what the other had been waiting for. Now was the next step of their journeys, would it lead back to each other? Would this be the last time they ever truly embraced?

"I'm going to shower up and then finish packing, I know we have to be at the airport in a few hours and I always like to be there plenty early." Jason was raring to go from the energy transfer he was graced with.

"Sounds good sweetheart, I'm just going to put some things together for you. I want this whole trip to be as stress free as possible," Christina added as passionately as she was beautiful.

"I love you."

"I love you too."

Once Jason was showered and neat and trim for the flight, he walked into the bedroom and noticed Christina scribbling on a piece of paper.

"What're you up to?" Jason questioned with a smile that always made Christina melt.

"I'm finishing up a note I want you to read when you're on the plane, or when you get there; just some positivity to put you in the right head space before you become a Manhattan big shot."

"Thank you, you've always nurtured my wellbeing, what will I do without you?"

"You're going to grow, evolve and become better than you ever imagined."

"That's one of the reasons I love you, I just hope that I've been able to be a little of that for you."

"Are you kidding? If you weren't, do you really think I would have been with you this long?"

Jason smiled and nodded because he experienced feelings everybody on earth could and should have for each other, unconditional love and inspiration to become better.

They finished packing what was left and were ready to run out the door.

"I'll carry these two suitcases down to the car. They have important papers and some personal items in them. What I can't take on my flight, we can drop off at the shipper on the way to the airport," explained Jason, excited to get the show on the road.

"Sounds good sweetie, I'll grab some bags on the way down with you," related Christina, eager to help.

They lugged the suitcases down to the car that would fly out with Jason, and all the boxes they would have to try to cram in the backseat and the trunk.

"Do you think all this crap will fit in here? Do you want to leave some stuff here?" joked Christina, trying to achieve high score in the Tetris game that was before her.

"I'm not saying I won't come back, but this is a whole new life for me. I need to feel like I have everything I need to move forward, and not feel I have to move backward because of something I forgot."

"I understand, this isn't just a long business trip, this is good bye isn't it?" Christina inquired as a tear ran down her cheek.

"Don't cry baby, we talked about this. We can still keep in touch. I must move forward in life with everything I love, believe in and want to do, just like you're doing now with Shane Corp. I'm ready to start climbing up my ladder towards the truth that I feel."

"I know, I'm just scared a little, but it'll be okay."

They finished cramming what they could with care, and noticed it wasn't all going to fit. Christina would have to take the last half carload to the shipper herself.

"Is that all, can we grab anything else?" wondered Jason with all the fright, excitement and downright uneasiness that went along with the major step he was taking.

"I think that's all we can fit, I'll send out the rest tomorrow. Once I drop you off, I just want to chill at home and do nothing serious." Christina was already formulating coping mechanisms for when Jason was gone, even though he hadn't left yet.

"Sounds good, well I'm ready if you are."

"Well I'm not really ready, I don't think any of us are truly ready for the unknown, but we can't let that stop us from moving forward."

"That's true, we must move forward with positive intentions, thoughts and gratitude for what we have so we have faith in the process and let it work."

"Didn't your mom used to say that?"

"What are you talking about, she still does."

Jason walked Christina back to the apartment for one last look to see if they missed anything. He knew they didn't, but felt in the pit of his soul there was something he still needed to do, something unfinished.

"What are we doing, we have everything. If we're going to have enough time to stop by the shipper before your flight, we need to get gone," theorized Christina, wondering why Jason led her back up to the house.

"I just wanted to look around one last time, and do this." Jason grabbed Christina and kissed her long and deep, filling her with pure energy.

"Wow," Christina exclaimed, feeling intoxicated instantly.

"That's all I wanted, we can go now," remarked Jason as he led a wobbly legged Christina back outside and towards the car. They both got in and began the drive towards the airport, and Jason's destiny.

The drive took longer than expected because of a multi car pileup on the freeway. Jason wouldn't miss his flight, but Christina would have to go to the shippers after Jason left.

They parked in short term parking so Christina could walk Jason all the way to the gate. "How much is the parking fee?" queried Jason as he reached for his wallet.

"Don't worry about it, I got this. Why don't you just grab your bags and mentally prepare for the trip," cooed Christina in the thoughtful, beautiful and caring way she so often displayed.

"Thank you beautiful, I love you."

"I love you too."

Christina walked up to the booth to pay, and received a little slip from the agent to affix to the inside of the windshield. She was sauntering back to the car when Jason gave her one of those looks. Christina walked up and he gave her another of the deep kisses that filled them both with pure white light.

Softly floating down from the clouds, Christina barely remembered her own name, let alone to put the tag on the window, but she did.

Jason and Christina moved towards the baggage desk with their bags and wondered if their lives would ever be the same. Would they ever feel as happy and as united as they did at this moment?

Jason handed his bags to the guy at the desk and showed his boarding pass. "Your flight is on time sir, but you'll want to go through security now so you don't have to run to the gate," expressed the nicer than average airline worker.

"Thank you, we will," countered Jason as he and the guy exchanged handshakes that made Jason's energy surge; he knew this was another sign that was propelling him forward.

"That guy was genuine, like he really wanted to help guide us where we needed to go," observed Christina, very happy there were still humans who were nice, and cared about people.

"People come into our lives for certain reasons at certain times. Sometimes they come in for a short period, sometimes long and sometimes the length of time they stay is longer or shorter than we hoped. We have to remember that if we're honest with ourselves, we'll get exactly what we need, and the right people will come into our lives for the right reasons. I think that airport guy was supposed to show us that we don't have to worry. We can feel good because we're not only moving forward, but moving toward something that can be enjoyed much more if we don't rush."

Christina knew that when Jason talked this philosophically, he was acting as a conduit for the positive energy flowing through him. Jason was the type of person that needed to express himself when he felt something, which is why he loved writing. It was a way he could tell people certain things they needed to hear.

They walked hand in hand toward the gate, knowing the smile they felt on each other's faces was not only being projected out into the terminal, but imprinted on their souls.

Jason grabbed Christina by the hips, gave her a hug and tried to show her one more time the love he felt for her every day. "Let's sit down for a minute, that screen up there says that we have time to wait before the flight leaves. Security didn't even take that long, almost like we didn't go through it at all," Jason snickered as he and Christina both knew their entire lives were in front of them.

They sat arm in arm not saying a word, just enjoying being close to each other. Jason and Christina never wanted the moment to end.

"Flight 1879 to New York is now boarding, First class can board now." The loudspeaker boomed through their brains like a message from on high that this was it, whether they were ready for it or not.

"They booked you first class right?" Christina inquired as if she didn't already know because she was holding the ticket.

"Why don't you look in your hand?" Jason lovingly insisted, knowing she wasn't in her right mind because neither was he.

"Oh, so it is," Christina replied. She was trying to delay the inevitable just a few seconds longer.

Jason and Christina hugged and gave each other a kiss that touched the very core of their being. Even though they had to part, they knew they had to help each other grow. This was but part of that process.

"Well this is it."

"Afraid so."

Christina walked Jason to the gate where he would walk up the tunnel, and what she thought was out of her life. "I love you baby, give me a call when you land and let me know that you made it there safely."

"Will do, this is going to be fine. I'm scared, but excited at the same time. This is something we both know I have to do," contended Jason, trying to reassure her.

"I know you do. I love you"

"I love you too."

They hugged one last time, and Jason trotted down the tunnel toward the plane. What the next step was, neither of them knew. All they could hope for was the strength to continue building what was best for them. Their whole lives had been building to this moment, now it was time for Jason and Christina to become the people they always knew they were.

CHAPTER THIRTEEN

Jason arrived at the airport in New York at the same time Christina was having pizza and beer on the couch they both sat on the day her phone rang.

"Hello?"

"Hey Christina, I just got in. How are you?" Jason called his love the moment he landed, just like he promised.

"How was the flight, was it bumpy? The weather didn't look too bad," theorized Christina, knowing this was the last person in the world she needed to make small talk with.

"The flight was good but the food sucked, what else is new," Jason sniped. They both laughed at the low quality of airplane food that never seemed to get better. "I'm walking over to the baggage claim, and I wanted to tell you I love you. I'll be off to the office in a little bit to meet my bosses, but more importantly Marty, who called and started this snow ball rolling."

"I love you too, you'll be fine. Just be yourself and they'll see the beautiful soul that I do. Once they talk to you face to face, they'll see the passion for truth and accountability that will make you the world's most important journalist," Christina enthusiastically orated, trying to build Jason up and send him off on a high note.

"You're too kind. I want to show them what I can do. I want to have Marty's backing when I go after those bastards in power that think they can destroy the world with impunity. There's a new sheriff in town, and that stuff just ain't going to fly around here," Jason declared as he and Christina had a good laugh.

Just then Jason saw his suitcase come down the conveyor belt and he picked it up, "they aren't going to know what hit them." He noticed a gentleman standing fifty feet away holding a sign with his name on it. He also had ears to hear every word Jason was saying, and a smile that showed he agreed. "Hey baby I have to go, it looks like the office sent a car for me. Judging by the guys little hat, it looks like a limo."

"Awesome, I haven't ridden in a limousine since my high school prom. Well you're in with the high rollers now, so you better get used to it. Just do me a favor, don't get corrupted by everything you see. You might be tempted one day to do something you know is wrong but do it anyway because you think you couldn't possibly get caught. Well please Jason, and these will be my parting words for you, don't become who you're trying to stop. Never forget why you went to New York, and what you're trying to accomplish," implied Christina, feeling the energy Jason helped build up over the years.

"I will never become the person I despise. I love you baby, you have been the most important thing in my life, and now I'm taking the next step. I couldn't have done it without your help," expressed Jason, attempting to describe the love and passion emanating from his soul.

"I love you too. You're about to become busier than you've ever been. When you have time, call me, I'd love to hear from you and know how things are going. I want to stay part of your life."

"You will Christina. I don't think I could ever not have you in my life. This isn't good bye, it's see ya later."

Jason hung up the phone and walked toward the funny hat wearing guy holding the sign, who had an expression like there was some place he would much rather be.

"I think you're here for me, how you doing?" Jason inquired of the man who was going to be his ride into the next chapter.

"I'm good, you're Jason?"

"Yes I am."

"What's your name by the way?"

"Bryan with a y," rendered the driver, very proud of his name.

"Huh. My mom was going to name me Bryan with a y because it was different. At the last minute she chose Jason instead," pronounced Jason, feeling connected to something he knew was just getting started.

"Crazy, well it is a small world. I'm here to give you a ride, the boss wants to meet you right away. We can keep your bags at the office and then take them to your place afterwards. Oh yeah, and welcome aboard."

Feeling like he boarded a ship that will take him from the port he's in now, to the port he's supposed to go to, Jason followed Bryan into a stretch limo waiting on the street outside the gate.

"These things have a full bar, probably wouldn't be cool though to show up and meet a new boss smelling like booze," Jason cajoled, trying to lighten his mood.

"Yeah probably not, but don't worry, I don't think your initial meeting will take that long. Afterwards, you can indulge while I take you to your place. I'll show you where the good places to eat and drink are too."

"That would be great thank you. I'm a little nervous, I've never been to New York, let alone been inside one of those big newsrooms."

"Don't worry. If you can produce another story like the water park murder, you'll be more than able to hold your own."

"Thanks for the kind words."

Bryan started the new Lincoln limousine and drove away, well not away from something, more like toward something.

Jason relaxed, and closed his eyes. He needed to assess what's transpired to this point, and what was going to happen in the meeting. Was he ready for this? Could he even live on the east coast, let alone New York City with all its extreme weather? If this was the town that never sleeps, Jason was going to make it the town that never knew what hit it.

They arrived at a high rise that looked like any other, but this one felt different. Was it because this was Jason's first professional reporting job? Or was it something else? Was this the place truth came from? Was this the place that would help him take down everybody and everything that was contributing to the deterioration of mankind? There was only thing Jason knew for sure, that he was called for a reason not fully clear, but one that was guaranteed to slowly reveal itself.

They pulled up to the Democratic Republic's parking garage, and Bryan flashed an ID badge to the guy working the guard shack. After some small talk about the guard's kids and how his wife never stops nagging him, Bryan and the guard shack guy felt at ease.

"Is this the guy they've been talking about, the one who thinks he can change things," chided the guard in the shack. He was trying to look through the darkened glass in the limo at Jason, even though he knew he wouldn't be able to.

"Yeah, they really wanted this one, and spent a pretty penny to get him. I hope he's worth it because I've never heard Marty build up anybody like this," Bryan articulated, looking just enough in the rearview mirror so Jason could see his eyes.

Just as Jason was about to join the verbal volley, the two men who worked together for years waved, and Bryan meandered through the lot to a spot marked especially for the limo.

What was that interaction back there? Was it because he's the new guy and Democratic Republic spent all this money hoping he could prove himself? Did anybody know what was going on?

Jason was exhausted by the thoughts rumbling through his head, but he had to hold out hope that the answers would come in time. Maybe this was the way it was supposed to be. Maybe this is how it is with all new hires.

He knew that whatever happened he had to be himself. He had to stay vigilant as to why he came to New York in the first place. He believed everybody should see each other in themselves because of their humanistic beliefs of accountability. To keep people in all positions of power accountable, he had to keep love and peace emanating through his work. Jason knew whatever story he investigated, or whatever tips he received about shady activities, he'd have to stay strong because this was the big time.

Jason remembered what his dad told him, "If you're going to do something, don't do it half ass. If you are going to take the time and energy to do something, actually do it. If you aren't going to spend the time and energy required to get the job done, why do it in the first place?" This would hold as Jason's mantra as he entered this new phase in his life.

"Well follow me," Bryan prodded, as a personal assistant came and grabbed Jason's bags. "Can you bring these to the waiting room outside Marty's office? We can keep them there until he is done."

Jason and Bryan ambled over to the elevator for the ride into Jason's destiny. "So you're the limo driver, and my personal "show me around" guy?" probed Jason, noticing Bryan's seemingly utility status.

"Yeah, I do whatever the big guy needs. When Marty asks, I do. He's a great man on a mission to do great things for humanity. I think that's why he brought you to New York.

He believes you can help move his ultimate vision forward," Bryan announced with utmost honesty and respect.

"Really, he wants me for all that?" Jason ruminated with surprise but also inner joy that he and this Marty guy might be on the same page. Somebody with influence helping him so he could get things done. "I'll do whatever I can, my mission seems to be the same as Marty's. I want to bring truth to the masses and show them what's really going on. When they see what's been swept under the rug, they'll stand up for each other like never before."

Both men got on the elevator with an immediate respect for one another. Was this what Jason should expect from everybody at Democratic Republic? Or was this just something Bryan was spouting that he was taking out of proportion? Jason knew only time would tell.

When the elevator reached the thirty-ninth floor, the doors opened to a hallway with only one door at the end of it, and it read Marty Jackson across it in gold letters.

"Well this is it man, good luck. Just be yourself, let your true thoughts come out, and you'll be fine," encouraged Bryan with an authentic want for Jason to do well. He knew what could be accomplished if this partnership took off.

"Thank you, I really appreciate that. Thank you for making my introduction into a completely new place a lot less nerve racking. I'll tell the boss you deserve a big raise," Jason bantered. They both laughed knowing they were not only on the same level, but were pretty much the same kind of person. "Take care of yourself man."

"You too and again good luck, even though you won't need it." Bryan, who led Jason through this high rise office, disappeared back onto the elevator, and returned to the ground level.

Jason knew at this moment, he literally needed to take the next step into this office to physically take the next step. He then remembered the note Christina wrote him. He pulled it out of his pocket and started reading, "You are my love, and you are my life. I couldn't truly love you if I didn't want you to succeed, which I completely and utterly do.

If I was a more selfish woman I would keep you all to myself, which I kind of want to do. I must share you with the world however, because you have a really important mission while you're here.

You must do well. You must take it the next step. You must leave this world better than how you found it. If you can get people to think about what's going on around them, and prove there's a lot more they can agree on then they can't, you'll know you served a great purpose on this earth. You'll be able to die a happy man. I love you, and may you continue to grow and evolve into an even better human being than you already are. I don't know if our paths will cross again, but if we stay open to what's really important, they just might. I love you, and this isn't good bye, it's see you later."

Jason folded up the note and put it back in his shirt pocket so it was close to his heart. He knew this wasn't going to be easy, but nothing in life worth doing ever is. He took a few steps, a few deep breaths and opened the door that said Marty.

"Oh come right in. Welcome, Marty has been expecting you."

CHAPTER FOURTEEN

Jason wasn't sure what to expect when he walked into Marty's office. Would it be a welcoming space that said hey, you're a valuable new member of the team, or would it say you're as replaceable as the next fifty people lining up?

Marty's secretary led him into a very ornately decorated office. There were paintings by world famous artists, along with artifacts from historical places that Jason was sure held some sort of philosophical significance, like Marty was trying to make a statement.

"Come in Jason, have a seat," invited Marty in a very welcoming, but busy sounding voice. "There are quite a few things to look at in here. It has taken me a while to amass them all."

"You do have some amazing pieces. I think you're trying to convey a message, because each item is from a different revolutionary period. They must give you strength and motivation," Jason profoundly remarked in a confidently inquisitive voice.

"Nobody has figured that out before. I knew we picked you for a reason, you're perceptive and can pick up on things the average person overlooks."

"That's just my nature," replied Jason, feeling like this was a test of his questioning fortitude.

"That's good you'll work out very well here then."

Marty sat behind his big fancy redwood desk, a position of power he felt he earned through years of toil. Jason was seated in front like a new underling the bosses only see as a means of production.

"Well let's get down to brass tacks. We wanted you here for a specific reason, and the water park story is a big part of it. You uncovered a conspiracy some of this countries most respected journalists didn't because they were either too embedded with certain interests to investigate deep enough, or they were so hard up for a scoop they glossed over what would have led them straight to the truth." Marty was covertly letting Jason know he was special without coming right out and saying it, he didn't want to boost Jason's ego too quickly. Marty wanted him to prove that he wasn't a one hit wonder, but somebody who was in it for the long haul.

"I just did what my heart and gut were telling me to do. Not that I shut off my brain, by no means I'd never do that. To figure something out that doesn't make sense, I drop any preconceived notions I have because they prevent me from seeing what I'm blinding myself from." Jason felt his confidence build and hoped Marty was on the same level.

"If somebody can't at least attempt to be objective in a story, what chance do they have to tell the complete and unadulterated truth the public has a right to know about."

Jason was going to enjoy working for somebody that seemed to "get" how it all worked. Was this going to be the opportunity he had been waiting for? Could he flourish in a place that respected him, and the good work he produced without thinking of him as some little piss ant that shouldn't be taken seriously?

"So, I've only ever worked for a daily and weekly newspaper, never a magazine. How long do we get to produce stories? What are the deadlines so I know how long I have to investigate things? Sometimes it takes longer than intended, but if stuck with, it usually leads somewhere," speculated Jason hoping he didn't sound too pushy.

"We've followed the columns and freelancing you've done. We even looked back at the older stuff you wrote when you were just starting out so we could see the full evolution of your work," Marty explained as he leaned back in his chair. "As far as how your assignments, we're a monthly so you do have more time to construct a story. This gives you the time to look into something as deeply as need be. If a story takes a few months to bear fruit, that's okay as long there's a payoff in the end."

Jason liked the sound of that. He always felt the daily and weekly news reporting he did never gave him enough time to fully figure out why something happened. Not that daily stuff wasn't important because it was, it's just the answers he gained were never satisfying enough. Jason knew the public had the right to know what was going on around them, because when they were informed, the world ran much more smoothly.

He liked the fact he'd be able to go after the big fish he always wanted to yank from the pond. There were a lot of people that needed to be taken down a peg, and he wanted to do his part.

Jason decided to test out his theory, what did he have to lose? He knew Marty liked him already, so why shouldn't he be completely open? Maybe by going what he thought was too far, would be just what they were looking for in an investigation. "I have a few ideas rolling around my head, things I can look more into, or did you have something you wanted me to work on?"

"Well, we usually assign a story if something big is going on. However, if there is something that you know is good, we'll back you. With your first story, I'd like you to choose whatever you want to cover. It's a trial we have for new people. We know that if they pick their own story, produce good material that nobody else can, or writes from an angle nobody else does, than we know they have what it takes." Marty uttered. He spoke with confidence because he'd been through this kind of initial meeting many times before. He wanted to show new people they were valued, and even though they might have done great stuff in the past, it's all about what have you done for me lately."

Jason sat back in his chair, not quite leaning back, but in a much more comfortable stance than he had when he entered the room. "Cool, I like the sound of that. Does this place have a good legal department when things get hairy? I mean I'm prepared to go to jail if need be to protect my sources, just as any journalist worth their salt would be. I just want to know you guys aren't going to flop on me."

Marty wasn't quite as stunned by Jason's question, as he was intrigued that he asked it in the first place. "We have some of the best lawyers in the country on our team, and we fight tooth and nail to protect our reporters. I love the fact you'd even ask me that, you must have a few tricks up your sleeve?"

"Not so much tricks up my sleeve, as much as journalistic fundamentals to take down powerful and influential people that think they're completely above the law and won't ever get caught. I want to show them that we're watching and they will be held accountable.

One of the best quotes I remember from school was in the code of ethics of an organization I can't remember the name of anymore, "be vigilant and courageous in holding those in power accountable." I just want to do good in this world so when I leave it, I'll know I did what I could to make it just a little bit better." Jason was feeling his full energy flow through him. He knew nothing could stop the truth that flowed out of his pen and keyboard except him. He knew if he could get past himself and really open up, the sky was the limit for what he could accomplish.

Marty liked everything he heard. The more he listened to Jason talk about what he believed, the philosophy behind his reporting and the reason he believed truth was the most important public service anybody could provide, he knew Jason would fit right in. "See, this is exactly why I called you and said we needed you right away.

We don't really have any open positions, and yes we're financially hurting just like every print media outlet out there. Regardless, someone like you that's passionate about holding those in power responsible for their actions is something that has been lost in the shuffle. I know they teach that in journalism school, it just seems like nobody is paying attention anymore."

"It's all I know. It's the truth I feel within my soul. The way we help the world and humanity positively evolve and move forward instead of backwards, is by proving in plain language that everybody is the same at their root. What makes us human and binds us together is our accountability to each other. Without that, we're just monkeys running around looking for the next tribe or herd to dominate and decimate," Jason ranted, letting it fly like he was hanging out with his friends back home. Of course it was a deep conversation like this that he and Christina had the first day they met.

Marty rubbed his chin for a second before he spoke, "We need to realize there are always people out there watching. I'm not talking about just the powerful watching the powerless, but also the powerless watching the powerful. If the people at the top thought they couldn't get away with half the crap they do, the world would be a very different place."

Jason and Marty sat back in their chairs so they could marinate in the thoughts that just went back and forth. They both knew what they believed, and what they stood for. Now it seemed the person sitting on the other side of the desk from them did too.

"Okay, well I always like to ask some initial questions to see what our new hires are thinking. It gives me a sense of where their writing is at, and where it's likely to lead." Marty gave Jason a nod, knowing they would produce evolutionary material together. "I think that's enough for today, you're probably tired from your flight and the nervousness about walking into a big and intimidating building for the first time. I'll have Bryan drive you to your new place, that way you can relax for the rest of the day. We can start fresh tomorrow."

"That sounds good, I am a little tired. I must say I'm still kind of in shock. Here I am, never been to New York, and now I'm about to take a limo to my new apartment in

Manhattan so I can get a good night sleep before I go to work in a giant skyscraper," exclaimed Jason with an exasperated, but excited look on his face. "Thank you again for the opportunity. I won't let you down."

"I know you won't, that's why I hired you. I'll show you your office tomorrow as well as around the building so you know where everything is," revealed Marty with a slow growing smile. "I know this is a big change for you, and you aren't fully sure of what to expect. I do promise one thing, that if the passion in the words you write comes out as courageously as when you speak, everything will fall into place. See you tomorrow how's 9am?"

"I like it, not too early," related Jason as he gave Marty a smirk who gave him one right back.

Just then the same driver that picked Jason up from the airport, walked into the room ready to whisk Jason off to the next step of his new life. "Are you ready?" quizzed Bryan.

"As ready as I'll ever be," replied Jason. He was scared, but excited about the next unknown he was about to experience.

"All your bags are already in the car. Let's go."

Jason waved at Marty one last time with an excitement that only came from being fully who he was. Jason followed Bryan down to the parking garage and got into the waiting limo.

"Just to make sure again, this bar is stocked right?" Jason chuckled as he reached for a drink.

"It sure is, and now that your meeting is done enjoy it. The drive to your place can take a while with traffic. This city can be a nightmare. The good stuff is in the little compartment below the ice," Bryan responded, knowing Jason needed libations to calm his nerves.

"Thanks, I've always had a taste for good scotch," revealed Jason as he reached down and grabbed a bottle of eighteen year and poured a nice belt. "This should do it, good end to a good day."

Jason took a sip from the crystal glass and let his mind wander. There was so much to take in, but he knew he was on the right path. He was drinking eighteen year old scotch in a limo, riding to his plush Manhattan apartment after having met with his new boss that seemed to have an immediate respect for his thoughts and skills.

Jason knew it would only get better from here specifically, because he expected the next new thing to be just around the corner.

CHAPTER FIFTEEN

A limo pulled up to a shiny high-rise at about 4pm carrying the world's newest reporter with something to prove. Jason looked out the window and thought about everything in front of him. He had been through adversity before, and had long dealt with self-sabotage, but he knew things were looking up. He knew as long as he stayed positive, and didn't take anything for granted he could use this opportunity to do what he always dreamed of.

As they pulled up, Jason couldn't help but express his excitement. The Jefferson's theme song immediately started playing in his head. "This is still a shock for me. I mean it's one thing getting an out of the blue phone call from Marty offering me all this, but it's a whole other thing to actually experience it."

"Just take a few deep breaths, and take it all in. Don't take any of this for granted, but also don't cling to the material success currently surrounding you. Don't let it work against you, motivating you to gain more material. Never forget what's really important and why you're really here, which is to help the world consciously and positively evolve by holding those in power responsible. You have a great opportunity, don't blow it," Bryan retorted as if he said it before to someone that let him down.

"Thank you, it's important to hear that from somebody who has gone through this with other people. It puts me at ease." Jason felt good about the start of his first day in a new place. "It's because of people like you that I'll succeed."

Bryan gave Jason a wink in the rear view mirror, before exiting to get Jason's bags out of the trunk.

The building was pretty big, not as tall as the office building which was Jason's new work home, but definitely bigger and taller than anything he lived in before. "What floor am I on?" Jason queried very intently, apprehensive about walking up a million flights of stairs.

"You're on the 25th floor. Don't worry though, this place has the best working elevators in the state," relayed Bryan after seeing the exasperation on Jason's face.

"That's good, because I don't want to carry all my crap up a ton of stairs. I always tried to live on the first floor, because the thought of moving my stuff up a flight of stairs, let alone 25 doesn't sound appealing," Jason shot back as a small amount of relief washed over his face. "When my girlfriend ships out my stuff, do I meet the guy down here? I've never lived in such a big place before, I have no idea how it works."

"No, we'll have somebody sign for it," answered Bryan with a sense of confidence. "We'll call when it arrives, set a time that's best for you, and bring it up."

"That sounds perfect," Jason emphasized with a growing sense of ease in his new surroundings. "You guys really have thought of everything."

"Well not everything. Marty believes you can think of things we haven't, or he wouldn't have been so adamant about bringing you here and offering you all this." Bryan helped Jason load his bags onto the elevator. "We can take this up to your place, I'll show you there."

Bryan was feeling less like a driver, and more like somebody that would be integral to Jason's success down the road. He hit the button for the 25th floor after they sauntered over to the elevator.

The ride was silent, which was weird considering how talkative Bryan and Jason were since their initial trip from the airport. Jason felt something great around the bend. He knew he'd get there because he finally allowed himself to be open enough to receive it.

The elevator door opened to a hallway that went on and on and on, but had only two doors. "Why are there only two doors on this floor?" Jason noticed with a real want to know.

"It's because there are only two residences on each floor. Here we are, apt 25b," Bryan responded sarcastically as they walked up to the door.

Jason started feeling nervous, similar to when he was younger and was afraid of moving forward with his life. He was very comfortable with the way things were. He tried to accomplish things, but he tried just hard enough to make it look like he was moving forward, without actually taking the proverbial next step to make it happen. He knew he couldn't let that happen again.

"Ahhh, here we are," proclaimed Bryan as he grabbed a key from his pocket and stuck it in the doorknob. "I hope you enjoy. This place is furnished, and we made sure the fridge and cupboards were stocked so you didn't have to go to the grocery store right away. Also, we left the best and most extensive take out catalog in the city. Any kind of food from anywhere around the globe, you can order with the touch of a button."

"That sounds great, thank you," expressed Jason thinking about all the great food possibilities he had to try while in one of the biggest cities in the world.

"Also, here is a company credit card for living expenses. As long it doesn't get out of control, you can use it for whatever you want as long as you want. We also left some financial information in case you were thinking about investments." Bryan turned the knob and opened the door into Jason's new world.

"Wow, this place is unreal," exclaimed Jason, amazed he'd come far enough to deserve a place like this. "When I was coming up, I never dreamed I'd be in a place like this, and now, here I am."

"Yes, here you are, and welcome. I'll be by in the morning to pick you up. I'll serve as your driver, personal assistant and adviser. If you need anything, someone to bounce ideas off of, or just someone to have a beer with, I'm your guy," Bryan pointed out, very confident he was talking to the world's next big thing.

"It makes me feel way more comfortable to know somebody has my back."

"No prob, that's just what I do and who I am. I'll see you in the morning."

"Ok, sounds good."

Jason and Bryan shared the same hearty handshake that all people did when they start an adventure leading to somewhere great.

Bryan left while Jason walked in the door, instantly wanting to put up his feet and get comfortable. He tossed his shoes and socks in the corner so he could feel the carpet between his toes, and make fists with his feet. He hadn't lived in a place with real carpet since he was young and living with his dad. He always had the crappy short carpet that belonged in an office. Now he had the real stuff that could actually be vacuumed, even though along with everything else they provided him, he was sure there was probably a maid that did that too.

Jason's beautiful apartment featured two large bedrooms, a beautiful kitchen with an island, and an energy that begged to be cooked in. The living room featured leather couches and recliners, Jason's favorite. The décor was modern but not overly so. It was decorated, but Jason knew that when his things arrived, he could put his own flavor on it.

He sat on the couch and pulled out the take out catalog and noticed Bryan was right, it was very extensive and featured every ethnic food from around the world. Wanting to try everything while he was there but not wanting to rush experimentation, Jason decided to go with something he knew and so he gravitated towards the Cuban section.

Jason picked out a restaurant, called them up and ordered some pork sandwiches and some sides that would make the meal special. There would be enough food that he wouldn't have to leave his place the rest of the night.

After the order was made and the food was on its way, he hung up the phone and stared off into space, which happened to be the big window that looked out on the city. He walked closer for a better look, and noticed a small balcony, so he decided to check it out.

It was a nice spot with a table and a couple of chairs, along with an overhang that was perfect for chilling under when it was raining. Jason felt like he would make it, and this would be his start. Of course he also knew life was a journey, and not a destination. He was living the meaning of "there is no there, there."

He sat down at the kitchen table and pulled his phone from his pocket, causing a bit of paper to fall out. Jason picked it up and noticed there was writing on it. "To Jason, welcome to New York, may this help ease your transition a bit." Jason looked down and saw two little joints.

This could have been Marty, but Bryan must have been the one that slipped this into his pocket, what a nice guy he thought. He lit up one of the joints and decided to call Christina and tell her everything that happened so far.

He dialed Christina and it rang a few times before she picked up. "Hello."

"Hey baby this is Jason. I made it and am chilling at my new place right now."

"That's great. So how is it, is it everything you thought it would be?" Christina inquired with a very strong want to know the details of everything.

Jason told her about Bryan picking him up and quizzing him on what he thought about being there. He spoke of the garage guy at the office and Bryan chatting back and forth about him, like he was the talk of the town. He told her about Marty, and how receptive and supportive he seemed to be to all of his ideas. He told her about the ride back and how Bryan helped him to his place and just happened to have a name his mom almost gave him, not to mention being someone he knew he could count on.

"Now I'm chilling on the balcony of my beautiful and amazingly huge place that is 25 stories up, looking at a great view of the city waiting for some Cuban food to get delivered while smoking a joint," blurted Jason feeling like he was talking a million miles a minute.

"Wow, that sounds awesome," Christina fired back feeling happy for Jason, but at the same time feeling the more excited and happier he was to be there, the less likely she was to see him again. "It sounds like everything you've ever dreamed of."

"It kind of is, they're completely supportive of my fight to hold those in power responsible and accountable," related Jason eager to tell her everything, but also wondering what was going to happen next. "Marty said they have a great legal department, and would totally have my back in case something crazy went down."

Jason and Christina talked for a while longer about the weather and the latest stupid thing the Senate did. They both knew this was leading to something great, even though it might keep them away from each other.

"I have to go the doorbell just rang, I think my food is here. I'll call you tomorrow. I start at nine so I'll call you when I get home."

"Sounds good to me, have a wonderful night sweetheart I love you. Just remember, I've always loved you and will always love you. You're the greatest man I've ever met, and I wish you all the success and happiness in the world," remarked Christina like she was saying her last words.

"Why are you talking like that, I'll talk to you tomorrow. I will keep in touch no matter how busy or crazy it gets here. I could never forget the most beautiful woman in the world," acknowledged Jason in the most reassuring voice he could find.

"Okay sweetheart. Have a wonderful night and we'll talk soon."

"That's right, soon, as in tomorrow," Jason reiterated with a worried smile in his voice.

"Sounds good to me, good night."

"Good night."

They each hung up the phone with a feeling of love and warmth towards each other, not knowing that this was the last time they would speak for a very long time. They say long distance is hard, but becomes even harder when two passions are pointed in opposite directions, even if they're headed to the same place.

Jason walked up to the door and recieved his food from the delivery guy. "Here is the money and an extra twenty for you."

He walked over to the couch, set the food down on the coffee table and began to contemplate. Was this what the next few years of his life were going to be like? Would he be able to move forward with what he saw as important? Would he be able to hold onto his principles?

Not knowing the answer to everything, Jason dug into the delicious food in front of him. He knew there was no way he could figure it all out right away, but an amazing pork sandwich was a great place to start.

CHAPTER SIXTEEN

If breath taking views and delicious pork sandwiches were any indication of what New York was going to be like, Jason knew he could make it. Deep down, he knew this was only the beginning, the start to something big. Whether it turned out good was up to him and his evolutionary ideas.

Jason rolled out of bed and walked into the bathroom. He threw some water on his face while looking in the mirror. Was this where his life was leading, being some big shot reporter living in New York? Was he going to uncover something major?

How was Christina and how was her work going? Would she get to investigate something big? Jason and Christina were destined for great things. They and everybody around them just didn't know what they were yet.

Jason hopped in the shower, which wasn't a normal shower. It was normal in so much as the water flow could be adjusted and would rinse you off once soaped up, but this one was different. The water cascaded out of a nozzle that shot down straight down on top of his head, instead of in front of his face. Jason had seen these fancy showers on TV infomercials before, but never used one, let alone every morning before work.

He worked in Manhattan and lived in Manhattan, a place he thought he'd never be. He was about to start his big job in the big city uncovering conspiracies. He could feel in his bones that he was going to take down somebody big and influential. Who would be the first person in Jason's cross hairs?

He didn't know where this life was leading, but Jason knew he was going to write about it. He worried that when he started investigating somebody, and they caught on that he was following them and/or trying to trip them up, they'd come down hard and be ruthless in their actions. Marty said the Democratic Republic had good lawyers that would fight tooth and nail to protect their reporters, but what about the inherent danger that comes from trying to unseat somebody from their comfortable seat of power?

A million possibilities were swirling around Jason's melon as he stepped out of the shower, and proceeded to dry off and get dressed for his big day. He wasn't sure if he had to wear a suit or just a button down shirt or what. Marty didn't mention anything about a dress code yesterday, so he thought why not just go casual and see what happens. Marty seemed like the kind of guy that didn't care what his reporters dressed like, as long as they produced.

Jason threw on his most comfortable jeans, and one of his many t-shirts that featured a clever saying. This wasn't to impress people in the office. Jason could care less about that. This was about being who he truly was and seeing if anybody picked up on it.

Jason walked into his living room and opened the mini-fridge when the phone rang. "Hello."

"Hello Jason, good morning. How was your first night in the new place?" Bryan inquired without a robotic I don't really care attitude because he actually wanted to know.

"It went great, just a little scary, being in a new place and city and all. It was very comfortable though, I ordered some take out from that menu thing you were talking about," Jason replied, wondering if Bryan was actually trying to build him up, or if Marty was trying to institute control by giving him things and then taking them all away? Did the Democratic Republic want Jason for his skills? Did they want to give him free reign in his writing because they saw his passion for evening the score with the top dogs?

"What restaurant did you get from?" wondered Bryan curiously.

"I got some pork sandwiches from a Cuban place. They were awesome. I love Cuban food. Heck, I've never had half the stuff in that book so I went with something I knew."

"Sounds like you're starting to settle in. Better material is produced when people feel comfortable. Marty really knows his stuff. If he thinks you're worth the trouble, he must see the makings of the best within you."

"The best is yet to come. I get invited to work at my dream job and am set up like I never imagined, how could I not work my ass off? It was basically an offer I couldn't refuse, except instead of a gun at my head, Marty held a bunch of money, a big office, and this amazing place," Jason sniped with a slight chuckle. He sincerely wanted to know where Bryan was leading him. Were they going to ask him to sell his soul or something?

"Well, we have to get to the office. I'll be there shortly, I'll ring when I'm downstairs," stated Bryan like he had to keep a tight schedule. This might just be a test to see what Jason was all about. It was hard to say who was being tested. Maybe Marty was testing himself, trying to see how truly good he could be when he had massive power and influence at his disposal.

When Bryan arrived, Jason made his way down the elevator to the familiar black limo waiting in the garage. Was this what it was going to be like every day? Get some food that's paid for by somebody else, and stay in an apartment that was paid for by somebody else after being transported to and from work in a limo paid for by somebody else? Was this his life now?

"So I get a limo ride every day?" Jason queried with a curious grin as to why the rollout. "Am I this special? I feel like this kind of thing is reserved for the big wigs."

"Marty wanted it this way," Bryan explained as honestly as he could. "He thinks if he gives you the experience of having everything, it will motivate you to take down those who deserve to be taken down, because you'll know how they live, act, and what they do in their free time. That way, you'll be there to catch them when there schemes implode and they fall on their asses. Or should I say when you trip them up."

"I didn't think of that, but it totally makes sense," responded Jason as he thought more about everything that happened since he arrived in New York. "So basically, I have to know my enemy before I attack? Didn't Lao Tzu, or Sun Tzu, or whoever wrote "The Art of War" say that?"

"That's right, it was Sun Tzu. He said that you have to truly know your enemy and everything about them, so you can learn what their weak spots are. This isn't a conventional war, more of an ideological one, but the art of war still applies. The irony is that while an ideological war is taking place, if money changers catch wind that you're after them and actually have a chance to stop them, they will use real war tactics to stop you."

"The S.E.E.R. program trained soldiers in torture by putting them through all the methods they'd endure if they got captured. Marty wants to make sure that I'm ready, and won't crack. I will not crack."

"Good, then you'll succeed."

Jason jumped in the back of the limo and got comfortable, while Bryan got in the front and warmed up the engine. "The only part I can't figure out, is why the limo, and why pick me up every day? Why not ride the bus? or subway, or drive for that matter?" Jason theorized.

"We wanted to make sure you can get to work. The subways can get confusing making it very easy to get off at the wrong stop. The buses are okay, but they stop at every little place and go through some pretty rough neighborhoods. It's not that public transportation is inherently bad. It's just that everything can be much better than it is now.

As far as driving, have you seen the traffic in this city? It would take you three hours to get to work, and you'd definitely get lost. Most importantly, we drive you because we want to keep you safe. When you start in on these people, they will discover you, they always do. They will make an effort to come after you. They could harm you. All of this is meant to watch your back, because if it's going to get to that point one day, then why not start like that from the beginning?"

"That's true the powerful don't want their power taken away by the powerless. Can I request that I be picked up in a different car though? I just don't know if I feel comfortable in a limo, at least at this point in my career. Any other nice car will do, just not a limo," Jason remarked, starting to feel confident enough to stand up for what he believed. This skill would serve him well in not only his reporting and news career, but throughout his life in general.

The ride to the office took less than twenty minutes as there wasn't much traffic. The streets were reminiscent of any big city, skyscrapers, people walking, homeless begging on the street and big trucks honking and blasting black smoke out of their tailpipes. As Jason looked around, he knew this is exactly why he never moved to a city. He wasn't a city person.

He came because of the offer. How could anybody refuse? He had to believe he arrived because of the important work he needed to do. If he couldn't produce the high quality material they pulled him all the way across the country to produce, all of it would disappear. He'd go back to a small Podunk paper in a small Podunk town and hope someday he got another big break.

Bryan pulled the limo into the garage as leisurely as Jason was anxious about his day, his sweaty hands were an indication he almost couldn't handle it, but he did. He had to. He was in New York to be positive in the face of negativity, and to take down the powerful while apparently living it up in luxury. Jason knew he had to be careful about that last part. He never wanted to be super rich. He just wanted everything taken care of so he didn't have the everyday worry of paying bills. He knew that when you hit a certain income level, a whole new set of problems introduced themselves. Jason didn't want to struggle financially anymore.

Bryan pulled into the same spot they pulled into yesterday, and exited the car. "Well here we are. I'm not going up with you this time I have a few things to take care of. Go up to Marty's office and speak with him, he wanted to see you first thing," Bryan exclaimed with a bit of excitement because of all the possibilities transpiring. "Here is my card, call me if you need anything."

"Thanks man, I appreciate everything you've done so far. You've definitely made my transition to this new life much easier. Thank you," Jason remarked in a sincere voice that made Bryan believe there were a few good people left in the world. Jason rode the elevator up to the 39th floor, and found the door that said Marty on it.

Before he walked up, Jason pulled the note from Christina out of his pocket and read it again. He knew yesterday was just the introduction, this was the start of the real thing and he needed to read Christina's beautiful words one more time before he entered his new world.

As soon as he was filled up with as much good energy as the note could fill him up with, he knocked on the door. "Come in, Marty is waiting," stated the secretary that was a nice person, but not nice to look at. If bosses screwing their secretaries were a problem, it wasn't even a question for Marty. Jason suspected his wife picked her out so he wouldn't be tempted.

"Thank you," answered Jason as he proceeded to walk in to Marty's office.

"Good, you're here. I'm glad all the stuff we provided didn't freak you out, causing you to hop on the first flight home," Marty sniped, testing to see how Jason reacted. "I'm glad you stayed, we have a lot of work to do."

"That's good, because I'm rested, well fed, and ready to take down some power-hungry crazies. What do you have for me?"

CHAPTER SEVENTEEN

If Jason was ever interested in taking down people who either beat the system, or built the system so they could beat it, then now was the time. Was he ready to act instead of endlessly dreaming? Could he take the step that would advance him toward what he wanted to accomplish big picture?

"You ever heard of the people in Congress that do insider trading?" inquired Marty, testing the waters for the story he was going to pitch.

"Yeah I've heard of them, it's pretty much called all of Congress. Let's not forget the Senate too, judges, lawyers, everyone in Washington seems to work by their own set of rules," Jason fired back as he felt his energy rise.

"That's for sure, they all do stuff that would send me or you to jail in a heartbeat. If the person with all the gold writes down the rules, then the person who makes the gold available, is the one who creates the rules," expounded Marty, feeling like he was standing on one of his soapboxes.

"What's your point?" demanded Jason, very eager to see what Marty was building to.

"I got wind of a new scam that Congress-people are pulling. They take disseminated information and make as much money as they can off of it."

"That doesn't sound new to me, they do that all the time, probably every day of the week."

"Right, but the difference this time is what they're doing with the information."

"Okay, so what are they doing with it?"

"They're taking it and making a lot of money off of it of course. Then when no more can be squeezed out without people catching wind, they start shell companies. Well not shell companies in the usual sense of being a front for the CIA or something. No, they are just a means of creating information. That way, they receive inside information on a guaranteed and regular basis, cranking it out like their own personal ATM."

Jason sat there for a minute, trying to absorb it all before he spoke. "That's crazy, but not totally unexpected, greed knows no boundaries. Is this something they all do? Is there evidence leading towards one individual we could go after because you figured out their weak spot?"

"This is just stuff I've noticed for a while. After the market crash and all the crazy radicals made their way into the capitol, the gloves are off."

"What do you mean the gloves are off?"

"I mean the rule book was thrown out the window, and new plans are being explored." Jason took a deep breath as Marty continued. "I've hit up some of my best sources, and as expected this is something that's always happened, except now corrupt politicians want to do things out in the open because their egos have grown so big.

To do it on the grand scale they want, they have to expand their reach, but with everybody having a camera in their pocket and the internet being everywhere, they had to rephrase it. Instead of insider information, they call it doing their homework. Instead of stealing information, they're gaining ground on their enemy that wants the entire system to fall.

Instead of committing financial crimes that should land anybody in federal prison for many years, they say they're only being smart about where the world is going and don't want the money to fall in the wrong hands."

"So it's a classic example of double speak, them saying one thing but doing another." Jason looked up at Marty and saw that he was nodding in agreement. "They really are making this world a little more like 1984 everyday huh?"

"It certainly seems like it," expressed Marty with fright about where the world was heading, but excitement because the intelligent, and passionate young man sitting across from him was getting what he was throwing down.

"I'll ask again, what do you want me to do with this?"

"I want to see what you can dig up. Now is the time to test your journalistic skills and see what you can discover. I know you're new to the city, and it can take a while to build up trustworthy contacts, but I want to see what you can do. That water park story was one thing, but we're talking about corruption on a global scale that will bleed this planet dry."

"I'm up for that, its sounds like quite the challenge. I've been waiting my whole life for an opportunity like this to take somebody down that deserved it Thank you I will not let you down."

"I know you won't, because that's the kind of person you are. Just keep me updated on what you find and when you have material to print. We'll give you as much time as you need, but we want to make sure this isn't going on forever without a payoff. Just keep me in the loop."

"I will Marty, thanks. Thank you for everything, the limo from the airport, the place to live which is amazing and better than I ever imagined. This job is what I've dreamed of since I was little, so again, thank you."

"Okay let's end this emotional outbreak before we both grow lady parts," Marty quipped causing them both to have a big laugh. Jason was glad Marty had the same sense of humor as him, and vice versa. "Before I send you off to the races, I have to show you to your office. I would say new office, but I don't know if you've had one before."

Not wanting to sound too excited, but wanting to express gratitude in as professional and clear a way as he could, Jason spoke, "I've never had a real office, but I always work better and more productively when I have a space dedicated to finding truth. That's what it comes down to for me, finding what people in power don't want you to know, and then telling the masses so they can tell everybody they know.

It keeps spreading and spreading until the powerful who thought they could always get off scott-free, can't find anywhere to hide. They cower in the corner knowing they can't pull one over on the people anymore."

"That's exactly it and once again reaffirms my hiring you. I want people with intelligent minds to go into easily understandable detail when they're articulating the problem. There are billions of people in the world that need to know. We must make it so that everyone from your liberal commie uncle, to your conservative aunt who worships Ayn Rand understands. Basically, something that breaks down walls and is for the benefit of everybody."

"I'm so down for that, show me to my workspace and I'll get started."

"We could go back and forth about this all day, but there is plenty of time for that later. Your office is this way, follow me."

Jason and Marty got on the elevator and hit the down button. When they got off, they walked down a long hallway with doors on either side that opened up to various break rooms, copy/fax rooms and office supply areas. The Democratic Republic was all business, but there was something about it that exuded energy, built for people to produce as much truth as possible.

"Here is your new office. I even had your name put on the door to make it more official," bantered Marty, pointing to the name tag inserted on the door. "If you stay here long enough, we might even paint it on."

Jason got the joke and they both chuckled, but just a little because it included a lot of truth. "Don't worry, I plan on staying as long as I have to, until I feel it's the right time to move on."

"That's what I hoped you would say. Go on in and get comfortable, it will be your home away from home. If you need anything, I'm only a phone call away. You can come and go as you please as long as you produce results. This stuff can be taken away just as fast as it was given. This isn't my first rodeo."

"I completely understand, I'll talk to you soon."

Marty wore a smile that said "show me what you're made of kid" while he walked down the hall for the elevator ride back up to his office. Jason stood there for a minute and tried to take it all in. When he was younger and did sports reporting and column work, he wondered if he'd ever be influential. He also spent a lot of time lonely and wondering if a woman would ever love him, then along came Christina. Life is funny sometimes in that it provides you with what you need when you need it, even if you don't know it.

Instead of standing in the hallway all day, Jason decided to turn the knob, walk into his office and into his destiny.

CHAPTER EIGHTEEN

Jason walked into the wonderland that would be his life for the next chunk of time and wondered if he could handle it. Would he feel the support of Christina who always stood by him when he was unable to journey forward with his dreams? Would he feel the love from his mom who always set him on a course to succeed the best she could, always making sure he could bounce ideas off her and talk to her about anything?

Almost as if he was scared to cross the threshold, he paused for a minute. They say your whole life flashes in front of your eyes the moment before you die. Jason was experiencing this sensation because he was taking concrete steps towards what he knew in his heart and soul he always wanted.

Was this real? Was he dreaming? Would he wake up in a pool of sweat next to Christina and wonder why he was given such a message? Jason knew his whole life had been building to this moment and he had to take advantage of the opportunity. The whole world was at his fingertips now, he had to move.

Jason walked around his office and was simply amazed. There was beautiful, real carpeting on the floor, not the usual ugly office stuff. Original paintings tastefully adorned the walls, which he knew could be replaced if he was going to call this place home for a while.

Jason walked toward a beautiful old oak desk with a shine he could see himself in. Behind it sat a chair fit for a king, and leather bound too. He sat and looked over the office, scanning his surroundings. He moved the laptop sitting on his desk to the side so he could observe everything. He proceeded to spin around in his chair like he would have when he was a little kid, but immediately stopped when he looked out the window.

Jason had a beautiful view of the city from behind his desk where he could see almost the entire skyline. He knew the 29th floor was high up, even though there were buildings in this city that seemed like they had 129 floors. Jason knew he made it, he arrived inside his dream. Now he had to make this chance at greatness that was thrust upon him worthwhile.

He started opening the drawers in the desk and found regular office supplies, ink cartridges for the printer, stapler, paper clips, pens, paper etc... One of the drawers had a phone in it, and chargers for every possible device. There was also a booklet for restaurants in town, which was the same that was in his apartment.

Jason felt like it was almost lunchtime, but he really didn't care if it wasn't. If he was going to take on the powerful that didn't like to be challenged, he knew he couldn't do it on an empty stomach. He pulled out the company credit card and flipped through the restaurant book. There was the Cuban place and many Mexican and Puerto Rican places, but Jason wanted to try something different. Not crazy different, just something he never had in the city.

There was food from any country he could think of, many of which he had to try at some point. Ethiopian, Afghani, Iraqi, Russian, German, the choices were endless. He knew he would have to spend a few weekends with some of the good stuff Bryan gave him and just have a munchies fest.

What was tickling Jason's palette today was something from a famous Jewish deli. He was always a sucker for a Rueben, and wanted to see how good they made them in the Big Apple.

He called up the Carnegie deli because it caught his eye. He had been to one in a Vegas casino years ago and figured they knew how to serve it up right. He ordered the biggest Reuben they had, along with some matzo ball soup for later. Jason knew it would never be as good as his mom's, but it would have to do for now.

Jason had a nice fridge, microwave, oven and stove with a sink on the side. He never saw an office with a kitchen and couches in the corners, almost like Marty knew he'd be spending long hours in there and wanted him to be comfortable. Jason felt that with all this, how could he not be?

The food came twenty minutes later steaming hot and smelling amazing. "How much do I owe you?" Jason stammered with his mouth watering at the thought of sinking his teeth into the deliciousness.

"That will be 15 bucks," replied the delivery man that wasn't interested in where he was or who Jason was, he had been in an office like this a thousand times. It was all in a day's work.

"Cool, do you take visa? Can I put the tip on there?" Jason wanted the delivery guy to know he understood what it was like working for tips as he had done so many years ago.

"I do and yes," cheerily answered the delivery guy, knowing he would be compensated. He pulled a phone from his pocket with a card reader attached to the top. Jason gave the guy his card which he proceeded to slide in what looked like any card reader you'd find at a store. The driver also had something attached to his belt which was beeping. All of a sudden the thing lit up and started making noise. Jason was amazed at what was happening before him.

"Wow, so you slide my credit card on your phone and print me a receipt from your belt, crazy the technology that's around now. I remember delivering pizza way back and we never had anything close to that," Jason exclaimed, amazed by what he was seeing.

"Yeah, I've been doing this for a while but we only got these new units a year ago. It's a trip, but it does make things a lot easier and much more mobile. It seems the whole world has gotten in to some big damn hurry, like they want everything yesterday. I must say, at least its job security," the delivery man bellowed with passion, yet apprehension about what the world had become and where he thought it was leading.

"It's the instant gratification culture we live in. People aren't satisfied with what they have and always want more. It's what I've spent my whole writing career trying to address. I'd love to show the world's population that if they're thankful for what they have instead of upset about what they don't, they will be happier throughout the day. They will have the motivation to sustain them so they can achieve what they never thought possible." Jason felt his energy pouring out, hoping he wasn't boring the poor delivery guy too much.

"I couldn't agree with you more, and couldn't have said it better myself," the delivery guy shot back with an authentic smile on his face, compared with the halfcocked "oh do I really have to smile" smile he walked in with.

After the receipt came out, Jason signed it, gave the guy a twenty dollar tip and handed it back.

"Thanks man, I appreciate it. Good luck with your whole trying to fix people thing. There are a lot of sick people that need to get their priorities straight, whether you're talking about Joe Shmoe walking down the street, Senators, Congressman, Governors or Presidents, we could all benefit. People need to realize politicians don't fall out of the sky. We're the ones that create them and their bad thoughts, which only get worse as they reach high office because they are us. So thank you, and good luck with your work. The world could surely use more people like you."

"Thank you, I appreciate the compliment, and I'm ready to go to work. The world needs saving, and I'd like to do my part while I'm here. Thank you again and take care."

"Take care as well, and remember, when we take care of ourselves, we do it so we can take care of the world, not in spite of it. See ya."

"See ya."

The delivery guy strolled out the door, as Jason clutched the Rueben and soup and returned to his desk. What a great random conversation he thought. It seemed like it was happening more and more since he arrived in the city. The more he opened up to all of life's possibilities, and let them happen instead of making them happen, the more easily they flowed through him. If this was any sign of the future, Jason liked what he was seeing.

He sat down at his desk, put the soup in the fridge for later, and took a big bite of the Reuben, causing Swiss cheese to ooze out the sides. Mmmmmmmm he thought, this was quite possibly the best Reuben he ever tasted, and he has had quite a few, as many as anybody who really loved corn beef brisket would expect.

He looked out the window of his shiny new office and contemplated where he came from. He started writing for a newspaper while he was still in high school, cranking out stories late at night to be turned in the next day before class. Hunched over his dad's computer while the internet was still wearing diapers was when Jason first got published.

Then there were the columns for the paper after he got his diploma, and was living near his mom. Crammed into her little studio apartment, Jason would beat himself up over what to write, how he would say it and how he could possibly have something to say the world would listen to.

Then Jason went to college, and everything changed. He wrote for the school paper and the school magazine. He discovered his love for writing that would really take off, once he put his full effort forward.

After he graduated he was lost for a bit. He found a job at a local paper, met Christina, and then did a story about a water park and a murder that happened. Which Jason only witnessed, because he was riding down the same water slide where the murder happened. Now, he was sitting in his fancy office, looking down at a view of the city, eating a

Rueben ordered off the company credit card and wondering where all the time went. More importantly, where was it all leading?

While Jason finished his sandwich, he recalled all the bad pay for crappy stories, and the struggle to get respected in the business had led him to this moment now. Would he take advantage of it, or would he let it fall by the wayside?

A grin broke out on Jason's face because he knew he was the leader of his own destiny, he was the only one that could make choices for himself. He was the one that decided where his life went and what he spent his time on, nobody else.

He got up from his desk, poured himself a scotch out of his office mini-bar that was stocked with only the good stuff, and walked back to the window.

As he took a sip, Jason knew this was it. He would grow from here, this place, now. He looked out at the city and ideas of where to investigate insider trading started flowing.

Jason knew he was getting a chance to leave his mark, to make the world just a little bit better.

CHAPTER NINETEEN

When people get away with something for long periods of time, they feel confident in their life choices and the positives they appear to bring. Jason knew this fight wouldn't be easy, but it was something he had to do.

With the scotch gone and his ideas flowing, Jason decided he better get to it. He knew Congressmen and Senators made billions off insider trading because for them, it technically wasn't illegal. They also weren't going to like somebody snooping around their cover ups.

Jason grabbed the laptop and set it on the desk in front of him. This technological marvel had been given to him by Marty with all the bells and whistles, the fast processor, tons of memory, but most importantly, the ability to ghost itself so it couldn't be traced. Jason knew being anonymous was vital once he started digging. The necessary research he was never able to do before, was now possible.

He opened the laptop and turned it on. While it warmed up, Jason began to envision what was he was embarking on. He was about to investigate the richest and most powerful people in the world, how would he handle it? Jason still felt a hole where Christina used to be, he felt she was gone and it pained him. He began to think love might not find him again, forcing him to endure many unsatisfying dates and one night stands he knew would be as unsatisfying as they led on to be.

In the past, Jason would go after things he knew would make him unhappy in the long run, because they made him feel happy in the short run. Now was the time for change in that dynamic, which consisted of healthier choices in each area of life.

All these thoughts were rushing through Jason's head while he was thinking of which direction to search. Who should he go after, Congressman, Senators, Judges, the President himself? The people that most deserved to be brought down he figured was a good place to start.

Jason knew many insider traders love to take advantage of cheap labor, so he started researching what Senators and Congressman had the loudest anti-immigrant voices. He knew people that spoke the most passionately against it, were usually the people participating in its subterfuge. Similar to the way a closet homosexual espouses hate for gay people, because they can't accept themselves for being gay. Anti-immigrant folk lash out so they don't have to deal, which is much easier than looking inward for answers.

Jason started poking around and wasn't surprised by what popped up. He found the usual amount of politicians speaking about supposed illegal aliens invading the country to steal American jobs.

It appeared some senators were gathering to speak against immigration in the city later that day. A coalition Tea Party, Conservative, Radical, anti-immigrant rally was being held to promote mass deportations. How they were going to round up twelve million people and then take them all home, Jason had no clue.

Jason knew this way of thinking was based on not actually thinking at all. The politicians spewing this bile counted on people not thinking, because the second a critical thought came in, everything fell apart.

Jason needed help and a ride to the rally, so he phoned Bryan because he knew he could bounce ideas off him. "Hey Bryan, what's up man, how you doing today?"

"I'm pretty good man, just been working hard, you know the tune," Bryan chuckled because he was used to punching a clock. "How are you doing?

"I was just sitting in my office having a drink, thinking about where to go with this story idea Marty gave me, and figured you could help," explained Jason, hoping Bryan would provide fresh insight. "Marty told me about Congressman and Senators and the insider trading they get away with because there's no direct law against it."

"There definitely should be a law against it. If you or I even thought of doing half the stuff they do, we'd end up in real prison, not the club fed they'd go to for six months."

"That's true, that's why they must be stopped. I'd like to see a few of them go to real jail, and for the first time in their lives pay for the crimes they committed."

Jason knew he and Bryan were on the same page. He thought it was great Marty provided him a driver that was his assistant, advisor and just about everything else.

Jason wondered though if it wasn't real, and if Bryan was planted there to spy on him. He feared the actions this line of thinking might produce, but he always had it in the back of his mind. He knew the powers that be were ruthless, and if they did hurt you it would be from the place you least expected, the people close to you.

"Swing by my office when you get a sec. I want to tell you my ideas, including where I want to go tonight," stated Jason with hopeful excitement. While it was true he was suspicious about Bryan and his motives, he also knew he had a history of sabotaging things meant for his benefit.

Jason poured himself another drink because he wasn't driving. Not that he was getting drunk, but Jason knew a little liquid courage would be helpful before he walked into the belly of the beast with somebody he didn't know watching his back.

Twenty minutes later, Bryan sauntered in. "What's up man, I was just about to go home, it's almost four in the afternoon," Bryan commented like he didn't want to talk that long, but also wanted to show Jason support. "What can I help you with?"

"You know how I told you Marty said I should look into insider trading?"

"Yeah, that is the root of a lot of evil doings," answered Bryan, wondering where this was going, but couldn't deny that he was intrigued.

"I was sitting at my desk sipping on a beautiful scotch and thinking, what creates so much money for insider traders? What's the one thing they need to keep their conglomerates working and profitable? How can they keep making their millions and billions while keeping labor costs as cheap as possible?" Jason inquired, testing Bryan to see what he would say.

"I'd say illegal immigration. The powerful need cheap labor to work in their factories and fields so they can make lots of money while having few complaints about working conditions over fear of being deported," Bryan blurted out. He was just getting warmed up, but needed to slow his roll because his breath was almost gone. "Sorry, I get fired up over that stuff."

Jason flashed him a smile, feeling this would be the right guy to work with, because he had equal passion for what was right and what was wrong. Jason also knew that to move forward, and accomplish what he wanted he needed a partner in crime. Somebody he could go back and forth with that had his back when the powerful came threatening. He knew it would happen when they got close, but the fear of danger never stopped Jason from doing something that would make society as a whole better.

Locked in his head for a minute, Jason felt he should say something before Bryan thought something was wrong. "I agree with everything you said. The cheap labor that fills factories is the grease that keeps companies making money so Congressmen and Senators can insider trade in the first place," Jason blurted out as he saw Bryan nodding in agreement. "Once we start mining, tentacles will shoot out in all directions, uncovering all sorts of heinous crimes. I want to make sure that when stuff comes to light, insider trading is made illegal for everybody."

Jason and Bryan imagined all the possibilities and very real challenges they would face in the near future. If they were both ready for this only time would tell.

"So when you called me over here it sounded like you needed a ride somewhere. I assume now it has something to do with illegal immigration," queried Bryan in a very supportive, but let's get down to business tone of voice. "What do you got?"

"There's an anti-immigrant rally tonight and I don't know the city, so I was wondering if you could drive me there?" Jason hoped that Bryan would act not just as a chauffeur and adviser, but also a partner in crime helping him to figure things out, an equal partner on the team. "I was thinking we could poke around a bit and see what we can find."

"We could mingle amongst the people and see what kind of dirt we can dig up, or just what flows out freely," added Bryan, liking the idea.

"I was reading they have an open bar, so when their alcohol fueled passion gets fired up, there's no telling what will spill out. They say you're more truthful when you're drunk. Well let's just see what kind of vitriol spews forth once their filters are gone, and they think they're amongst a bunch of like-minded people," spouted Jason, knowing it would be enlightening to walk behind the curtain.

"Sounds like a plan. Follow me down to the garage, and don't worry it's not a limo this time. I thought about what you said, it is a little conspicuous driving around the city in a limo, especially if you're trying to blend in."

Jason and Bryan got down to the garage, and in the spot marked for the limo, was a jet black 61 Lincoln convertible with suicide doors.

"How did….."

"When Marty and I were looking at your profile, you listed this car as one of your favorites, and one that you'd love to own," exclaimed Bryan, watching the smile take over Jason's face. "We were thinking about the 67 corvette because that was your number one, but that's something you want to play in, not work in. This car will be our home away from home while we're on the road."

"I don't know what to say, this is awesome." Jason could barely contain his excitement over uncovering government schemes in of his dream cars. "This is real right, I'm not dreaming?"

"You're not dreaming man trust me, this is for real. It'll get a lot more real shortly, are you ready for it? Are you ready to walk in to that rally and do what you were brought here to do?"

CHAPTER TWENTY

Jason and Bryan were tooling down the road to the rally when a song came on the radio that sent Jason into a flashback.

"This was Christina's and my song," lamented Jason, remembering fond memories. "Well not really our song, but my song for her. It's Crazy On You by Heart, who is amazing live by the way if you ever have the chance. Talk about women that can really rock it. Her song for me was Magic Man by Heart."

"That's funny, you like classic rock, me too. Have you been to many shows?" quizzed Bryan, eager to see what Jason had been up to before he rode into the city on a wave of optimism.

"I've been to a lot. As a nice Jewish boy, I even worked maintenance at a Lutheran camp one summer to save up money. Except I didn't save any and saw ten concerts instead, it was amazing and something I'll never forget," remarked Jason.

As they wound through the city, all the familiar sites Jason had seen pictures of were there; the Empire State Building, the Chrysler Building, and a bunch of others that he couldn't remember the names of.

This was the big apple he thought, this was it. Was it the cutthroat, winner take all, I'll stomp on you if you get in my way place he heard about? Or were tons of people just trying to make it amidst a constantly changing and evolving world, learning each day how to handle chaos like all humans before them?

"Here we are, the Elks Lodge," Bryan bellowed as they pulled in to find a parking spot.

"I didn't know they had these in the big city, you see them all over back home. I guess they have them in not only small town and middle America, but also in the city that never sleeps. Do they even know what an elk looks like around here?" snickered Jason said as he started to laugh.

"They know what an elk looks like because they shoot them from helicopters, no wait that's wolves," teased Bryan who always knew how to take a joke too far, even though there was usually truth in what he said that needed to be explored.

Jason and Bryan pulled into a spot and got out. They would act as reporters, not undercover people trying to infiltrate an organization to see what they were up to. Jason decided the best course of action was to ask questions, ones that didn't step on anybody's toes, but questions that said, "I would like to know, but I'm not going to pester you for an answer because I'm an information conduit."

There were a lot of cars parked out front even though the building looked like it would seat 100 at most. Traffic was whizzing by, stopping, and then moving again just like it always did. There was a strange air around this building and Jason could feel it. He knew something was up and was going to find out what.

"When you get this many anti-immigrant people together, somebody in the crowd always says something stupid, we can start from there," sniped Jason, trying to lay down a game plan. If he and Bryan were going to walk into a place with hostiles but didn't want to be seen as hostiles themselves, they needed to blend in and act like they were just reporting on the rally; not use evidence they find to link a politician to insider trading.

"That sounds like a good idea. If we don't go in there with a strategy, they'll sniff us out and make it ten times harder to find the next leg of the spider web," stated Bryan. He was glad that Jason thought of something, and that he might work out after all. He did seem to have a passion that drove him forward no matter what.

They walked toward the building as scores of people arrived. Some had funny hats with tea bags hanging off of them. Some wore t-shirts with racist sayings, but all were carrying signs, stickers and flags signifying what they believed in and were only so happy to tell you all about.

"These illegals need to go home and stop trying to take our jobs," yelled one guy to Jason as he walked in the building with his wife.

"Why do these people come here when they got a perfectly good country of their own," spouted another as Jason and Bryan got closer to the door. "They think they can just do whatever they want and suck on Uncle Sam's tit forever. That's not going to happen if I have anything to say about it."

"These people are very passionate," Jason whispered in Bryan's ear, not wanting to start a fight before they got in the door. "They seem like the type that if you question what they think or why they think it, they won't be able to answer. They'll stumble on their words and then walk away, or think you're out to get them because you disagree with them. Which is funny because disagreements are one of the reasons we ask questions in the first place."

Bryan let Jason finish his diatribe because he looked like he needed to get it out, he could tell the new guy not only had something to prove, but was fired up and ready to go. By the time they reached the front door, they had to wait in a line, so they decided to talk to a few people while they had a minute.

"Hey I'm Jason and I'm here reporting so more people hear about the cause and what they can do about it. Would you like to comment?" Jason inquired of the clean cut man behind him who was wearing an expensive suit, despite dirty tennis shoes.

"Yeah, I'm here because immigration has gotten out of control. This place will just let anybody in and say hey, come here and live. Take our benefits, use our schools, hospitals, and drive on our roads, but don't pay any taxes, or vote in our elections, or even have descent American values. They don't know what it's like to make a real and honest living, they don't know what a hard day of work is like," spewed the man aching to express himself.

Bryan looked at Jason like, here we go. He thought Jason would go off on this guy by how strong his opinions were when they were talking amongst themselves in his office and the car. He was worried Jason would mess the whole thing up, and they'd have to go back to square one. This was Jason's first real test as a reporter, to see if he could handle people in a professional manner to get at the heart of an issue; which was the only reason he would even think of coming to a rally like this in the first place.

"Is there a way we could fix this problem, something we could do to teach them the American way of life?" Jason theorized, leading the man on. He felt the secret to taking right-wingers down in verbal combat was just letting them talk. They would eventually say something to disprove the point they just made, basically the conversational version of set it and forget it.

"We could build a wall with gun turrets and a moat along the whole length of the border. We could even plant land mines, but none of that would work, they would just find some other way in. We have to stop them. We have to throw out politicians that don't want to push any meaningful security measures through. They're the lousy pinko commies that want to let anybody in with no rules, and let it be a free for all.

You think crime is bad now, just wait and see what happens if we keep sitting on our hands. See what happens if we keep electing politicians that say they want to stop illegal immigration, but then turn around and do nothing. They are the real problem. They are the real people we need to get rid of. Why do Congress people say illegals are a bad thing, then, when they have a chance to do something about it, they don't? What are they hiding, and why and where are they hiding it?"

Jason thought it was mighty interesting somebody on the complete opposite end of the political spectrum as him, could probably agree with him a lot more than he thought. It's amazing what can be seen when you get to the root of what's wrong.

This guy wants to take down politicians who aren't tough on immigration when they say they will be. Jason wants to take them down because they support illegal immigration when it keeps their fields and factories filled with cheap labor because it makes them more money. Then, they insider trade with the information of where people are and the best way to hide them and put them to work. They might come from two different places, and might think of the perfect world as two different locations, but on this they might come together. Was this the key to the whole thing? Could people come together when they see their end goals are basically the same by virtue of being human? Could they see that what they want is the same, and what they think they want has fogged over their critical thinking skills?

"Well thank you for your thoughts sir, and I agree something has to be done about Senators and Congressmen who say one thing and do another. It's poisoning the whole political landscape, but the more people like you that ask questions, and get to the root of what nobody wants to talk about, the better off we'll all be. See you in there," responded Jason as he waved at the guy, who waved back, and then disappeared into the building.

"That was quite something, but I see where you were going. We can use that guy for what we want to do," deduced Bryan, pleased by Jason's craftiness.

"It's not so much using him, as much as coming together where we agree. He wants to take somebody down, and so do we. If we can help each other, not use each other, not only will we take down corrupt politicians, but we will unite people. If we have any hope of taking down the powerful, we need numbers. We need people to see who the real enemy is," Jason orated as the words flowed out of him like they came from somewhere else.

"I couldn't have said it better," conferred Bryan as he nodded at Jason because he fully supported him and had his back. Marty was right, Jason was special. He could be the next great journalist. Or he could be just a nice, honest and conscious guy that wants to do good in the short time he's here. Either way, Bryan was excited to have Jason on his team, and was very much looking forward to what was coming next. Right now however, it was time for them to go into the rally and be surrounded.

"You ready for this man, you ready to be engulfed by the other side?" Bryan teased with a smirk.

"In a situation like this I'd usually say I'm as ready as I'll ever be, but instead I will just say yes, I'm ready to take the next step. Let's do it."

CHAPTER TWENTY ONE

There were so many American flags in the Elks lodge it looked like Uncle Sam projectile vomited all over the walls. "What do you think they would say if I walked in waving a Mexican flag while handing out free burritos?" Jason snickered softly under his breath.

"They probably wouldn't like it too much, and might have to prove how American they think they are. The word American means different things to different people, but I'm pretty sure this crowd has no idea what a true American is. Then again who knows, it's a big crowd," Bryan retorted back, feeling the need to say something.

Jason and Bryan walked around a bit before they located seats to watch the guest speakers. There were booths with people selling all matter of American flag gifts, everything you could cram a flag onto was there; ashtrays, shirts, hats, stickers, cups, magnets, etc.... There were also items that would be considered by some to support their anti-immigrant stance, but to others they would be downright racist.

All types of people attended, young, old, rich, poor. There was something missing though and Jason noticed it immediately. "Have you seen any black or brown people since we walked in?" Jason theorized because it seemed to be true. "It's a sea of white."

Amongst the souvenir booths, were numerous organizations handing out information in an attempt to swell their ranks, or at the very least accept some donations. These groups ran the gamut of your basic protest group to para-military vigilantes readying for the war they thought was coming.

Jason thought there were many people they should talk to, so with Bryan at his side, he started talking. "How you doing man? Nice to see so many people out here for a worthy cause," Jason observed, hoping to score some points even though his words couldn't be further from how he actually felt.

"There are a lot more people than last year. I guess with a gridlocked immigration bill and politicians doing nothing about it, a lot of people are ready to take action," responded the man under a banner of his group No Browns, the word browns was circled and had a line through it. "We're here to drum up support for our cause. With twelve million people needing to get the hell out of here, we need all the help we can get."

Jason took one of the guy's pamphlets and nodded at him as he and Bryan took their seats. There was a small stage at the end of a very big room with a dozen booths scattered around what looked to be a couple hundred chairs. "Can you believe what these people will say, I feel like I'm in the heart of darkness right now," espoused Jason not knowing exactly what to do next, so he decided to wing it. "Groups of many different white hues are here, but we should go after the militant ones that will actually commit violence, and not just talk about it."

Bryan fired back, "yeah that No Browns guy talked tough, but I don't think he'd actually do anything. To me, the giveaway was how freely he spewed his ideas without animosity. There was no actual hate in his eyes. Some of the people here do, we just have to look for it."

"The vigilante types are probably linked to the corrupt politicians, who both stand to lose equally if immigrants were made legal. The politicians would lose the status quo of cheap labor they can take advantage of, and the vigilantes would have to deal with a multi-racial society."

It's an amazingly simple thought process that could lead somebody to the level of rage and pent up frustration Jason felt in the room. He knew these opinions were mostly built on the idea of the "other", those thought of to be different, or people just not thinking at all. This rally and the whole idea of booting out immigrants or throwing them in jail, only makes complete and perfect sense if you don't think about it.

"Do these people think about anything, I mean really think," Bryan inquired. He wondered how a person could be so against somebody because of what they looked like, or where they came from. "Seems like something they should have learned in kindergarten or something, you know, treat others like you'd like to be treated. Everybody is different. We come from different places, eat different foods, speak different languages and come in all shapes and sizes. Oh yeah, and we all look different."

"That's it, they don't think. They don't think outside their circle or about consequences to the next generation if they keep doing what they're doing," bellowed Jason, wondering what was going to happen once the speakers actually started speaking.

Jason grabbed a program of the event from under the metal fold up chairs he and Bryan found themselves sitting on. "Looks like there are ten speakers. Some locals that run Tea Party and anti-immigrant groups, then a couple

Congressmen trying to shore up their base for the next election," explained Jason as they waited for the first speaker to come out. "I'll bet the Congressmen speaking here would be a great place to start looking. Anybody who supports the violent upheaval of happy and hard working families has to have something up their sleeve."

"They just might have that fifth ace of defending the status quo while acting like they want all illegals out. They talk tough so people will come to their side, and then they keep things the way they are to protect their profits." Bryan answered slyly. "Maybe we'll get a good recipe for pure white bread while we're here?"

The crowd really started to fill in because the speakers were slated to start any minute. Jason and Bryan knew it would be difficult to see who actually supported the cause and who was faking it. Most of them were big talkers, too comfortable in their own bubble to be bothered with difficulties that didn't directly concern them.

"Maybe if we get some good leads, we won't have to stay for the whole thing, just being here makes my skin crawl," exclaimed Jason. He was trying to figure out how to handle being in the middle of the crazy anti-immigrant crowd he always felt were a bunch of nut jobs.

"I agree with you, we shouldn't stay any longer than we have to," Bryan countered, agreeing with Jason on his uneasy feeling. "We just have to remember why we're here. We're trying to prove that some people say they want illegal immigration to stop, but really want it to continue so they can make lots of money."

"If there's one thing that makes disparate groups link up, it's the all mighty dollar. I had a journalism teacher once tell me that if I wanted to find the truth of any story, I had to follow the money, because it always pointed to who was responsible."

A man and his wife in their seventies saw two empty seats right next to Jason and Bryan and sat down. "How are you doing son? It's good to see young people still care about this stuff and not just old farts like us," chuckled the man to Jason.

"Speak for yourself, I may be old, but I don't fart nearly as often as you," the man's wife volleyed. "Don't let this guy fool you, he farts all the time."

The four of them laughed out loud, what a great way to start things off Jason thought. Which he also felt was interesting, some of these people might have crazy opinions he definitely didn't agree with, but they were human, they made the same stupid jokes all people of a certain age did. There are cute old couples that have been married a few hundred years on all sides of the political spectrum.

If people could see the immigrants they were disparaging and trying to kick out were just like them with the same needs and wants, most of the problem would disappear.

"This thing gets more interesting the longer I sit here," Jason sniped, excitedly awaiting the first speaker.

"This is a great place to be amongst people who say whatever is on their minds," expressed Bryan trying to make a point. "Within any movement there is always disagreement about ideas and levels of involvement. A lot of people think the world is painted black and white, when really it's drowned in a grey hue."

The first speaker on stage was a twenty something college student that looked like somebody Jason hung out with back home. The guy regurgitated the tag lines about how immigrants were taking our jobs, how they all needed to go, how we needed more guns, security and definitely a wall, all the stuff one expected Jason thought. Then just like the guy he talked to outside, the man said something that made both he and Bryan ponder.

"While I firmly believe these people coming into our country want nothing more than to take what they can because they can, I also think something else is going on," noticed the speaker, immediately grabbing Jason's attention. "We have politicians who talk a good game. Some of them are even here today trying to build up their street cred by making promises. The trick is however, they'll never actually keep them. When a politician says they'll look into something, it means they just threw your request for help straight in the garbage can."

The crowd erupted in cheer, nothing like a strong "politician's suck" line to really get the crowd going Jason thought as the man continued.

"Whether these Congressmen are against your values or are completely dead set on supporting them, they always have a sinister motive. They'll say whatever they can to whoever will listen if it helps them get elected, and puts more money into their campaign coffers.

They might say immigrants need to leave, and that they'll even drive the bus back to Mexico. The truth is they won't lift a damn finger because their interests are leading them in the opposite direction. Politicians worship the almighty dollar, and that's the only thing they care about. If lying will make them a buck, they'll be all about it."

As he and Bryan were listening to this guy go on and on, Jason had an increasingly strong feeling he had seen him before. "It seems like I've met him somewhere," whispered Jason softly so they could still hear the speaker. "I don't know if it was in passing, but he seems really familiar."

"Maybe we can talk to him after this is over. He sounds like he thinks more than most people here, but critically deficient enough to fit in," Bryan responded as quickly as he could so he could also continue listening.

"These politicians are only interested in making money and will say anything to get it, like a crack-whore but without the sex," the guy joked to explosive laughter throughout the room. "They will do anything to make the people think they believe a certain way, like they're constantly trying to pull one over on us."

"What's the point man get on with it," some guy yelled from the audience.

"I will get on with it if you let me," as the crowd began to grow testy, the speaker remained calm and spoke from his heart, or where one would usually be found.

"Basically, if politicians say anything for money, people will think they hold certain positions when they really don't," the speaker pointed out, not giving an inch to the crowd.

"I know I've seen this guy before, it's on the tip of my tongue," remembered Jason as the guy continued.

"When they take these positions, you must always be skeptical. For instance, when a politician says they want to deport a bunch of people, many times they really don't." Some mysterious men in dark suits and sunglasses were motioning the guy at the microphone to cool it, but he pressed forward anyway because the energy from the crowd kept him going.

"So if a politician is only in it for the money, and say they want illegals to leave, is there a possibility they don't want them to leave? Is there a chance they really want them here because immigrant labor is cheaper than American? Are politicians making money hand over fist because the companies that employ immigrants make truckloads of it themselves and therefore contribute more to campaigns? And on and on the circle of shit goes, no wonder we don't ever get anywhere....."

By this time the dark suited big wigs were getting majorly pissed, almost like he said something he wasn't supposed to. They started yelling that he better stop or he was going to have his mike cut off, but he wasn't affected. This rally was starting to get a lot more interesting Bryan thought. He was more intrigued the more fireworks that happened, which meant they might be getting somewhere with the story.

"Some of the politicians here today are probably the ones standing in our way and aren't supporting us like they claim. They might be the ones that............."

Instantly his mic was cut, and the man was whisked off-stage like he was on the gong show and his act was terrible. If he pissed someone off Bryan thought, he must be getting close to the truth.

"I knew that guy looked familiar, I think his name was Bob or James or something, I'm not sure. Hell it could have been Sean for all I know. I remember I had a couple classes with him in school back home. We didn't agree on much, but when we did it was because it was universal and would help everybody, not just one side of things," Jason reminisced with eagerness because he was getting close to something. "Our story about this whole thing starts with him I just know it. We must find him."

CHAPTER TWENTY TWO

Jason and Bryan's mystery man was forcefully escorted behind the stage. The whole crowd grumbled like a hippie spontaneously started playing protest songs about how war sucks and rainbows are cool.

The organizers knew they had to do something, so they introduced the next speaker, thinking he might be able to calm the mob. The gentleman was in his late fifties with the scars to prove he had been in some violent battles, but wanted to keep fighting as long he had people beside him.

The man spoke like he authentically wanted people to listen. "How y'all doing today?" he sniped as the crowd let out a loud groan. "I know that last guy isn't what you wanted to see. I'm here to tell you my focus isn't on the politicians. While I definitely believe some of them should go, I think the actual illegals should be our main focus. I mean if there are less illegals, then we wouldn't have a problem right?" the guy theorized as the crowd lusted for vigilante acts that could stop this scourge on the American way of life.

"They don't understand us, so why should we even try to understand them. They're sucking us dry and must go if we ever hope to move forward as the glorious Christian nation we were always meant to be." The guy went on and on about how immigrants sucked and we should either shoot them, kidnap them, drop them back off in Mexico or just disappear them somewhere.

"This is exactly what I thought would happen, some guy gets on stage and starts spewing hate. As the crowd listens more intently, he gets angrier and angrier while detailing how he would dispatch the alleged menace to society," Jason stated with uneasiness, knowing the more the crowd got whipped up, the more careful they had to be with their words.

"I couldn't agree more, that's what I expected too," commiserated Bryan. He was trying to comfort Jason, while at the same time trying to remind him why they were there. "While the crowd is all whipped up, we should go find where they took that guy you know. Maybe he can help us. Maybe he is someone from the other side who isn't completely insane."

Jason and Bryan hurriedly wove through the crowd that was yelling, screaming, clapping and getting out all the feelings they'd been suppressing for years because they didn't think about their actions.

They finally made it to the back of the stage and stopped a security guard to ask about Jason's friend. "Hey man how you doing," inquired Jason of the guy wearing a bright yellow security shirt with a look that said he'd love to bust some heads. "What happened to that guy they booted off stage earlier? What did they do with him, did they kick him out?"

"That guy was a distraction to the ideas meant to be articulated at an event like this," the guard sternly replied as if Jason was challenging his passion for the cause.

Noticing the guard was a little agitated by his first question, Jason tried to smooth things over. "I agree that guy needed to go, he was spewing hate that no red blooded American needs to hear," Jason quipped, knowing how ridiculous that phrase always sounded to him. If somebody was an American, of course their blood was red, they're human aren't they?

"This is the fifth rally I've worked and the crowd gets bigger and bigger as support grows for what needs to be done," expressed the guard, beginning to think Jason was on his side.

"What do you think needs to be done?" wondered Jason very curiously.

"Well they either have to round them up and put them in jail because they broke the law. Or they just need to line them all up and shoot them. We have tons of bullets in this country that could easily get the job done. If we send them back, they'll just return with three more brothers and five more kids. They must be stopped by any means necessary before there's nothing left of the country we used to know."

Jason knew this backwards type of thinking, never held up to the smell test if you thought about it for more than five seconds. You can't just kill twelve million people unless you want to turn into the Nazis. If they shoot them all, more would return anyway. There are a lot of people in the world who want a better life for themselves and their families. They come here because the United States was built by immigrants. This was an argument he knew the security guard wouldn't be comfortable with, it was never a good idea to compare anything with Nazis.

"That's true, we have to do something," Jason sympathized, trying to reassure the security guard that he was on the right side, without actually saying anything racist or bigoted. "That guy you drug out earlier, I would love to give him a piece of my mind. I want to let him know what I really think of people like him," Jason blurted passionately, hoping to be believable. He also knew he could agree without actually going into detail. He wouldn't be lying, Jason wasn't a liar.

"I feel like giving that guy a piece of my mind too," the guard added, very eagerly licking his chops. "They took him around back and did what they do best. He might still be back there."

"We should go check," Bryan motioned to Jason, wanting nothing more than to leave the building and all the virulent ignorance it represented. "You think they beat on him?"

"They might have, in which case it might be a struggle to get to his car," Jason replied in a very worried tone.

"I hope y'all have a great day. When you find that guy, you'll see what we do to agitators. We must let nothing stand in the way of our cause. What was done to him was the tip of the iceberg of what we have planned," retorted the guard, while trying to keep an eye on the crowd at the same time.

Jason shook the guards hand right before he and Bryan walked around the back of the stage and out the back door. It was extremely strange to see the daylight after experiencing all the darkness floating around, but still a welcome sight.

Very few cars were in the back, none of which appeared occupied. There was nobody lying on the ground seriously hurt or dead they could see. They did spot marks in the dirt lot that looked like somebody was dragged before crawling off.

Jason and Bryan followed the marks from the backdoor toward the line of cars. One of the drag marks led to one vehicle in particular. "That car looks very familiar," Jason observed, pointing at the blue Trans Am sitting right in front of them. "I know it from somewhere."

"You think it's our guy, the one you remember from school?" queried Bryan as they both approached slowly.

The car wasn't running but the windows were all fogged up, like somebody was in it. Jason started to think, what if this was the guy's car he was thinking of? Would the guy even recognize him? Would the guy have happy memories? Or want to beat him up for something he didn't remember he did?

Jason looked into the Trans-Am's window and couldn't see anything except for a figure he could barely make out through the icy frost. "Aaron, is that you?" Jason inquired as memories started flooding back to him. "It's me Jason from school."

The silhouette in the car started to move, but very slowly. Bryan walked over to see what was happening. "I guess you remember the guy's name, is he moving at all?" Bryan worried, trying to sound concerned for somebody Jason knew, even though he knew they had to question him, and follow the inevitable lead he produced.

"Yeah it's me, who are you again?" demanded the man in the car that Jason thought was Aaron. Until he stepped out, Jason couldn't know 100%. "What do you want?"

"It's me, Jason. We went to school together back on the good ole west coast. I remember this Trans-Am like the back of my hand, bright blue with that big eagle on the hood. As soon as I saw it, I knew it had to be you. I had to say hello," Jason responded trying to get the guy to step out of the car for friendly conversation.

"Hold on I'm coming out, but I'm moving a little slow so bear with me," Aaron expressed, attempting to extricate himself from the car without much success.

"I'll bet they roughed him up as a warning to never step out of line," thought Bryan, hypothesizing three steps ahead.

The Trans-Am door creaked open, and there in the flesh stood the man Jason knew as Aaron. "What's up man, is that you," solicited Aaron, trying to get his eyes to focus. "What are you doing here?"

Aaron had deep purple and red bruising on his face and arms from being kicked, and punched over and over and then thrown out the back door, just like one might see in the movies.

"I got a job with Democratic Republic, I'm an investigative reporter," acknowledged Jason, happy to see a friendly face, even if it was beat up. "This is my partner Bryan."

"Nice to meet you."

Aaron and Jason embraced like friends that hadn't seen each other for an eternity. They wanted to ask each other a million questions immediately, the least of which was what the other had been up to.

"Bryan and I were researching a story, and we saw you dragged off stage, what happened?" Jason probed with genuine concern for Aaron's wellbeing. Life is funny sometimes, especially when people show up unexpectedly from a past they thought was gone forever. When Jason left school he stopped calling people back, his life was leading in one direction and his friends another. He missed hanging out with Aaron ever since.

"I was speaking and all of a sudden they grabbed me, threw me in some backroom, punched and kicked me and then tossed me out like garbage," exclaimed Aaron. He was glad to see Jason, but felt he was owed an explanation for his friends escape.

"What are you up to now, you look like you could use a drink or four," bantered Jason, trying to smooth things over. "I'd love to catch up and talk more about this rally. They seemed to be with you at first, but when you pulled the focus off immigrants, the crowd had to think for the first time in their lives. Needless to say they didn't like it."

"That sounds about right. I think they kicked me out for making them think too," deduced Aaron as he nodded in agreement. "I was trying to inform them about the root of the problem, but if they aren't being told how evil brown people are, and what has to be done to stop them, they don't want to hear it. The reason I even showed up today was to show them a different way, a less violent and more efficient path to achieving their goals. Talking to these people though, is like trying to explain how global warming causes an ice age. Either you believe it, or think it's a conspiracy, there is no grey area."

The three of them had a hearty laugh, causing Jason to recollect why he enjoyed hanging out with Aaron in the first place.

"We never agreed on everything, in fact that's what made our conversations so stimulating. We could always find common ground and agree that politics were the problem.

Bryan and I are researching a story about insider trading. We located this rally because illegal immigration was our first step, because of pretty much everything you orated on stage. Certain elected officials want to keep things the way they are because they're making money hand over fist, which Bryan and I believe causes them to insider trade." noted Jason, very happy to meet up with an old friend he hadn't thought of in a long time. "I know this great little place around the corner from my office if you want to cruise by. We could have a few drinks and just chill, catch up and you know, fix all the world's problems."

"I'm down for that, sounds like something we could definitely work on together. That is after a few Pb&Js, and I ain't talking about peanut butter and jelly," Aaron cajoled as he and Jason shared a laugh that brought them each a flashback of easier times. "Let me clean up a little and I'll follow you. Then after we have drinks, you can show me your fancy new office, I would love to see how far you've come."

CHAPTER TWENTY THREE

The Blue Fox tavern was rode hard and put away wet for years as the cities favorite watering hole for lost journalists trying to find their way.

"This looks like the place," Jason indicated as he and Bryan pulled up in the Lincoln, followed by Aaron in the Trans Am. "Let's park over there, two spots are together."

As they exited their cars and walked towards the swinging saloon doors, Jason knew this was going to be a moment he'd analyze for hours after it ended. It's not every day an old friend pops out of the wood work to give a speech at the very event you're investigating, what could it mean?

The three of them located a table and sat down. "Are the PB&Js good here, I've only had a few since the last time we hung out," recalled Aaron, contemplating simpler times when all politicians weren't corrupt, and the string pullers were much more distinguishable. Then Aaron remembered politicians had always been corrupt, they just evolved alongside technology.

"Well PB&J's don't really change from place to place considering it's just a shot of Jameson and a Pabst Blue Ribbon," Jason shot back with a chuckle. He ordered it so much at his favorite bar back home that the bartender knew it was his drink, and automatically asked him when he walked in if that's what he wanted; well that and if he wanted to have a drink first or smoke a bowl first. Jason loved that.

Sauntering up to their table was a cute little barmaid, a typical 22 year old coed that was eyeing Jason up and down like a piece of meat. "Three PB&Js please," proposed

Jason. The waitress elevated her boobs so much she was practically sticking them in Jason's face.

"You got it hun, be right back," responded the waitress with depraved eyes indicating she wanted Jason to ravage her.

"I think she likes you man," whispered Aaron with a little smirk on his face. "Seems you've become more attractive to women since I saw you last."

"I had an amazing girlfriend back home I really loved, but had to leave her behind because I knew how important this opportunity was. I had to take it. Now I'm just following clues, and they led me and Bryan here to this rally, and to you."

As a look of wonderment mixed with tons of questions washed over Aarons face, the incredibly well-endowed waitress returned with their drinks. "Here you go boys, I'll open a tab for you," she declared as she placed the drinks on the table, and bent down one more time to give Jason an obvious invitation to look down her tiny red shirt that was being stretched to its limits.

"Oh she definitely likes you," teased Aaron, not remembering Jason being a ladies man.

"You think?" retorted Jason as he flipped over the coaster under his drink to reveal a phone number. "I would love to give her everything she's been deprived of, but right now I'm investigating a huge story with my new partner and an old friend. She can wait."

"Suit yourself," countered Aaron in disbelief that Jason would turn down a beautiful big breasted woman, who obviously wanted to pull him into a bathroom stall. He must have really changed Aaron thought.

They each raised their drinks and toasted to the chance meeting that brought them together. "Cheers to meeting up again after all these years, and coming together to take down some greedy bastards," stated Jason with a proud smile because he knew the two people next to him were down for the cause. "Let's get down to brass tacks, how long have you been speaking at those rallies? I know we didn't agree on everything back in the day, but we knew we were on the same side. Have you turned all crazy now?"

"Not crazy, just more libertarian," answered Aaron. He knew Jason could work with anybody because he was a pragmatist who knew mutual agreement is achieved once all the bullshit fades away. "I spoke at those rallies because I thought they were starting to see things my way, that yes, we should have more legal immigration. Apparently they don't agree that their favorite politicians are standing in the way of that, and will profess how tough on immigration they are until they're blue in the face, then turn around and defend the status quo."

"They're making way too much money to stop an endless gravy train," explained Jason with a comment like a dialogue bubble in a cartoon. "The whole system is built on fear and ignorance. When you brought up how their friends in high places might be screwing them over, it was too much for their brains to process. They didn't believe you, and you immediately became the enemy."

Jason knew drinking cheap beer with friends while figuring out the world's problems, was how to start the next revolution. If they figured this thing out, they could be the next crime fighting trio, but maybe that was just the alcohol talking.

"Since we have an idea of what's going on, we should look into the Congressmen at the rally, and see if they have anything to do with a cover up," Bryan interjected confidently. There was a clear mission in front of him, and he believed he was doing the right thing. "There was a Congressman from Florida, and a couple from Arizona and Texas."

Jason thought for a minute how everything happened for a reason when an idea popped into his head. "Aaron, where do you live now man?"

"I live in Arizona, why do you ask?" Aaron thought it was a little strange, but then again Jason might just be attempting friendly conversation.

"I'm curious, how is your life is going man? I like to know how friends of mine are progressing," conveyed Jason sincerely.

"Man, after school I must have called ten times, you never called me back. Now all of a sudden you want to know about my life. Why the sudden interest? Do you actually care, or are you just interested in a story?" interrogated Aaron with an edge in his voice, but not so much it would make someone throw a punch.

"I just needed to get away, for me. Whether it was real or not, I felt that my good friends and I were all headed in different directions. I was going somewhere they weren't, and I needed a change. So I came to a beautiful small town, where I could write for a newspaper and report until

I got my big break. It was nothing personal. I just needed a fresh start for me and my sanity. Then I met Christina, and I knew I made the right decision."

Aaron and Jason took a drink of their beers and noticed they were both on empty. "Another round of PB&Js please," requested Bryan of the waitress who was walking by.

"You got it boys," she responded, giving Jason the strongest come fuck me eyes any of them ever saw.

"Thanks man, I appreciate it," expressed Jason to Bryan, as his partner pulled put some money. "Let me get the next one."

"Oh she wants you bad," Aaron needled, as he started to settle down. "I hope you didn't get offended by my questions, I just wanted to know."

"You have every right to know man." Jason gave Aaron a look without muttering a word that said he still gave a shit.

The voluptuous waitress came back with their drinks and set them on the table before strolling off. "Thanks hun," Bryan piped up, hoping she'd pull him into the bathroom instead of Jason. "Where should we go from here, I was thinking one of the border-states Congressman?"

"Yeah, they probably are involved in immigration schemes," Jason answered, as he took a sip of beer and raised his shot glass. "Here is to the beginning of a good working relationship. May we show these unscrupulous politicians it's possible for their kind to get caught, and it's impossible for them to succeed without first looking over their shoulder."

The guys downed their shots because that's what you did after a hopeful toast. "Now that I think about it, there was a guy who might be a good place to start," remembered Aaron, thinking about who was slated to speak right after him. "Right before I went on stage, I noticed this guy behind me. I think he was a Congressman or Senator, something official. He made a few comments that led me to believe he wasn't the same guy he was poorly attempting to portray himself as."

"What did he say to make you think he wasn't an upstanding citizen?" Jason inquired with a sarcastic smile.

"We talked about what we wanted to change with the immigration system, and how we had to stop people from coming into the country illegally. He said we needed to make sure that if somebody wants to come here, they have to do it the right way," detailed Aaron as he took a drink and continued. "He then said son, how do you expect we're going to do that? What should we try that we haven't already failed at miserably? I've been trying to persuade Congress people for years to come up with solutions, nobody listens. I just have to keep at it though, I mean that's what the voters sent me to Washington to do right, fight for the people?"

"What doesn't sound on the up and up with that? We should always be skeptical of politicians that say they'll fight for the people, because they don't mean it half the time. What makes you think that Congressman wasn't one of the good guys?" Jason cross-examined, putting Aaron on the spot.

"It's what the Congressman said next that really made me go, what?" echoed Aaron as he took a drink of the lovely

PBR sitting in front of him. "He said he was one of the good guys trying to fight the good fight, and it was all the other Congressmen who were doing wrong. He told me about a guy he worked with that had a good idea to make a lot of money, and how could he turn that down."

"Okay, a politician telling another politician that he wants to make a lot of money, that's not a surprise, that's what they do. Why is this even a story? Why do you think this is the guy we should go after, the one that's going to give us our in? Cause once we start down this path, they're going to know we're after them and will start coming after us," Jason indicated, trying to make Aaron get to the point.

"This has to be our guy because he started talking about the owner of a big construction company who was convicted. He'd bring in cheap, illegal labor from any country he could get them from. He would even make his wife sleep with those who made complaints," replied Aaron as he uneasily adjusted himself in his chair.

"That sounds like something I've heard before, continue," responded Jason, now thoroughly interested in what Aaron had to say.

"If the people making the complaints didn't want to sleep with his wife, who wasn't bad looking I have to say. If they didn't want to sleep with her, he would have them killed. The Congressman said the guy owned a water park or something."

"Oh shit really." Jason wondered if this was the same story that brought him to the big city. "What did he say happened next?"

"Well, he said the guy killed somebody who complained too much. He said the complainer was going to turn him into I.C.E. for bringing in all these extra workers, and paying them nothing while treating them like dirt. You know how they say the people who pull the strings are the ones in the shadows? They rarely peak their head out for fear of getting caught."

"Yeah I know that one, who doesn't," countered Jason, wondering where this was going. Then it dawned on him, but Bryan was quicker on the draw.

"I'll bet the Congressman you spoke to backstage was the construction guys connection for getting his workers into the country. He had to be the one that made the whole thing possible."

CHAPTER TWENTY FOUR

Bryan's revelation stopped the guys in their tracks. They didn't notice their scantily clad waitress wander over to the phone behind the bar.

"Hello, Bill? It's me Mary at the bar. The one thrown out of your rally, that guy you wanted me to look out for, he's here drinking with a couple people," explained the experienced waitress whose endowments allowed her to get anything she wanted. "You want me to hold them here? What would you like me to do?"

"Stall them for a little bit longer until I have Mark strike fear into them. He'll be there soon," responded the commanding voice on the other line.

Bryan, Aaron and Jason were more than prepared for another round as Mary the waitress walked up, even more eager to stick her chest in their faces than the last four times she freshened their drinks. "Need anything else boys?" she seductively propositioned, while shooting them all a come get me look.

"Just keep the drinks flowing, and we'll make sure you get a big tip," Aaron suggestively stated as Mary smiled and walked away to get their drinks. "Either of you think it was a little weird she looked at all of us like pieces of meat?"

"Hadn't she been doing that already? Is something wrong with a beautiful woman imagining your piece of meat? Has it been so long that your tube steak has turned into jerky?" sniped Jason as he and Bryan laughed their asses off.

"No dumb ass, your mom and your sister weren't enough for me last night, oooh the things they did," bantered

Aaron, knowing it would get a rise out of Jason, but also get him to listen. "Okay in all seriousness, it was a little strange when that waitress was here the last time, oh wait shhh, here she comes."

The t-shirt exploding maiden set their latest round of drinks on the table and walked away. She didn't even look at them, let alone give them the eyeball gangbang she beamed a minute ago.

"See, that was a little weird right, that's what I'm talking about," Aaron observed, while looking at her ass as she walked away.

"You're still checking her out though," Jason blurted like a first grade student.

"Just because I think we're about to get screwed over, doesn't mean I can't gander at the fine ass that's doing it," remarked Aaron as he took a big gulp of beer.

"What are you saying, just spit it out," Jason demanded, tired of Aaron's game playing.

"I think those boobs I mean I think this lady is keeping me here for some reason. I don't know why, I just feel like something is going on. Remember me mentioning the Congressman at the rally talking about that guy he turned down," expressed Aaron knowing how vague he sounded, so he tried to expound.

Just as Aaron's explanation was about to exit his mouth, a hand tapped him on the shoulder making him jump out of his pants like something out of a Dr. Seuss story.

"Fancy seeing you here Aaron, this isn't your usual watering hole is it? Mind if I sit?" insisted the confident, dark suited man as he sat down like he owned the place. He made all the guys uncomfortable but intrigued at the same time.

"Don't I know you from somewhere? How would you know this isn't my usual place for a drink?" wondered Aaron. He was curious if the guy had been following him or was just a dick.

"Come on man, you can't be that drunk already," cajoled the man as he peered right at Jason with an evil eye that inferred this chance meeting, was no chance.

"I know you, you're that guy who was going to speak after me at the rally. You're that Congressman, Mark Ridell," remembered Aaron as he cautiously stuck out his hand to see if the Congressman would shake it.

"Yes I am, sorry you got ejected. I told them they shouldn't have done that, he's going to run to our enemies for help," the Congressman remarked while purposely not shaking Aaron's hand. He continued to glare at Jason like he was going to choke him with the Jedi mind meld.

"Yeah, what was that about? I thought we were on the same page. We both want to make change, or is it something else? Do you have other interests?" Aaron interrogated, yearning for a path to the truth.

"While it's true that we must stop illegals from coming here, we are a country of laws and we have to abide by them or we're left with chaos. We can't just go around doing and saying whatever we want, it could make somebody look bad to the people they work for. I can't

~ 189 ~

imagine what that feels like," fumed Ridell, whose face was visibly getting red with the anger building inside him towards Jason.

"What's your point man? Why are you staring at Jason like you want to eye fuck him to death?" Aaron implored, trying to regain his manhood that floated away when Ridell sat down at their table.

"I don't like interrupting my busy schedule to tell little piss ants what they should and shouldn't be doing. I have way more important shit to do then sit here and talk to you in this pit. Stop poking a hornet's nest. You never know when you'll get stung. You'll never discover what you're looking for because we wield all the power and influence. What do you have, some cheap beer and whisky? Please," Ridell chortled, who was getting angrier the longer he sat at the table.

"You were the one that had me thrown out? You want to fight me right here? You tough enough to get into an old fashioned bar brawl? Don't come in here and threaten me, nobody threatens me. I'd love to knock you down a peg, take you off that high horse you're sitting on," Aaron fired back as his own anger was building.

"You think I've made it this far in the game without being able to handle somebody like you," Ridell smoothly replied as his anger disappeared, and the unyielding coolness he walked in with returned. "All I'm saying is watch your back. Whenever you're walking down the street and feel a breeze, think about me nipping at your heels. Think about me knocking you down a few pegs from the lowly place you're already at. I should actually thank you for working hard and making me so much money.

My friends and I have had countless exotic vacations and truckloads of cash bestowed upon us because people like you will always have to provide for your stupid families. You will put up with whatever crap pay or working conditions we put you through. Just keep working worker bee, you can't beat us. You can't risk your own survival to enter this fight. You will lose and you know it. Come at us if you want, but only if you feel like leaving this earth. Just remember, there are a lot easier ways to kill yourself."

Ridell didn't take his eyes off of Jason the whole time, and after he felt he made his point he got up and walked away. "See y'all, and don't forget to vote in November."

"What an asshole," Aaron thought. "Dude thinks he can walk in here like he's above the law just because he is supposedly elected by the people to create the law. He was preaching for the one percent, and needs to be taken down more than a little bit."

Jason sat there quietly, deep in thought. Why was that Congressman staring at him? What did it mean? Did anybody else notice and think it odd? As he asked himself more and more questions, the wheels started to crank and a few ideas sprang up.

"I think I had a thought," interjected Bryan.

"Hey man I haven't known you that long man, but you stay silent the whole time and then you come up with that? What are you going to say next, that you see something you can smell?" responded Aaron trying to be a dick, but a not a total dick; the kind of dick that always gives out a light hearted ribbing, what guys always do as a means of respect and acceptance into the group.

The guys roared with laughter as they were all a little buzzed, several Jameson's and PBRs will do that to a person. "I'm going outside to smoke. I need some nicotine after all that, and some green. What do you say man, want to spark one up for old times' sake?" queried Aaron looking a little bleary eyed, but still the same trustworthy and passionate for justice person Jason remembered from school.

"Sure man, that sounds great, I'll be out in a minute, I just want to talk to Bryan for a sec," answered Jason, really wanting Bryan to say what he tried to say earlier.

"No prob man, after you two are done making out, I'll be outside," Aaron drunkenly slurred as he stumbled out the door. He didn't care how loud his voice was, or that half the bar turned around to stare in unison.

"You figured something out, I think I did too," stated Jason, somewhat clear-eyed to Bryan, which was strange considering the amount of drinks they had consumed.

"What is it man?" Bryan questioned not with brotherly concern, but with curiousness that only a journalist hot on the trail of a juicy lead could have.

"Remember the water park story?"

"Of course, it's the whole reason Marty brought you out here."

"Well when I took down that construction owner with all the illegals, it came out in court that he bribed some politicians. They pulled strings with local law enforcement so he could bring his new "slaves", I mean workers into the country. Nobody ever got close enough to prove anything against this string puller. I mean nothing, not even the guy's name or address. He was covered in so much insulation, it was impossible to find him."

"What's your point?"

"I believe this is the guy, and I think he just told us to back off or we'd get hurt, you know the stereotypical threat. You know what that means? It means we're getting close. It's no coincidence Ridell showed up, he must have followed us. How else could he know exactly who we are and where we'd be? Anyway, when somebody feels threatened they emit a certain energy that surrounds everything they do."

"Why was he staring at you like you were a hot pizza when he came in here to talk with Aaron?"

"Don't you get it man, he's the guy; the DJ who made everyone dance to his beat."

"Yes, a powerful dick that thinks he is invincible, I know the type."

"This guy is the same, but different. When I looked into his eyes I saw rage, the same rage a momma bear has when trying to protect her cubs. I've messed with him before, and he knows I'm going to do it again. Don't you get it Bryan, he's the guy. He is the key to this whole thing. He is the one that pulled the strings at the water park, and now is trying to make us give up. That's not what we do and that's not who we are. He will pay. He is the Congressman that made the construction guy's scheme possible. He is the next leg of the spider web."

Filled with confidence, Jason and Bryan walked outside. "Where's Aaron, I don't see him," wondered Bryan as he and Jason couldn't spot him anywhere.

"I'll bet he got tired of waiting for us and took a cab home. We can meet him for breakfast in the morning when he comes back for his Trans Am. Can you swing me home too, I'm feeling tired myself," Jason declared, ready to end the day and start a new one.

"Marty would be proud, your first time out and we already have a Congressman threatening us. We must be getting somewhere."

CHAPTER TWENTY FIVE

How do you expose a secret? Should a trustworthy person be told about the clues in-case information falls into the wrong hands? Or should one sit back, let the whole thing unravel and just watch the show? This was the dilemma facing Jason because he was hot on the trail, but didn't know what step to take next; except maybe having a discussion with Marty.

"We should go back to the office and tell Marty what happened yesterday," Jason articulated as he took a big sip of coffee, hungrily awaiting his pancakes.

"I don't know why you picked this place, the food isn't even that good," Bryan asserted with a less than satisfied look. "We should have called for take-out, and just brought it to the office."

"Yeah we could have done that, but we're here now. The food might not be the best, but when I'm sitting in one of these booths I feel close to the people. If we have any hope of cracking this thing wide open, not only do we have to be imbedded in the community, we need sustenance that sticks to our ribs."

The waitress brought them each some pancakes, a few fried eggs, bacon, sausage, hash browns and toast. "Okay I see where you're going with that whole sustenance thing," related Bryan as he inhaled a strip of bacon. "This isn't half bad."

Bryan and Jason ate their breakfast without saying anything, both knowing this case was unlike anything they ever saw. The spider web unraveling before them would only do so if they were vigilant, and courageous. The web would completely fall apart once they figured out how it all fit together.

"Alright let's finish up and then go see what Marty has to say," Jason affirmed as he took a couple more bites of pancake and then got up to go to the bathroom. "That Ridell guy will never know what hit him. I've been waiting my whole life to take down someone like him. He won't get away with this, I won't let him."

"You feel strongly about this and that's good," Bryan emphatically uttered, trying to reassure Jason because he knew the fight ahead would be long. "You must channel your energy so we can focus it on who really deserves it. If Ridell was linked to the water park guy by pulling his strings, there's no telling who is pulling Ridell's strings. The people usually controlling things are no name, no face people who never show in public. Remember, Ridell is probably the tip of the iceberg."

"That's true. No matter how deep this thing goes, we have to keep digging. At the same time, he's a good start. Let's focus on Ridell before we think about the bigger fish, I think he's the key to finding what we're looking for at the current moment. Right now, I have to make an evacuation," explained Jason as he excused himself to use the bathroom.

"Just do what you got to do so we can get back."

As Jason was relieving himself, Bryan thought about what he was going to tell Marty. Was he going to tell him that he and the new wonder boy found evidence of a vast conspiracy to funnel illegals into the country? That they must have been getting too close because they were not so secretly threatened? Bryan had been around long enough to know, that when somebody threatens you, especially in a position like Ridell's, they always have something up their sleeve. He might simply tell Marty that Jason was exposing himself to danger, and would get himself killed if he went any further.

"You ready to go back to the workshop where Gepetto can turn you into a real boy?" giggled Jason as he exited the bathroom with a relieved look on his face. "He might even make a girl for you, but only if you ask nicely."

"Keep joking, that Ridell guy and his henchmen undoubtedly will turn you into wood," Bryan expounded, hoping Jason wouldn't turn this into a dead horse beating because he thought it was the joke that kept on giving.

"Yeah I got some wood for you," Jason pestered with a smirk on his face.

"If you're done talking about your wood, you ready to go?"

Jason and Bryan strolled out of the diner and stepped into the Lincoln. "I really like that place, they have a good eye opener, decent specials, but most of all I like how the waitresses call you hun. It gives you a real salt of the earth kind of vibe. Being amongst the people is where I feel most at home."

"It does help when you have the best assistant and friend money can buy," Bryan grated with a sinister look on his face. "Just make sure that when we solve this, you won't say something stupid like, I'll bet he won't be coming back for seconds. Or hasta la vista or something else out of a bad action movie."

"Leave me and my cheesy one-liners alone, they'll always be funny. I mean hell, what would half the movies today be if there weren't witty one-liners?"

"If that's all that's saving movies these days, no wonder Hollywood is in so much trouble."

They pulled up to the office around ten and leisurely walked in. Jason knew he had a big day ahead of him and was glad he had food in him to make it through. The chance meeting with Aaron yesterday threw him for a loop, at the same time he's glad it happened; it led Bryan and him to Ridell. If Aaron wasn't thrown out of the rally, and they hadn't met for a beer when and where they did, they might not have the information they do.

"Come on in boys, how was the rally yesterday?" solicited Marty as Bryan and Jason walked into his office. "I'll bet it was filled to the rafters with intelligent and insightful people huh?"

Jason knew it was time to prove his chops, prove he could hang with the big boys. Bryan gave him a look that said this is your shot to help move our species forward.

Jason spoke knowing his career was on the line, not to mention the huge scheme they had a chance to blow wide open; he had to treat it just right. "The rally was good, lots of nut bags just as expected. There was a random assortment of speakers, ranging from all level of tea party, conservative and libertarian. Everybody with a loud mouth and a closed mind seemed to be there."

"Did you find anything to lead us in an insider trading direction?" Marty continued inquisitively.

"There was actually." Jason took a gulp, he was nervous about speaking to Marty, but also confident because he knew he was working his passion and the sky was the limit. "Obviously we're looking at illegal immigration, that's why we went to the rally in the first place."

"Right, I know."

"So we're there and a guy starts spouting how they're taking our jobs, how we have to build a fence, and throw out all illegals because they're sucking us dry economically and giving us diseases. It was his reason for why our economy is in the toilet and can't seem to recover."

"Okay, so the usual?"

"Yeah, the usual vitriol you'd expect to hear. The speaker then said something that struck a chord with me."

"You got struck by something at a tea party rally, I'm going to remember you said that," Marty razzed with a chuckle.

"He said politicians talked tough, but didn't really do anything to combat the immigration problem. They insure the system stays the way it is because they're making too much money to stop it."

"Okay, now I'm interested." Marty sat up in his chair as a light bulb went off in his head.

"Once he brought up two-faced politicians which any thinking person knows has always existed, he was forcibly exited from the stage. Bryan and I went to investigate, and found him around the rear of the building covered in bruises like he was beat up and thrown out the backdoor.

The guy was actually somebody I knew from school, and we all met up for a drink after the ordeal just to catch up."

"I hope this is leading somewhere," Marty impatiently added, like a guy who didn't have time for unimportant details.

"We were minding or own business having some drinks and laughs remembering the old days, when this guy comes up and taps Aaron on the shoulder." Jason felt like he was reporting to his commander on one of those cops shows his mom likes to watch.

"And then what?"

"The man that tapped Aaron on the shoulder wasn't just anybody. It was the Congressman that was going to speak at the rally right after him. He said Aaron shouldn't have been thrown out because he'd run to their enemies for help, all the while staring at me."

"Why was he staring at you?"

"He wasn't just staring, he was glaring into my soul, like he was trying to make me spontaneously combust. He sat there and threatened Aaron for a bit while Bryan and I sipped our beers."

"Does this story have a point, my patience is wearing thin?"

"We think this Congressman was staring at me because he knew me. Or should I say knew of me. Remember that water park story?"

"Of course, that's why I brought you here."

"That's funny, that's the same thing Bryan said. Anyway, because he was talking to Aaron but glaring at me, I knew there had to be a reason. When he finally left after ten minutes, it dawned on me. When I brought that construction guy down for smuggling illegals and murdering troublemakers….." exclaimed Jason, tooting his own horn a bit.

"Of course I remember that, and?" Marty fired back, waiting for the punchline.

"When I took him down, I heard about a Congressman who was bribing cops and lawmakers to get illegal workers into the country. Basically, he was the string puller that made the whole operation possible."

"How do you know he was the guy? What's your evidence?"

"Call it a gut feeling. I know you'll say that I'm too young and inexperienced to have gut feelings. I'm telling you the way this guy scowled at me I must have made him feel threatened, which really pissed him off."

"You must have."

"So what should we do? Should we start investigating the Congressman? What would you do?"

Marty leaned back in his chair for a minute. "You boys care for a belt of scotch?"

"It's 1030 am, isn't that a little early?" Jason queried since they were at work. It wasn't as if a family friend offered him a beer at 8am because they were helping move stuff out of a house.

"Come on, what are you going to do, tell the boss? Oh wait, I am the boss. So just shut up, and drink," Marty demanded welcomingly, but forcibly because he wanted to make sure the boys didn't take this lightly.

Jason and Bryan relented and were handed glasses with some of the finest twenty one year old scotch money could buy. "So what's so important you have us drinking when we should be having a midmorning snack?" Jason blurted trying to prove he was still on his toes.

"This guy you've described, this Mark Ridell is a nasty individual," recalled Marty as he gulped down his drink and poured another. "I dealt with him in the past when I looked into polluting factories that bribed regulators so their safety inspections would look better than they actually were. This guy was pulling all the strings behind the scenes, the guy that made everything run smoothly."

"So the middle man?"

"Kind of, more like a facilitator. Like everything had to pass through him, or it wouldn't get done. It didn't matter if it was a chain link fence that needed to be built, a new steam stack, or somebody needing to be paid off or silenced. He was the guy that made sure it happened.

Does he have somebody pulling his strings? Probably, that's how spider webs function. You think you've figured them out, then you find a leg that goes somewhere you didn't expect.

For now, I'd focus on Ridell. It can't be a coincidence he reappeared, there must be something big going on. Go after him."

CHAPTER TWENTY SIX

Jason and Bryan walked out of Marty's office with heads full of confidence they could accomplish something great. The material they found and the story produced would put everything they previously did to shame.

"This is it huh, my big break?" theorized Jason as if he didn't already know the answer, and just wanted Bryan to say the words.

"Oh, you mean besides you coming here," reacted Bryan as he gave Jason a no shit look. "You need to prove you can not only run with the big boys, but beat them to the punch and put them down when they deserve to be put down."

"That's true, and I appreciate your help with everything so far. I wouldn't have had such a good start without you."

"No problem man. I want to do some good too, ya know?"

After the both of them had enough of a chick moment, they rode the elevator down to Jason's office to come up with a strategy.

"Where should we go first? What should we look into? Should we go straight for the Congressman, or somebody else at the rally?" Jason hypothesized, trying to put all his options on the table while walking in the door. They hadn't even sat down on the amazingly comfortable leather furniture before Jason spoke again.

"Okay listen, before we get started, we have to make sure we have each other's backs." Jason wore a caring but serious look on his face that let Bryan know he meant business. "If we're going to unravel this spider web, I need to know that when the spiders start coming at us, and they will, hell they already have with Ridell back at the bar. I need to know that when we get closer to the truth and they get really pissed, that you'll be there, I need a partner in all this."

"Of course man, I got you, don't worry," Bryan reflected as reassuringly as he could. He was worried Jason might crack under the pressure, but worried that he might too.

"Let's go over the material we have and see where it leads," shared Jason. They poured over all the notes and literature they had from the rally, the Congressman, the waterpark, everything. "We should start one of those Beautiful Mind things on the wall, so we can see how it all fits together."

"That's a good idea." Bryan grabbed some papers and pinned them to the wall. While Bryan was constructing what he hoped would be the downfall of the powerful, Jason's mind started to wander. How was Christina he thought? With him doing so well in New York and hot on the heels of uncovering something he always dreamed of uncovering, he realized he hadn't thought about her much until now. What was she up to, how was she? Was she getting along okay? Was she moving up at her company? Was she able to work on exciting cases where she could uncover something incriminating to take down some powerful people?

Jason thought the most amazing woman in the world would surely have a master plan. He also wondered if she ever thought about him, because he was consciously trying not to think about her. He needed to focus on the next step in his career.

Sometimes Jason felt empty inside, a void where Christina used to reside. He missed her so much he wondered how he could go on, or why he should even get out of bed. He then remembered something she said right before he left. Christina told him that no matter what happened, she would always be with him. He would always be able to feel her spirit and energy as long as their souls stay connected. Jason smiled and knew that wherever she was, she was doing okay, because he was too.

"You going to help me man, or just sit there?" Bryan questioned flippantly because he was doing all the work.

"Sorry man, I was daydreaming a bit," replied Jason feeling a bit dazed.

"You were thinking about Christina huh," Bryan observed as he gave Jason a look that said don't bullshit a bull-shitter.

"Yeah, I just miss her that's all. I know she'd want me to do this, because the actions you and I are about to take will be for the betterment and positive evolution of the human race, or at least take it the next step."

"Taking down a Congressman would definitely do that," deduced Bryan trying to come off as experienced, but knew he had never succeeded in taking somebody powerful down.

"Alright, here I come."

Jason and Bryan worked for the next few hours pinning up pertinent information to the case. They had full color brochures from the rally, news clippings about the event, and endless anti-immigrant material published by groups fighting for and against it in the area. They also had Congressional minutes Bryan obtained years before from a source he wasn't sure would ever be useful. He felt now was as a good a time as any to find out. Once everything was spread out on the wall, they tied strings from points in certain stories that connected to others, almost as if they were creating something.

"I always said if you want to unravel a spider web, you have to construct one yourself," Jason illustrated, knowing he never said such a thing before, but should have. "Oh look at the time, we should order some food."

Jason called up for some of those amazing Cuban sandwiches he loved. It was one of the first happy memories he had in New York. He thought it poetic since he was entrenched, and needed all the good energy he could get.

"Looks like our Congressman's been speaking about illegal immigration since college, way before he ran for office," Jason noticed while reading the bio on Ridell's Congressional website. "Also looks like he was forced into the family construction and farming business because his dad was a dick, and wouldn't let him be a dancer like he wanted."

"A dancer, really, it says that? That's the most stereotypical thing he could say to a tough marine father who fought in multiple wars and very passionately wanted his son to toughen up." Bryan was beginning to see why all this was coming up now. "I remember collecting material on Congressman Ridell before he was a big wig on the anti-immigrant scene. Whenever I wanted to do a story about illegal workers, I could always look to him for sharp insights."

"So basically, he wasn't manly enough for the dad who wanted his son to follow in his footsteps. How did he end up becoming just like him, or at least do what his dad wanted him to do, portray the illusion of toughness?" Jason speculated, wondering what Bryan knew.

"When I came to town a while back, it was my shot at the big time, kind of like how it is for you now. I was a young hot shot with something to prove. I wanted to uncover all evil doings. I wanted to take influence and power from people that should never have had it in the first place."

"Ok, so you were just like me. Except I didn't come here to take power and influence, I came here to help humanity with its next evolutionary step. We do have many of the same goals, that's the reason we're working together I'm sure. What changed?"

"I caught wind that Ridell's dad was killed under very suspicious circumstances, and decided I should investigate. There I was, young and dumb and thought I could just leap into a world of murder and nothing would happen. That couldn't have been farther from the truth."

"Why are you just telling me about this now? Why didn't you tell me you had a history with this Congressman while Aaron and I were trying to figure out what the hell was going on?"

"I don't know, I'm sorry about that. Now that he's around though, he probably has unfinished business. I knew once we started digging, everything would come together like it was supposed to. I can't go into this thinking there isn't a reason for everything, that's where I screwed up last time.

I thought about all these random events, and failed to see how they were interconnected. You, me, Aaron, even Marty had dealings with this guy. Since it's all coming to a head now, there still must be lessons to learn. Maybe we're being pulled together because we opened up to the possibility that life was more complex than it appears," Bryan blurted out in a fast paced verbal up-chuck.

"Okay, I get what you're saying. Everything is interconnected, and we have to keep our heads in the right place to see how it all plays out. Continue with what you investigated before."

Suddenly there was a knock, and from the smell emanating under the crack in the door, Jason knew what it was.

"I love that smell, hey man, lunch is here," declared Jason, eager to answer the door and bring the smell from thought into reality. "I'm a good Jewish boy that loves pork, sue me."

Bryan chuckled, "how much do I owe you man?"

"Don't worry, this one is on me, or should I say it's on Marty," Jason countered as he held up the company credit card he had been using for expenses.

"Nice, food always tastes better when somebody else pays."

"I fully agree."

They sat down and ate like a pack of wild hogs, but Jason's mind kept rolling. "So tell me more about this guy, I want to know about your link to him."

"Okay okay," relented Bryan as he took a big bite of his sandwich. "Damn this is good."

"It sure is."

"Anyway, I was investigating who killed Ridell's dad. I poked around and talked to a lot of people as I would in any investigation. Once I interviewed some of the dad's friends, I discovered he had quite the temper, and liked to be rough with Mark. Normally he would just beat the mom, but when he got really drunk he'd take it out on his son. When he got tired of hitting the boy, he would sexually abuse him, because that's what every father of the year does right?"

"Then what happened?"

"One night Mark waited for his father to fall asleep or pass out from drinking too much, and then bludgeoned him to death with a sledgehammer."

"Brutal man, damn."

"Brutal is right, apparently it took them weeks to clean up all the blood because it splattered everywhere. So as I'm checking into it, I start thinking about what I would've done in that situation. If my dad had been beating and raping me, I would probably beat him to death too. I started feeling sympathy."

"That makes it hard to be objective, that's why they say to not get personally involved with your stories and sources."

"I know, but once I realized he was only preventing himself and his mother from being beaten and raped more, how could I help the cops find him? How could I with good conscience report everything I knew? They'd lock him up and throw away the key. Even though his dad was dead, Mark would still be controlled by him. Hell he'd be spending the rest of his life in prison because of him."

"So what did you do?"

"I made sure he didn't get caught by planting evidence that led the cops towards arresting another guy who had a warrant on rape charges anyway. They convicted him to life in prison.

Afterword, I kept investigating Ridell, and found out he was involving himself with all sorts of shady underground characters. Basically he was cool with anybody that showed him at least the illusion of respect. He started committing all sorts of awful crimes, and the more power and influence he gained, the harder and harder it was to get close to him.

Now that you and I are investigating him for this conspiracy stuff, It makes me upset I didn't bring him down back then, it might have prevented all this from happening."

"It might have, it might not have. I mean if it wasn't this Congressman behind a big scheme, it would be another.

I want to prove to you, Marty, myself and the world that when human beings are presented with information that makes the powerful less so and the powerless more so, they will stand up. When we take this guy down, and we will, it will be because we knew we could, because it was the right thing to do."

"You're right Jason we need to go after Ridell. We need to take him down before he hurts anybody else."

CHAPTER TWENTY SEVEN

Congressman Mark Ridell used to be human, now he's whatever the quick and vast accumulation of money and power calls for. To say he's a whore would be too light a term. To say he's the epitome of what's wrong with society is a little more in the ball park.

Bryan and Jason were working the case as well as they could for an entire day now, but they still needed evidence to tie Ridell directly to the schemes they both knew he orchestrated.

"So what's our next step? How do we go after this guy," Jason questioned, not sure what direction to take. "I'm sure you don't want to see him because he abandoned you after you got him off the hook. What a bastard, saying he didn't owe you anything. Does he have an office? What do you think about me just showing up and talking to him?"

"You're just going to stroll into his office and ask him to what, give himself up for the good of humanity?" sniped Bryan with a bit of sarcasm. "Do you really think he'll crack that easily? He didn't climb high up the corruption ladder without covering his tracks. Don't you know they teach how to cover things up in Politician 101."

"They have a Politician 101?"

"Of course, it's right next to bull-shitting class, and across the hall from how to steal from the poor and give to the rich class. You know the usual political prerequisites."

"Yeah I bet they take all that," Jason sardonically uttered with a laugh, knowing that humor was essential in what they were about to undertake. "Don't those classes come right before they receive their get out of jail free card, and right after they get their above the law card."

One of the reasons Jason and Bryan worked so well together is they both knew how ridiculously corrupt the whole political system proved to be. It provided mountains of material to use for articles, features, and taking somebody down who deserved to be taken down. All of it was easily accessible, they just needed to show the world.

"What about that friend of yours Aaron? It seems like we parted ways pretty abruptly once you and I got what we needed," relived Bryan, trying to steer the conversation back to the task at hand. "Is he staying locally, or did he just come in for the rally that didn't go so well?"

"I think he's around, I'll try giving him a call. When we were hanging out, he told me he'd really like to help us. I'm not saying that because he's an old friend and I'm trying to play catch up for something bad I may or may not have done. I'm saying it because he has a strong passion for this stuff."

"At this point, I have to trust your instincts. We're hotter on the trail of Congressman shithead than I've ever been. I can't wait to see how it all plays out. My hope is that it ends with a corrupt politician in jail."

"Before we break out the champagne, let me call Aaron. Maybe he has found something to help track Ridell."

Jason picked up the phone and dialed Aaron's phone number to ask for help, when all of a sudden it felt like déjà vu. He was having a flashback of when he and Aaron were both in school and he'd call to see if they should go out drinking, or just chill at home with beers and look at the stars.

Jason was unnerved that he left Aaron behind, but their paths weren't the same. He hadn't thought about him for years. Then once he was speeding down his own path, he ends up finding Aaron traveling the same path. The whole thing seemed like the ultimate black and white definition of synchronicity, but that's why Jason needed to call Aaron. He needed to see if there was any more purpose behind their one chance meeting. Was Aaron going to help Bryan and him take Ridell down?

"Hello," Aaron slurred like he had been woken up.

"What's up man, how you doing today?" queried Jason, hoping Aaron's friendship was all he thought it was; his intuition had never been wrong before.

"I'm all right, just waking up. That was a crazy one a couple days ago. I don't know how today could possibly top it, but if you're calling this early, I'm sure it'll be a doozy."

"You give me way too much credit man. We had so many good conversations back in the day. We would talk about politics, sports or whatever was going on in the world. When I moved, I felt everybody was on a different path then me. I had to try something and some place completely new. It's funny how I thought we were on different paths, but now here we are both going after the same thing."

"I did wonder just what the hell happened to you. All of a sudden you weren't returning my calls when you always had before. At this point we could spend all day arguing about what happened, whose fault it was and who is different than who. In the end though, does it really matter?"

"Of course not."

"Right. So what do you say we go after this sorry excuse for a human being and take him down? We were brought back into each other's lives for a reason, this might be it."

"Cool. Can you meet me at the diner on the corner of 5th and Starkly? It's right around the corner from my office, and has the best breakfast in town. Well I think it does, of course I haven't tried every single restaurant in the city, but I think it measures up pretty good," perceived Jason. His mouth was watering for food, and his passion was yearning for humanitarian brownie points.

"Sure, that sounds good. See you in twenty?"

"Ok, see you."

Jason and Bryan arrived at the diner before Aaron, so they got some coffee and waited. "For a little place they have really great coffee," proclaimed Jason who was beginning to be happy in a city, something he never thought possible.

After sitting for twenty minutes and Aaron not showing up, they decided to order because the decibels of Jason's stomach rumbling was deafening.

"Where is this guy? What was all that stuff about wanting to help find Ridell, maybe he changed his mind. Maybe he is just as much bullshit as the politicians. Hell, maybe they're working together and both laughing at us right now because we haven't figured it out," Jason deduced, trying to contain all the thoughts burning in his brain.

"You said Aaron was very receptive, especially when you apologized," recalled Bryan trying to make Jason feel better. He also wanted to remind Jason of the actual obstacles in front of him, not just what his mind was tricking him into thinking was in front of him.

"Maybe, I don't know what to think anymore, everything seems to be moving too fast," Jason added, nervous about his path forward.

"Did you expect it to be slow when we went deep?"

"I always knew the whole thing would speed up, it's just hard with that whole expect the unexpected thing. By definition it makes it hard to prepare."

As Jason took a sip of coffee, his cell phone rang. The caller ID said it was Aaron. Maybe he finally dragged himself out of bed Jason thought, and realized the greasy spoon chosen for their morning meeting, was great at curing hangovers.

"What's up man? Where are you at?" Jason spouted, curious about his friend because he really wanted the chance to hang out again.

"Awwww, you must be Jason," answered the voice on the other end that definitely wasn't Aaron.

"Who is this is? Where's Aaron?" clamored Jason, whose curiosity feelers went up immediately.

"We've been following you for some time. It's amazing you've gotten this far. It's a testament to your talent."

"Who are you? What do you mean you've been following me? Where is Aaron?"

"He's safe for now don't worry. What you should do is back the hell off. Don't stick your nose where it doesn't belong. We know about the rally, we threw Aaron out for losing faith. We know he met up with you afterward.

Hell, we even know that because you broke some water park story you were brought to New York City. Now you are a pain in the ass on the east coast just like you were on the west coast. We should have stopped you back then. If we did, your so-called fight for justice would have been written off as the maniacal ravings of yet another conspiracy theorist. If that dumb-ass wouldn't have committed murder with a million witnesses around, we would be in a very different position."

Jason was stunned, this guy seemed to know about his journey and rise to stardom. He knew about Aaron and how he turned into a supposed traitor. Jason also wondered if this guy knew about Bryan and Marty. Judging by how things were going so far, he wasn't ruling it out.

"I don't know what to say."

"You have nothing to say? Some guy calls you on an old friend's phone, and tells you he knows everything about you and your friend's lives, and you're not a little curious?"

"Oh I'm curious I'm just trying to process."

"Let me break it down so it will be easier to digest. Since we are always watching, it was easy to take Aaron, who is safe for now. He's being held where you can never find him. Back off. Stop digging. Stop trying to find out who is behind keeping illegal immigration illegal. Stop trying to see how much money is being made by keeping those filthy mongrels picking oranges, peaches, building stuff and whatever the hell else they do. Bottom line, if you back off, we'll let your friend go and you can start trying to be friends again.

If you screw with us though, and try to threaten our power, not only will you never find Aaron, but you and everybody you know will be put through such a living hell, you'll wish you were all dead. Do I make myself clear?"

"Crystal. How do we know when we've backed off enough? When will we know if we've gone far enough for you to free Aaron?"

"That's the thing, you don't. You also don't know if I'm lying. That's just how the game is played. When you sat at home with Christina and wondered what your life was going to bring, you wanted to do something, but didn't know what. You dreamed of taking down people like me, people who commit heinous crimes because we know we'll never get caught. You're going to have to forget that dream Mr. Jason. Forget something like that might be possible, because it's not."

"How do I know Aaron is okay? Is he even still alive?"

Jason's phone instantly vibrated with a multimedia message, which meant a picture. "There. I'll call you in a week, if you've backed off, I'll think about letting your friend go."

The line went dead, and Jason just sat there wondering what to say. What could he possibly say to Bryan to make him understand what just transpired?

"What happened man, is he coming for breakfast?" speculated Bryan with an innocent look on his face. "I'm getting pretty hungry."

"No, no Aaron isn't going to make it."

"Did he already eat or something? Maybe we can meet up with him some other time then. If his passion is half as strong as yours, then it will be smooth sailing when we make these shitheads pay."

Jason just shrugged his shoulders. "They took Aaron," Jason responded as he showed the picture to Bryan. "They threatened me and everybody I know because they think we're getting too close. They knew everything about me. Maybe they're tapping my phones, my place, I don't know. Apparently they've been watching me since the waterpark, and have been keeping tabs to make sure I don't get out of line."

"Well that sucks, but all I can say is now you've arrived. Once you and your inner circle have been threatened by a nameless and faceless entity for getting close to revealing a major kink in the system, you have truly arrived. They only threaten when they feel threatened. They're lashing out because they know we actually have a shot. If they know Aaron, who you are and what you're about, then they know me and everything I've done also. It's just one more leg of their spider web."

"So what do we do, how do we get Aaron back safely?" inquired Jason, very eager to rescue his friend.

"We go at them full force, we attack and don't let up. We must find hard evidence, something that can be proven in court, or at the very least be used to threaten them with.

Holding leverage over their heads is exactly the blackmail crap they always pull, maybe we can make a deal to get him back," suggested Bryan, trying to offer a solution.

"You want to make a deal with them? Isn't that like selling your soul?"

"I'm only telling you from experience it's going to get really ugly. You think it's bad now because they took your friend. It gets so much worse from here. I want to make sure you and I are prepared. Once we enter this fight, there's no turning back. The only way to really get your friend back is by taking them down. We could lose everything, or we could gain everything. They say life comes down to choices. Well we have a choice, and a chance to do something great for humanity," bellowed Bryan with as much passion as he could drum up.

"Well I choose to move forward, I choose to do good by getting rid of trash that doesn't serve our collective and positive evolution."

"So you're in?"

"Oh I'm in. This is going to lead to where I've always wanted to go. I was born ready, and trained all my life for the chance. Let's do it, let's change the world."

CHAPTER TWENTY EIGHT

Jason and Bryan walked out of the diner exploding with the energy that only an authentic good versus evil battle could produce. The fight would be hard, but would provide the clarity to Jason's journey that he's longed for.

"So what should we do next? I want to do something right now, yesterday, now," Jason blurted very impatiently as he and Bryan hopped in the Lincoln so they could head back to Jason's office and game-plan their next move. "I feel like it's my fault they took Aaron, if they hurt him, it's on my hands."

"Look, I know you want your friend back, and we will get him back," related Bryan with a confidence that only came from somebody who pictured an endgame. "We have to calm down, breathe, and think rationally about our next move. The worst thing we could do is act without thinking. If we're trying to beat these people down, we need to strategically think about what causes them harm. We can't let our personal emotions get in the way. We're dealing with some heavy stuff here. If we show any weakness, they'll smell it a mile away and use it against us before we have a chance to mount an attack."

"Okay, okay, okay. It's just I am so anxious, scared, excited. Pretty much every emotion is coursing through my veins right now. I'm just trying to grasp onto something before I go spinning out of control."

"Well, that's what I'm here for. I watch out for you and you watch out for me, that's what partners do."

"That's what friends do."

The traffic was surprisingly light as they meandered through the city back to the office. Maybe everybody at the office was inside working or eating lunch at their desk Jason thought. Had any of them even thought about attempting something like he was about to? Where would he go from here? Was he going to look the answer up in the newspaper, a book, what? His mind was going crazy with all the possibilities of what could be, what could happen, and what would happen especially if his habit of self-sabotage took over.

Bryan pulled the Lincoln into the Democratic Republic's parking garage just after eleven. They sat at the diner for almost two hours before leaving. They both always knew that one day they'd be fighting corruption. Now the day is here, it's real, and it's time to show what they're made of, so what were they waiting for?

"What are you waiting for?" pondered Bryan because Jason had been sitting in the car for five minutes after Bryan had already gotten out. "You just going to sit there? Are we going to do this thing?"

"We're going to do this man, hold on. I'm just kind of shocked, I don't know what to do or where to go," explained Jason nervously, knowing his words sounded just as crazy as they did in his head.

"It's okay man, let's just go up to your office and plan some shit."

"All my life I've needed somebody to be there for me, to bounce ideas off of, to work with, and to bring me back down to earth when my mind floats away, thank you man."

"No problem man. You can thank me all you want when we bring down this untouchable Congressman, and your buddy is back safe. Let's stop on the main floor first, I want to talk to some people"

Jason finally exited the Lincoln and joined Bryan on the ride up to the main floor. They had barely gotten off the elevator when they noticed something crazy going on. Everybody was running around like chickens without heads, and even more so than usual.

"What the hell is going on around here?" shouted Bryan with a look of surprise mixed with a little fear.

"We got a call raving about how somebody here is under investigation for illegal wiretapping, and if that employee didn't stop, they'd close down the whole magazine, and throw us all out on the street. Not just out of a job, but if we live in employer bought housing, that is going away as well," Marty's secretary yelled back. She rarely saw Bryan on the newsroom floor, and started to wonder if he was involved.

"Who would make such a call? Who has the pull to make something like that happen? Would somebody actually do that because of one employee," queried Bryan, thinking of possibilities so far-fetched only a desperate conspiracy theorist would think them.

"I don't know, in all the years I've worked for Marty, I've never received a call like that. We've dealt with heavy hitters too, some real power brokers that lost their power directly due to some story one of our people broke."

"When they called and said somebody better stop wiretapping, did they give a name," Bryan honed in as he entered full truth finding mode.

"They didn't, all they said was that this person needed to stop."

"They said nothing else, even if it seemed insignificant? Sometimes the littlest details can break the case," Jason interjected as his ears perked up watching the whole chaotic scene.

"I guess there was this one weird thing. He said nobody can stop them, not even a critic."

Jason thought for a moment, and then it came to him. "Hey Bryan, let's go up to my office, I just thought of something. Thanks Barbara, you've been very helpful. Bryan and I will get to the bottom of this."

Barbara nodded as she walked away with a small smirk on her face almost too small to notice, but something Jason thought was interesting. What could that mean, how could she smile? No time for that now, he and Bryan had work to do.

"Sounds good man," added Bryan as they walked into the elevator. Once they exited onto Jason's floor, the guys knew something was off; they just weren't sure what.

"Something strange is going on I can feel it," expressed Jason as he and Bryan walked to his office door, opened it and went in. "It must be in the air."

"I think so. It was pandemonium in the newsroom, everybody running around yelling and screaming like 6 year olds on Halloween after too much candy," replied Bryan trying to lighten the mood a bit. "Up here, nothing, I don't hear anybody even walking around."

"Something is definitely up."

They walked over and sat down at his desk with a scotch poured from Jason's stash to think for a minute. "They must have been talking about me when they threatened the entire office. I'm just asking questions, you know, like any good citizen. Why are they doing this to me?" theorized Jason like he didn't already know the answer.

"Seriously, are you really asking me that right now?" questioned Bryan with a surprised look on his face because Jason didn't expect the absolute worst. "You think it's bad now, just wait. We have to work fast and be focused. We should get somewhere where we aren't being watched, taped, or followed."

"Somebody could even be listening to this conversation right now," Jason fretted as all his preconceived notions melted away. "I always knew it could get bad, but imagination and reality are two different things. Let's grab what info we have here, then hurry over to my place and grab everything there before they stake the place out if they haven't already. Do you have a safe house where we could post up for a few days so we actually have a shot at this thing?"

"I might have a place like that. We need to get there quick, we don't want them to find out where we're headed. It should buy us a few days to do what we need to do."

Jason and Bryan quickly grabbed what they needed out of the office, then raced in the Lincoln over to Jason's place and grabbed everything useful there.

Bryan and Jason arrived at the safe house in the late afternoon just as the sun was starting to set. "I'm getting hungry, think we can call that Cuban place for some sandwiches," Jason hoped, needing some food in his stomach before they brought down the vault of power. "I could really go for one right now."

"Are you nuts? We're hiding from the feds or whoever these people are, and you want to get food delivered so they can follow the delivery boy right to our doorstep? Or better yet pose as the delivery boy so we let them right in? Don't worry though, this place is my little bunker. I've stocked it with food, water and everything we need for at least six months. After I investigated Ridell the first time, I found this place in case I had to escape. I got caught up in the survivalist fad, but at least now it will serve the purpose it was meant for," expounded Bryan. He was happy to finally show his refuge to somebody ready to actually fight the power, and not just talk about it.

Jason grabbed a couple duffle bags from the trunk of the Lincoln, and followed Jason up a narrow staircase to a locked door. Once Bryan turned the key, Jason saw the door open to a small hallway with several doors. "What is this place, the labyrinth or something?" Jason sniped half joking but half not. "I know I should be expecting anything to happen at this point, but man, really?"

"Just follow me," Bryan relayed in a reassuring voice because he was trying to build Jason's trust, but also trying to keep himself calm.

Bryan unlocked one more door, which revealed a stair case that led down even further. After walking down what must have been three or four flights of stairs, Jason wanted to ask if they were there yet like an annoying kid on a family vacation.

"Here we are," exclaimed Bryan as he opened up the door at the bottom of the stairs. "Welcome to my home away from home."

"Its nice man, real crab-people esque." Jason was trying to make a joke he knew Bryan wouldn't find funny, but it made him laugh. "You like being underground?"

"Laugh all you want, but this is an old safe house the CIA abandoned back in the fifties after the Russians discovered it. It has passed through different corporate and private owners over the years, and then it came to rest in the hands of yours truly," explained Bryan proudly. "The feds won't come here because the enemy found its location. Since everything is so hi-tech now, they don't think they need bunkers like this anymore. They hide in plain sight and disguise themselves digitally, or so they think."

"Sweet man yeah, this place isn't bad. I was just giving you crap," Jason noted, feeling like Bryan was the partner he'd been waiting for. "Let's put all the stuff we have back up on the wall, there has to be something we missed."

"Sounds like a plan," agreed Bryan as he walked over to a little cabinet in the kitchen stocked with food. "First we must have a drink, a toast to a new partnership."

Bryan poured them each a two finger belt in some ornate crystal glasses he placed in his bunker for a special occasion.

"Is this eighteen year?" Jason queried as a smile broke out on his face.

"Actually its twenty one," answered Bryan as he raised his glass.

"It's good scotch, because that's what the good guys need, and we are the good guys," declared Jason, scared, but amazed he was about to do something he always dreamed of. "Here is to the continuance of a great partnership. May the powerless succeed over the powerful. May our actions reverberate so other people can stand up to their corrupt officials, and tell them exactly why they aren't going to take it anymore."

"Here here. Just because these bastards think they'll never be held accountable, doesn't mean they never will be."

CHAPTER TWENTY NINE

Congress is a funny place because you have to be accountable to voters, but you can also poke, push and prod people to attain what you want. You can pull strings and make people dance. Somebody can make you dance while you're making someone else dance, sometimes with or without your knowledge.

Jason and Bryan had a big task ahead of them. A task they could tackle as long as they stuck together, and didn't get sucked into the sabotage that was slowing down the evolution of humanity.

"You find anything man, all I'm seeing is a bunch of history on this guy. He was a trial lawyer before he was elected to Congress. Mr. Mark Ridell graduated Valedictorian from his high school and was the person everybody loved to hate," observed Bryan as he pointed to a picture from Ridell's high school yearbook he found on the internet. "Even back then people thought he was up to something. He would love you, and then screw you over."

"Crazy, seems like young shitheads really do grow up to be older shitheads," retorted Jason as he and Bryan laughed like only people who had everything on the line could. "I wonder what he did after that."

They scanned every inch of their evidence wall, while trying to research on their laptops for anything they could find.

"We have to ask ourselves who we're up against, what they want, and how we stop them. Sometimes a simple formula does the trick, especially when dealing with something really complex. It can reverse the cycle," intuited Jason as he looked at Bryan, expecting him to say something brilliant to lead them to the answer that would end this whole mess.

"That sounds like a good idea, let's sit down for a minute and consider our options," replied Bryan. He and Jason sat around what would be their kitchen table, dining table, poker table, and whatever else they needed a table for.

"So the guy is Mark Ridell?" theorized Bryan as he took a sip of scotch, "you want a beer man?"

"Sure," Jason anxiously answered, wanting to quench the dry mouth caused by over action of his brain. "So what does Ridell want?"

"He wants to make tons of money, while gaining as much power and influence as he can along the way."

"Kind of like every politician ever?"

"Yeah pretty much."

Jason gave Bryan a look like they were starting from the beginning. He sat there for a minute and thought about Christina, had she moved on? Had she found happiness without him? Amidst the whirlwind of thoughts of what used to be, Jason remembered something Christina told him when they first met. She mentioned a flower that would only bloom if you let it bloom on its own. Jason wondered why he was thinking of this now when it seemed to have nothing to do with anything. Then it struck him, Christina was saying if you really want to take somebody down, not only do you have to catch them in the act, but for them to stay caught, they must trip themselves up.

"You still with me man?" wondered Bryan because Jason looked like he had a flashback to another time and place. "You were thinking about Christina again weren't you? We have to stay focused right now. You do have to deal with her, but right now we have to deal with what's in front of us. We need something real to grab onto, I think it was you who told me that."

Jason paused for a minute before the right words came. "I was thinking about Christina, and you're right I definitely have some issues I need to deal with concerning me and her. It's just something she said years ago rushed back. It was about a flower, and letting it bloom."

"A flower bloom, we're trying to take down a Congressman for illegally smuggling people and who knows what else into the country, and you're thinking about flowers and your ex?" criticized Bryan, concerned Jason might not have the cajones to complete the job.

"A flower bloom yes, but it's what that bloom represented. For people to be truly held accountable, they have to walk into a trap with a full head of confidence that they'll never get caught. They must assume they will always be two steps ahead of their enemies."

"Two steps, what one isn't good enough?"

"When you are dealing with billions of dollars, you have to take all the precautions you can." It hit Jason like a ton of bricks. "We have to set a trap for Ridell to walk into. We can't always play defense against the steps he takes, so we have to go on the offensive and ensnare him like salmon in a gill net."

"That sounds like a good idea. I guess I never felt confident enough to do that when I investigated him before. He beat me every time I tried to do anything," lamented Bryan with a sad look on his face.

"Don't worry man, we'll get this guy," comforted Jason, trying to reassure Bryan. It seemed a much more natural role than the other way around, but what was he going to do, he was still the new guy.

"So the answer to our third question is figuring out what he wants. We know he wants money and power. We could pose as corporate executives and make him a deal or a bribe that would get him caught. Maybe we could pose as fake border patrol agents and make a deal with them as they smuggle people in. Maybe we could get hired as farm hands or factory workers and work our way in from the outside?" offered Bryan, trying to help the inspirational guy sitting next to him. What an amazing human being Bryan thought, feeling some of the energy Marty must have when he hired Jason.

"Well here's something," Jason noticed, pointing at his laptop for Bryan to look. "It says here Ridell proposed legislation this morning that would change zoning laws to allow a building for something called Moon Systems. Ridell was an executive there before he got elected. He worked his way up after starting fresh out of high school. It also says he didn't sell his stock in the company when he took office."

"Well he's definitely not the only person to ever do that," all politicians do Bryan thought. "What's your point?"

"My point is that he still owns stock. He's trying to pass a bill that will make his former company a boatload of money, visa vie making him a lot of money. It's the very definition of insider trading, somebody using information nobody else has to game the market."

Bryan sat in disbelief. How could Jason be getting this close this quickly? He looked into this guy on and off for years and had never been in the same ballpark of information. Was he really that good, or was he part of the problem? Was he a Ridell spy sent in to rot the plan from the inside? What did he even know of Jason before a month or two ago?

"So what do you think we should do," inquired Bryan, thinking Jason couldn't possibly be this good if he didn't have inside help. "You should go right up to Ridell, and say you know he's full of shit."

"I would love nothing more than to do that, and I probably will when he's being led away in handcuffs. Right now however, we need to focus on making our way into Moon Systems."

Jason and Bryan pondered for a bit, but nothing seemed to come. All the dust that got kicked up was settling, and they didn't know where to turn. It's like when somebody starts a journey and is very motivated to move forward. Then when they get halfway to their goals, they start losing steam, and wonder what can get them going again.

Out of the blue, the phone rang.

"Hello, is this the jerk that has my buddy?" Jason defiantly demanded because he saw on the caller ID who was calling.

"Is that anyway to talk to somebody holding your friend's life in his hands," questioned the guy on the other line who sounded like Ridell, but Jason wasn't sure. "Have you been behaving?"

"You threaten my office and say everybody will be thrown out of their jobs and homes, why should I behave myself."

"Did you forget I could kill your friend at any time?"

Jason received a picture message of Aaron being held with a knife to his throat. He couldn't see who was holding the knife, but by zooming in he could see an American flag pin on the captors lapel.

"Doing your own dirty work I see, what's wrong, couldn't find anybody to do it for you," Jason bantered, knowing what he saw and knew he had to stand up for himself.

"This is how it's going to be, a speech will be made next week about a new bill to rezone a certain piece of land. If it passes, I'll let you off the hook and release your friend. If for any reason that bill stalls or doesn't pass, I'll kill your friend and send you his body parts one at a time."

Jason was shocked and didn't know what to say. Bryan would usually consult Marty at times like this, but he recognized the voice on the phone. He would take care of this situation himself. Bryan grabbed the phone and let it fly.

"Who do you think you are threatening my friends like that?" Bryan interrogated, as he faintly heard the Virginia Cavaliers fight song in the back ground. "Just tell us where you're holding our friend, I promise I won't expose you?"

"Won't expose me, what could a little fly like you do to me?"

"A lot more than you think, Bill."

The only sound on the other end of the phone was a man breathing hard like he was going to say something, but then decided against it and hung up.

"Did you scare him? Did he hang up out of fear?" Jason guessed as he began to see why Marty brought Bryan to New York, he still had spark in him after all these years. "Who is Bill?"

"I guess I owe you an explanation," figured Bryan as he took a deep breath like he was about to tell his life story. "I recognized his voice on the phone, I don't know if you noticed, but it was a different guy from who called the first time."

"I didn't notice that. Again, who is Bill? Why did mentioning his name make him hang up?"

"Bill Shultz was majority whip until he got busted for insider trading some years back. Ever since he's been working his way through the business world, investment banking, hedge fund managing, fixing, etc...; basically making as much money as he can."

"Continue."

"He also graduated from the University of Virginia. I recognized the fight song in the back ground when he was on the phone. He was into funding non-profits through all sorts of legal and illegal means, special funds, shell companies, whatever got the job done. Now he is into the immigrant game, pulling strings for business leaders so they can get cheap labor for their factories and fields. He also pulls strings so Congressman and Senators pass the legislation they want passed. He is very good at making problems disappear."

"Basically he's a fixer with a brain, an evil and greedy man that only cares about money. Great, sounds like every politician in Washington, again we're at square one. How did you know it was him? How do you know this much about him?"

"He is a dangerous person that needs to be stopped. If he's the one holding your friend, I know where they might be. He has some holdings in Virginia, a few abandoned buildings near the university. I'll bet anything Aaron is being held there."

Jason was still baffled how Bryan could know all this, and was still wondering why he wouldn't tell him how he recognized Bill's voice. "Okay, say he is held there, great, how are we going to get him? We aren't cops and can't just go in with guns blazing. What about the Congressman?"

Knowing that he was about to be forced to fulfill his destiny like Jason was being forced to fulfill his, Bryan spoke, "Bill always looks for a good opportunity to make money, especially from politicians. They know he can pull the strings they need pulled. I'll bet dollars to donuts that Bill is working on the Moonsystems re-zoning legislation Ridell proposed. He must be facilitating its passage."

"Okay, so he's helping, but that still doesn't tell me how we're going to catch him in the act?"

"Listen, if Bill himself called and said they're holding your friend, it means he doesn't trust other people to do his dirty work. He's a firm believer in, you want something done right you do it yourself.

We should go to the warehouse where Bill and your friend could be. Since its Ridell's law he's fixing, Ridell is probably there too. The place is extremely insulated. People go in and out when they have something they don't want anybody to see. We'll get a bird's eye view of your friend to make sure he's in there, and see how many guards they have outside. We'll distract them with some loud sound effects played from speakers stashed in a bush nearby. When the guards leave to check what the noise was, we'll scoot past them and into the building. Once we're in, there is a certain room used for interrogations, I'm sure that's where he's being held."

Still not knowing what to think, Jason decided to just play along and see where Bryan was leading him. "Okay, so we get past the guards into the building and close to where Aaron is held. How will we bring them down? How will we make them pay?"

"Well with hidden cameras of course and recorders. I have the best equipment available. When we go in we'll be wearing some of the highest tech cameras and recorders the industry provides. They are made to look like pieces of clothing."

"So we slip in past the guards, covered in recording equipment, walk up and get them to confess? You really think they're just going to confess to us?"

"They're the type of people so confident in their ability to never get caught they think they never will be. They think because they're so insulated, they can beat back anybody or anything that comes at them."

"If we get them to admit what they're up to, great. How do we get out of there with Aaron and without them killing us? You think they'll just let us go?"

"I do because the cameras will be streaming a live video of the whole operation. Beforehand I'll send an email to the police and the feds with a link and how they should watch at a certain time, something I've done before. It's led to arrests on a handful of occasions. We stall Bill and Mark until the cavalry arrives to put them in cuffs, and take them to federal "pound you in the ass prison" where scum like them belong."

Now that the whole plan was laid out in front of him, Jason was beginning to think they might actually be able to pull it off. Since he had no other ideas or plans, he figured it was worth a shot. "Okay, let's do it."

"Great, so we do this tomorrow, the sooner the better. I have all the equipment here, and we can send the emails right from your laptop. Are you ready for this? You came to New York to take some people down, and now that opportunity has arrived, how do you feel?"

"My life is beginning to feel truly purposeful, tomorrow will be legendary" uttered Jason with a smile. He was truly satisfied with the path he and Bryan were on. "Tomorrow is the big day, awesome. Just one more question, again, how did you recognize that Bill guy? If I'm going to risk my life, I need to know all the details."

"He's my brother."

CHAPTER THIRTY

"Bill is your brother? You don't think that information could have been useful before?" Jason insisted, feeling slighted by the secret. He wondered if Bryan's loyalties were really with him and their operation. "Why keep this from me, considering what we're doing tomorrow?"

"I didn't know how you'd take it. Yes Bill is my brother, but we haven't talked in years. He went off the rails a while back and I didn't want to be involved with his schemes, let alone the people he was getting involved with," Bryan defensively stated with as much honesty as his body contained. "We parted ways because we had different goals. He wanted to improve only himself, because that's all he cared about. I wanted to help improve everybody's lives. You know the old saying, "we all do better when we all do better?" Yeah, that's kind of something I live by."

Jason wondered if he should believe Bryan. He was attempting the most risky operation of his life, and he had to be able to trust his partner. If their cameras were found before Mark and Bill confessed, Jason and Bryan could be hurt or killed and have nothing to show for it. Such the inner dilemma, but something Jason knew he could handle because he'd been preparing all his life. Leaving the beautiful Christina to move across the country was hard, but became easier when he remembered his purpose was to create peace by taking corrupt people down, starting with Ridell.

"I believe you, I believe you, it's just a lot to take in. The idea that my partner is the brother of the guy me and him are chasing, is a lot for me to process," stated Jason totally exasperated. He was trying to wrap his head around the concept by the signs on his face, which Bryan easily picked up on.

"You're trying to make sense of this, and that's a good thing. On those cookie cutter cop shows, they'd pull the officer off the case because they couldn't ask them to go after a family member," responded Bryan trying to prove he could be trusted. "I'll go after Bill, don't worry about that. He's been a blameworthy string puller for a long time and deserves to be held accountable. He might fix people's problems, but we'll put him in a predicament he won't be able to squirm out of no matter how powerful his friends are."

"It's good to hear you're completely on board. Just one last question before I pass out, who else is your brother connected with? Is there anybody that might come looking for him?" Jason pondered very inquisitively.

"Bill could be linked to anybody in the country, or around the world for that matter. Like I said, he's fixed a lot of things for a lot of people. However, if the gate-keepers bottom line isn't hurt, they won't care one lick if he disappears. Hell, we would be doing them a favor by tying up one of their loose ends"

"It really is all about greed. It's about how much money they can make, and screw anybody who stands in their way, huh?"

"Yeah, pretty much. We do have to remember that when we take Bill and the Congressman down, the gate-keepers interests could be hurt, and they might come after us."

"Just spit it out."

"When we take these guys down, the fight isn't over. It will lead us to someone else, who leads to someone else and so on and so on."

"When does it end?"

"Who says it ever does? We just have to do as much good as we can while we're on this earth. When we engage there's no turning back. We must dedicate ourselves, because once we open the door, there's no returning to a normal apple pie life, ever, this will shake everything up."

Jason wanted nothing more than to take down the powers that be, and build something more equitable and fair in its place to serve every inhabitant on the planet. Was he willing to sacrifice everything to pursue the common good? It's what his mom would want for him, what Christina would want for him, and most of all, it's what he wanted for himself.

"I'm definitely in. I was born ready to show power hungry elites they can't get away scot-free no matter how insulated and protected they think they are. As long as you have my back, I have yours," Jason expressed with the confidence David had right before he slayed Goliath.

"I'm happy to hear that, and of course I have your back as well," Bryan fired back with a smile. He knew he had a partner that was as down for the cause as him, and maybe even more so. Bryan was sure glad Marty brought this wunderkind out from California. "Let's get some rest. We have a big day tomorrow."

"Night man."

The next morning a slow sunrise lingered in the sky like an annoying neighbor that wouldn't go away. Maybe it was the sky, the environment, or the operation about to commence, but Jason knew today would prove if he could be everything that his dreams were telling him he could be.

"You sleep much last night man?" Bryan questioned Jason as he made coffee in the small kitchen built for one person. "I just thought it was easier if we crashed here till we finish this thing."

"Or like you were saying last night, until this part is done," Jason interjected while he was coming into waking life, and his mind was sharpening for the day ahead. "What time do we go over there, early morning? Or do we wait for the afternoon?"

"The earlier the better. If we can surprise them we'll have the advantage, and they won't have time to react."

"That's true," Jason echoed as he sat down in the kitchen to drink from the coffee cup Bryan handed him. "I have a question. If they've taken every precaution, wouldn't they have done some kind of electronic sweep on the building? Wouldn't they have some kind of device that disrupts live streaming signals and anything that broadcasts a signal?"

"Maybe, but these guys are more old-school. They have some gadgets, but they mostly use old fashion muscle and intimidation, you know how things got done before the internet. Besides, they'll do a sweep, but only once. They think doing it once will clear everything out, so when we enter with our cameras on, they won't sense anything is amiss. They don't realize an electronic sweep only disrupts things that are presently there, and not prevent things from working in the future. Basically, we'll be in the clear because they think they're in the clear, little do they know..........."

"Hell if we were doing this before the internet, we would have to charge in guns blazing, and beat the hell out of them so they wouldn't come back, which they would anyway. It's great we can use technology to our advantage."

Bryan liked what he was hearing. He could tell Jason was fired up and ready to go. "I have to check the equipment, make sure it works before we pack up and cruise over. I'd love to have this whole thing wrapped up before lunch." Bryan wanted to get this over fast, even more than his partner whose old buddy was being held hostage.

"You thinking pork sandwiches?" pondered Jason whose eyes lit up at the thought of expelling corruption, and eating some pig in celebration.

"Of course, and some really good booze. Plus some of the secret stash I've been saving for an extra special occasion, which this definitely qualifies for. The stuff I gave you when you first came to town doesn't even compare."

Jason remembered the weed being super skunky, and special coming from who he thought was his personal driver, but ended up being his partner and good friend.

"Sounds great to me," Jason responded. "We'll need some serious celebration when this is over. We have a lot of work to do before we break out the champagne."

Bryan knew Jason was right as they both put on suits with cameras sewn in. They were built in to the buttons, cufflinks, the lapel, and the handkerchief. The whole get-up was a special gift from an electronics expert Bryan knew. He also knew how bad it would be if it fell into the wrong hands.

"Looks like the first one works, and the second," observed Bryan with Jason's laptop in front of him, streaming images picked up by the cameras he was wearing. "It pays to have friends in high places, makes things like this possible. Sometimes we have mutual enemies which, also makes things like this possible."

"Why would you say that right now," exclaimed Jason, thinking it odd considering they were about to take down some people in high places. "Do you have other secret friends you aren't telling me about?"

"No, no other fixers. Well, no other people that concern this case anyway. I just have my sources like any good journalist. You of all people can surely respect that."

"I definitely can. When I was younger, my dad taught me the importance of having friends who were cops," acquiesced Jason, feeling that Bryan was in the fight for the long haul.

Bryan kept checking the cameras until he made sure they all worked. He then emailed the respective parties a URL, and when they should watch.

"All of them seem to be working. When we switch these on, the cameras broadcast live right to this link. Not only will it stream to the authorities so they can play their correct role as the cavalry, but also to a separate drive I've set up. That way we can build evidence against the entire system, especially when these people lead us to other people who lead us to other people."

As Jason wore his suit with a bunch of little cameras sewn in, fear overtook him because he knew his life would never be the same once he went after what he truly wanted.

"You going to daydream all day, or do you want to get this finished so we can have some pork sandwiches? Can't you smell them already?" lured Bryan with a smile. "We can do this man. We just have to play to their egos when we go in there, which as journalists shouldn't be hard."

"Definitely not, but I'm not going in like we've already won," remarked Jason, trying not to undercut what they were attempting. "I'll smell those sandwiches, when the cavalry bursts in to save the day."

"Well grab what you need and let's hit it."

Since Jason and Bryan were already wearing the suits, all they needed to grab was their regular reporting equipment; which included a pen, paper, laptop which would be left in the car, a soul and a critically thinking mind.

"Today this Lincoln is going to help rewrite history," orated Jason because he and Bryan were wearing high-tech gizmos he didn't even know existed until Bryan showed him. He knew the possibilities were there, but for them to exist in reality was earth shattering. That didn't matter now, what mattered was that he and a guy he trusted were about to take down some big fish.

They pulled up to a very rundown building near the UV campus at around 9am. Oddly, no people or guards were keeping watch. Maybe it was because the building was never used for anything on the books.

"You think Aaron is really in there," Jason wondered as he and Bryan exited the car and sauntered toward the building. "Why aren't there any people or guards out here for us to sneak past?"

"They probably stashed their cars, or got dropped off or who knows. What really matters, this is the place that I'd take them if I was Bill," stated Bryan, wanting to be as open and honest as possible, but not too much because everybody had their secrets.

"You ever brought anybody with you to a place like this, I mean other than to bust people?" theorized Jason, testing Bryan's reaction.

"Of course not. You don't trust me?"

"I trust you. However, the journalist in me needs to know all the angles."

"That's why you're the brightest up and comer I've seen in a while."

Bryan and Jason entered through a dirty and broken down door they had to put some muscle into to break open. Once they were in, there was a large open room and some additional smaller rooms near the back and off to the sides. "I'll bet anything they're back there," whispered Bryan as he pointed to the back with a befuddled look because there weren't any guards on the inside either.

"I think it's weird there aren't any guards in here either," Jason piped up. His comments took Bryan off guard because he was basically reading his partners mind. "I think they're leading us into a trap. Little do they know, it's actually a trap for them."

Bryan smiled because Jason uttered exactly what he needed to hear. He knew Jason was getting sharper and sharper as time went by. "Let's go man, that one back there, I'll bet Aaron is in that one."

Jason and Bryan quietly tip-toed across the greasy and metal strewn warehouse floor trying not to make a sound, even though Bill and Mark were probably waiting for them anyway. Jason opened the creaky door at the northwest corner of the building, and Bryan followed as they both walked in.

The lights were on, and it was only slightly cleaner than the rest of the factory. There was Aaron, chained to a big metal hook in the floor. Two figures were standing directly behind him. They immediately recognized Jason and Bryan.

"Hey brother."

"Hey Bill."

CHAPTER THIRTY ONE

"How long has it been, twenty years?" Bill the fixer snidely queried. "What took you so long? I thought you would've found me a lot sooner with this whiz kid by your side."

"When I found out Ridell was involved in a scheme that would only work if he had the right friends, friends who could push bills through to benefit only his investors, I knew you had to be involved somehow." Bryan expounded like he'd been practicing the line ever since he discovered his brother was who he and Jason were hunting.

"You're right I fix things, and Mark needed something fixed. I'm pushing this bill through so he and his friends can make a ton of cash."

Jason glared at Ridell who glared back with equal intensity. He was the guy Jason and Bryan most wanted to see go down in flames.

"So your plan was to do what exactly? You aren't cops, you don't have guns, and if I can remember correctly Bryan, you can't even fight. You haven't been in a physical fight since you were thirteen on the playground," Bill needled, trying to get under the skin of his little brother so he could figure out his plan.

"That might have been eighth grade, but I got a few good ones in," Bryan bragged as he looked at Bill causing them to both smile at the memory. It was as if a million different events didn't happen between then and now that completely altered their life paths.

"I hate to break up this stroll down memory lane, but what are you going to do with Aaron? Of what actual use is he to you? Is he your leverage so you can bring in more illegals?" investigated Jason. He wanted Bill and Ridell to fill in the details for the cameras so the cops could bust in, and that delicious pork sandwich would be down his gullet.

"Pretty much," answered Ridell who had been playing the silent observer. "You think you can just bust in and rescue your friend, you aren't superman. You're just some nosy reporter sticking his neck in a guillotine."

"Oh yeah, are you the executioner?"

"I might be, or Bill here might be. We were thinking of letting your friend go before you waltzed in. When we make a deal we actually keep it, but now having all three of you here has changed our game plan."

Bill walked over to Jason and Bryan who both could clearly see an Uzi pointed square at their heads. "Here, put these on. I'd feel more comfortable if you were chained up."

Bill threw a pair of hand cuffs to Jason and one to Bryan and pointed to two big metal hooks attached to the ground next to Aaron.

"I'm here to rescue you," explained Jason sarcastically, trying to get Aaron to smile if only slightly.

"Great, thanks man. I appreciate you coming back and validating that you're an actual friend no matter what happened in the past. I just wish you wouldn't have ended up in chains next to me," Aaron countered with a small smile that showed he was happy, but mostly sad because he figured nobody else knew what was happening.

Just when all hope drained from Aaron's soul and he started to think the inside of this dirty warehouse was going to be his final memory, Jason turned to him and winked.

Aaron didn't think much of it, probably just a friend trying to make another friend feel better, especially if this was the end for all of them.

"So, shithead," bellowed Jason to the Congressman, trying to rile him up.

"Now we're resorting to name calling are we? I thought journalists were above that, I thought that was something left to us evil politicians." Ridell retorted back because he thought Jason was consciously trying not to submit during these final moments.

"That's right, shithead. You don't mind if I call you that right, because that's what you are? How do you think you're going to get away with this? You think nobody will get wind of what you're doing," Jason prodded as Bryan looked at him like he was challenging the Congressman too soon, and didn't want him to blow the whole thing or worse yet be killed.

"We have a lot planned after we kill you for poking your heads where they don't belong," stated Ridell so confident, it was obvious he loved hearing himself talk. "You can't stop us, look at your chains, you aren't going anywhere. You three are the only ones in the world who know what we're doing. Who is going to find out? Who is going to be left to tell the story?"

"You're right nobody is going to find out. Just humor me. I know you're going to torture and kill us gruesomely or whatever. Just tell me what your scheme is so I'll know I haven't gone completely insane. Consider it a dying wish, or last request. I can't tell anybody anyway, what do you have to lose?" Jason blurted out, curious to see if his words sank in.

Ridell held the guys that could bring him and Bill down, but was this a trap? While his inner thought process was chugging along, Bill glared at Mark because he knew this was a bad idea.

"Whenever the villain divulges his entire plan, he always gets caught, and whatever he said is used against him. Do you really want to say anything more? Are you sure this is really a last request? Don't you think it's one last effort to take us down? Take it from somebody that's seen everything in every situation, this is not a good idea," Bill strongly urged. He was concerned Ridell would ruin his plan for getting rid of their mutual obstacles.

"I guarantee this is not one of those situations. The cavalry isn't going to burst in, rescue them, throw us in jail, and hold up these three like heroes for bringing us down. You really think that's going to happen? This isn't the movies," Ridell sniped with confidence that only comes from blind faith.

"Are you afraid to tell us what you're up to?" chided Jason, waiting for the answer that would send in the cavalry and commence down to the letter what Ridell had just described.

"I'll grant you your last wish, and then Bill here will take his Uzi and put a bullet in all three of your brains," Ridell maniacally agreed with confidence that came from false expectations. Jason knew an audience was watching with baited breathe for what was going to transpire. He was sure the cops had enough at this point, but like him, wanted Bill and Ridell to divulge as much as possible.

"If you're going to kill us anyway, just tell us, we'd love to know," added Jason wanting to spell it out so the cops would swarm in. He could already taste that pork sandwich.

"Okay, okay. So I think you already know Bill here fixes the issues I can't fix myself," Ridell acquiesced as he looked at Bill who continued to glare at him, but he forged ahead. "I enlisted his help getting a bill passed by forcing everybody to support it, and if they refused, he got rid of them. With his help it will be smooth sailing, and we'll be infinitely richer than we already are."

"You bring people to your side, and if they don't come willingly you kill them, or you have Bill kill them?" Jason continued, leading Ridell on as much as he could.

"Sometimes the only way is the direct way. So yes, I kill them or Bill kills them. I have the most fun when it's set up so the target meets an unfortunate accident. That way I end up with plausible deniability, and continue to be the shiny penny people can trust."

Jason laughed under his breath as did Bryan and Aaron, he could be trusted; yeah right, when hell froze over.

"Well, continue." Jason knew there were only a few more pieces to be revealed.

"Once this bill is passed, Moon Systems will build research and development facilities on environmentally sensitive land that has been rezoned, because fuck all the plants and animals. I hate all those people that want to defend the environment, I don't eat from there so what do I care? They're from the peasant class and always fight against me, but at the same time they have jobs and a living because of me."

"Illegals are then smuggled into this country and if they survive the trip, they're held against their will to work for slave wages?" Jason theorized.

Aaron and Bryan relaxed and watched Jason go to work on the Congressman. They might have been chained up with a gun to their heads, but they felt confident everything was going to be alright.

"The ones that make it are put to work and paid very little. We give them housing, clothing and everything they need to survive. They can't leave, but why would they want to?"

"That's true, so, modern day slavery?" Jason repeated.

"You hit that one right on the nose. Tell him what he's won Johnny. Yes, we need a workforce that allows us to expand and do whatever we want for as long as we want. We will grow this thing until we control the whole government."

"You're saying you're not the only one with a scheme like this?" perceived Jason, whose ears were perking up.

"Of course, for an operation this big we need lots of help. We are the puppet masters, controlling all the underlings that allow the whole machine to function.

We are also the string pullers, and we know what's going on all the time. You don't want to mess with us. Since you did however, you will die here today by our hands. We will tear everything down and make it look like you and everybody you know are guilty.

We'll blame everything on you so we get off scott-free and continue to grow and expand our operations. How do you think we've gotten so powerful with never a serious inquiry that amounted to anything? Sure, people have tried over the years, some string pullers have been brought in for questioning, but do we ever really go to jail? Do we ever really pay for their crimes?"

Jason knew what Ridell was saying made sense. The reason the world was constantly spinning more and more out of control was because the people behind the scenes have never felt threatened. They just keep pawning off the blame on somebody else, becoming more powerful each time.

"There are Six Entities and they....."

"Can't we just shoot these shitheads so we don't have to worry about them anymore," interrupted Bill who was growing impatient and worried about the details Ridell gave Jason, Bryan and Aaron.

"All right, go ahead," Ridell relented as he walked toward the door, almost as if he wanted his back turned so he could have plausible deniability. Bill was ready to go.

"It's been nice knowing you guys, maybe in another life we could have been friends. Brother, I will see you in the next world," Bill relayed as he raised the Uzi to Jason's head, wanting his brother to suffer as much mental torture as possible before his lights were permanently shut off.

Just as the hammer was about to go back and cause Jason's lights to go black forever, a dozen armor-clad S.W.A.T. team members burst in.

"You guys all right?" the team leader shouted at the three guys.

"Yes we are, take them away boys," retorted Jason. "I've always wanted to say that."

With guns out the swat team surrounded Bill and Ridell and put them in cuffs, almost exactly as Jason pictured.

"I knew it man, I knew it. Why did you open your big fat mouth, I knew they had something up their sleeves. I mean why would they just walk in here unarmed? No wonder people like you need fixers like me, you don't know your head from your ass," lamented Bill as he and Ridell were led into the waiting paddy wagon.

"In jail, you'll be taught the difference on a daily basis," bantered Jason as he, Aaron and Bryan were unchained and freed.

"Really man?" Bryan interjected while shaking his head. "We take down a corrupt Congressman and his fixer, and that's what you come up with?"

"Yeah, so," smirked Jason as a big smile broke out on his face, and the aroma of pork sandwiches filled his nostrils.

CHAPTER THIRTY TWO

"Did you really think it was going to be that easy?" Jason queried. He and Bryan got in the Lincoln to head back and tell Marty what happened, Aaron caught a cab home for some much needed rest. "I know we had suits with listening devices built in, but how did you know they would work?"

"That's the thing, I didn't," expressed Bryan with a happy but exhausted look on his face. "I've used the suits before and they've worked, but just because a person has the right equipment doesn't mean everything will go off without a hitch. We got lucky on this one. Since I never look a gift horse in the mouth, let's be happy about what we accomplished, and surround ourselves in gratitude."

"It must be nice to finally see Ridell led away in handcuffs though, you've been chasing him for a long time."

"It is nice, I guess, it's just one of those things. You spend so much time chasing somebody, and when you finally get them you think, it's over already, and you start missing the chase. It's okay though, something quickly gotten over with good company, good food, and some of the finest grade hydroponics in the city."

"Seems like I've heard that line before."

Jason's mind wandered as he and Bryan rambled back to the office. As they passed skyscrapers, taxi drivers, people yelling at each other and what seemed like hundreds of hot dog carts, he couldn't help but wonder about the six entities. Ridell had mentioned them before the swat team busted in. Was Ridell the head of this particular snake? Or was it somebody much more sinister, with even more power and influence, and a higher hierarchical position?

"What do you think Ridell meant by the Six Entities?" pondered Jason with a very inquisitive look that said this isn't over yet. "He mentioned them right before the cops nabbed him. Do you think they're part of a worldwide operation that involves multiple countries and governments?"

"Maybe," Bryan begrudgingly agreed. He was always interested in digging up dirt on corrupt politicians, but he was tired and thought it could wait for another day. "I've been playing this game a long time. One thing I've learned, when you remove one spoke from the wheel, not only are there plenty of replacements, but they're much stronger because they've had to compensate. Right now, I think we should relax and enjoy this victory, they don't happen all the time."

"You're right, there's plenty of time for the Six Entities later. It's not like they're going to get more evil and corrupt overnight, at least I hope not. Let's enjoy this one, plus all those pork sandwiches aren't going to eat themselves."

Just as they were about to pull into the garage where they always parked the Lincoln like clockwork, Bryan passed the entrance.

"You going somewhere?" Jason observed. He expected Bryan to take the familiar left turn into the same spot that might as well have their names painted on it.

"Yeah, the Cuban place. I thought we could actually get a table, sit down and enjoy a meal like normal people," sniped Bryan who needed to decompress after years of searching for Ridell.

"I don't think I've ever actually set foot in there. I don't even know where it is, but I'm always down to check out a new spot. Plus I'm eager to get a drink and some food in me."

"Maybe we could even smoke a joint in the alley afterwards."

"Sounds good to me," replied Jason. He knew that if Aaron was with them and not lying on his couch exhausted, he would definitely be down.

When the boys arrived at The Cubano, it was about one in the afternoon, perfect time for lunch. The place was packed when they walked in, popular joint they thought. The restaurant had a TV in the bar area with a bunch of people crowded around it, waiting for a multitude of dishes marinated in an amazing Cuban Mojo. The smell of it slathered on succulent pork as it slow cooked, was almost too much to take

"What's happening?" questioned Jason as he walked up to the crowd glued to one 25" screen.

"Looks like they busted this politician and some other guy, must have been his partner or something," explained the mid-forties man at the bar drinking a beer and nursing a shot.

"Does it say for what?" Bryan interjected as his ears immediately perked up.

"Just standard stuff, such as the investigation is ongoing and they're still collecting evidence. How they're portraying it though, these guys schemed to make tons of money, somehow illegal immigrants are involved, so is cheap labor, insider trading,,," the man trailed off because he was staring at the TV screen, not even attempting to make eye contact with Jason and Bryan.

"Crazy, a corrupt politician actually held accountable for something he did, sounds like a happy day?" Jason sarcastically retorted. He was trying to feel good about the miscreants they got off the streets, but also a little sad they got scooped.

Bryan could see Jason was starting to get visibly upset, so he motioned for them to sit at the empty table by the window, "no need to get worked up on an empty stomach," Bryan figured as he motioned for them to sit down.

Jason sat near the window and stared out. He was looking a little distraught even though the air was so caked with the smell of pork sandwiches, It smelled downtown Miami.

"What's wrong with you man, you should be happy about what just happened?" remarked Bryan, trying to make Jason feel better and himself too. He had just as much reason to celebrate.

"We spend all this time investigating a story, collecting evidence, talking to witnesses, coming up with a plan, executing it perfectly, and then somebody else gets all the credit. What kind of story are we supposed to write up for Marty, one that everybody already has? That thing only ended a few hours ago, and it's already plastering the news with background info and observations from everybody," Jason sadly relented as his thoughts poured out.

"Listen man, the 24 hour news cycle makes it hard for print journalists to break anything sooner than the major networks. One big network will report something, then another big one breaks it, and then another and then another. They utilize all their time trying to out scoop the other. Then if one of them gets a piece of the story wrong, the other networks then report on how they got it wrong. They stop talking about what actually happened, and start reporting on the reporting. Sometimes we just have to be happy that we did some good, and that one less vile office holder is on the streets."

Jason retreated to the dark recesses of his mind. While he was trying to wrap his head around anything, the waitress walked up to take their orders.

"Two pork sandwiches with the works, and could you bring us some of that delicious Cuban coffee after we finish eating? Just for good measure, could you also wrap us up two extra sandwiches we could take home and eat later?"

"You bet, anything else," suggested the waitress in perfect English. She looked at Jason with grave concern and female nurturing.

"He'll be fine he just needs some good food in him. Fuel for the body, is fuel for the soul," Bryan philosophized, wondering if the waitress would counter with a witty remark.

"Anything to drink while you wait for your food?"

"Yeah, a couple of beers, we need it."

The waitress winked in agreement as she walked away, while Bryan pondered why it was true. They caught some string pullers that really deserved it, and took riff raff off the street. The political world was now without the services of D.C.'s most well-known fixers.

Jason tried to fix his gaze on anything in the restaurant. He was totally out of it like he'd been hit with a truck, finished a fifteen round boxing match, and got dumped by his girl all at once. "You have something to say man, by that look on your face I don't know whether to hug you, or tell you to go take a shit?" Bryan teased half serious, but at the same time trying to lighten the mood.

"I can't help but wonder if this is all there is to life?" Jason pondered, about to go philosophical. "We go out, fight corruption and defeat it before lunch so we can get sandwiches. This just seemed too simple, like everything fell into place a little too easily."

"Maybe, but who's to say. All I know is that I'm going to enjoy this beer," Bryan reiterated as the waitress set down their drinks. "If life is really about balance so we keep in tip top shape, then we must balance work with play."

"You're right. I just need to loosen up."

Even though his words said it, his heart didn't believe Jason had time to relax. He had to figure out what all this meant and what was coming down the road. He needed to know it yesterday. What could Bryan say he thought? What would Christina think? Jason pulled out his cell phone and scrolled through his contact list, and stopped when he got to her.

Bryan looked over to see what Jason was doing and just shook his head. "You know this is what she wanted for you right?" Bryan questioned with a caring but much more serious look than he had just a minute ago. "She was the one that pushed you to come here because she really loved you, and knew this was your dream. She wasn't one of those women who holds her man back because she's lonely, has low self-esteem or because she can't be alone.

A woman you really loved and that really loved you pushed you to pursue your dream in a place where it was possible. We took down some very influential people today, which is pretty much the definition of that dream. All you can think about is what more could we have done. Remember, the best motivation in the world is being thankful for what we have, not being upset about what we don't."

Jason couldn't find his words. Even when he opened his mouth, they didn't come out right away. "You're right this is my dream. I just miss Christina is all, and would love to share this with her. She was the love of my life. I don't know if I'll meet anybody as special and amazing as her again, she was everything I wanted."

"She seemed like a great woman from everything you've mentioned, and you've mentioned a lot. Sometimes so much I wish you'd shut up about her for a minute," Bryan bantered. He was trying to make Jason laugh which apparently was going to take more effort. "You have to ask yourself, what can I do? You see what life has to offer, and figure out what you want to go after. Do you want to waste all your time worrying about things you can't change, or do you want to concentrate on what you can change, like ridding the world of ignorance and corruption? Just because we brought down one Congressman, doesn't mean there aren't truckloads more waiting in the wings. Hell, the new ones might be worse."

"I know what you're saying about feeling gratitude. I can only do what I can do, or I yam what I yam, like Popeye used to say," Jason uttered as he felt a weight lift by talking to somebody he was in the trenches with. "Christina was an amazing woman and still is an amazing woman, if I meet up with her again one day, great. If I don't that's okay too, as long as she's happy. All I want for her is to be satisfied, and to achieve her dreams. Her investigations will take down powerful people, just like mine did."

The sandwiches arrived just as Jason finished his thought, they were as beautiful as he imagined, and smelled even better. His mouth immediately started to water like he hadn't eaten in a week.

The guys sat there and ate in silence, just devouring the delicious melt in your mouth pork. It's not that good food doesn't make you talkative, because it does. It's just when good food is around, if people aren't talking it's because they're too busy eating. It was a good sign, and one that Bryan and Jason knew all too well.

They inhaled their sandwiches and sipped the coffee that always made them wired. It would make anybody wired, it was known for that. As they loaded back into the Lincoln, Jason had other plans. "Want to take the rest of the day off? We could go back to my place and drink and smoke some of that fine green you've introduced me to out here." Jason sounded a little more upbeat than he did in the restaurant, pork sandwiches always did that too him.

"After what we pulled off this morning, we deserve it. Besides, Marty won't care if you got out scooped," Bryan fired back with a smile as he turned the car around, and headed to Jason's.

"Marty won't care all those outlets broke the story before us? I thought that's why I'm here, to uncover big stories and write about them in his magazine, and scoop everybody else?" Jason deduced because the question had been burning within him since seeing the news at the Cubano.

"He just knows there's nothing he can do about being out-scooped. What he really cares about is we're okay and not hurt, but more importantly that we took some evil bastards down. That's what he really called you out here for," Bryan spelled out. He felt he had to tell Jason his real mission.

"He brought me out here to take down evil?" quipped Jason, a little surprised.

"Yeah, you take them down, the world benefits, and he pays you for the good work. You don't actually have to write any stories, you just take the bad guys down and expose them. Marty benefits because there is less corruption, and more accountability in the world. He made a lot of money a while back, and just wants to take down some string pullers down before he dies.

When I unsuccessfully looked for Ridell, Marty took all the stuff away from me he gave you because I couldn't produce results. You can. Today is an obvious example of that. Enjoy your role as the un-doer of inequities, and bringer of accountability. Taking down corrupt people and making the world a better and more equal and fair place was your goal, right?"

"Yes, it's just a lot to process," Jason relented, not sure what to believe.

"I know it's a lot, but once you fully comprehend that some rich guy wants to do good by paying you to take down king makers, you'll settle in. Marty knew you had the journalistic skill for the job. Now I do too."

"Thanks man."

Jason and Bryan pulled up to his place right about 418pm. "You know what it's almost time for?" Jason teased with a smirk.

"Uh, let's see. Could that be something green with hairs all over it, and smokes when lit?" volleyed Bryan, happy to see Jason was now in the joking mood.

"You got it buddy," related Jason, smiling from ear to ear. He knew the road ahead would be long, but with good people in his corner, he knew he could handle it. He couldn't help but wonder though, who was pulling Ridell's strings? Who was giving him orders? "Think Ridell had a boss?"

"You still obsessing about that? Forget about it for a bit, corrupt governments will be there tomorrow," Bryan needled as he and Jason parked and walked up to the elevator.

Jason wanted to have fun, but also knew in his gut there was more to this story, more that would be revealed once he started looking. Who was more powerful than the

Congressman? Who was giving him orders? Could it be someone from the capitol, or from 1600 Pennsylvania Avenue?

CHAPTER THIRTY THREE

Jason woke up on the couch and wearily peered at the clock which blared 10pm. Had he fallen asleep after parroting too much with Bryan, or was he just tired after the day he and Bryan had? Jason hoisted himself off the couch and stumbled into the kitchen to find something to drink. His cottonmouth was getting the best of him.

What was the point of all this? Why take down one Congressman if a more despicable one pops up? Wouldn't they wreak more havoc just so their pockets become fatter? Jason knew the mentality of all powerfully dishonest politicians were the same, even if their motivations varied.

Jason was tired and wanted to go back to sleep, but knew he'd be wide awake at 3am if he did, and wouldn't be able to fall back asleep. He parked his butt to relax and watch TV when the phone rang. "Hello."

"What's up man? After the Pork sandwiches and fat doobies we smoked you fell asleep, so I just decided to cruise home," declared Bryan, feeling good from the day but plenty tired. "I wanted to tell you, I'm taking some time off, I really need a vacation."

"You and I both man," reiterated Jason, happy his partner would be getting some time away, but also wondered what he'd do alone. "How long you going for?"

"Not sure, I need to get out of town and just go. I've been looking for Ridell for years. Now that he's going away I need to reassess everything, and make sure I'm headed in the direction I want for my future."

Jason always knew Bryan to be truthful, but knew he didn't feel the same pull to leave. "I totally understand. Sometimes we get burned out and need time to decompress. When are you leaving?"

"Tomorrow," Bryan answered with trepidation, but excitement that he was doing the right thing for his soul. "I know it's sudden, but I really need to leave and just be for a while."

"That sounds great man, you definitely deserve it." Jason was happy for Bryan, but also sad about losing their connection, just like when he left Christina for New York. He knew sometimes hard decisions had to be made for the benefit of a person's psyche. "I can't say I'll be happy when you're gone, it has been awesome working with you this past month or so. We make a great team. Since this is what you really want and what you really need, who am I to stop you? Just promise to keep in touch, okay."

"Of course man, you're a very special human being and the world definitely needs you out there saving it. There will be plenty of profiteers for you to chase and upend, just like you want and just like society needs. I wish you the best of luck in all your ventures. Just remember that if you ever feel burned out or need a break, take one. No problem is worth cracking up over. The world is too important to let some shithead drag you down."

"I will man, I will." Jason knew Bryan was right, he could use a vacation, but he was hot on the trail of the next puzzle piece and didn't want to miss out. "Take care of yourself man, and thank you for everything, I mean it. Send me a postcard from some crazy place you go. I want to know you're leading a happy and fulfilling life."

"I am man, believe me. Thank you for all the kind words. I know the world is a better place because people like you fight the good fight. Don't give up and don't surrender. Talk soon man, have a good night."

"You too man, take care, good night."

Jason hung up the phone with Bryan hoping they would meet up in the future which he knew they might, but probably not for a while. He and Bryan would attempt to keep in touch because that's what good people did when they have a connection. Jason also knew it's what you say to be polite, and in the end you don't really mean it. As soon as that person is out of the picture their memory slowly fades away, until you can't remember them; unless something jogs your memory.

Trying to process, Jason sat back down on the couch and switched on the TV. He channel surfed like it was going out of style. He continued for about ten minutes before he just gave up, and turned it off. As he headed to bed for a good night's rest, the phone rang again. Maybe it was Bryan again he thought. "What's up man, you forget to tell me something?"

"I don't know, this is Aaron."

"What's up Aaron, sorry I was just talking to Bryan. I wondered where you escaped to. It seemed like you were in a hurry to leave after we took the Congressman down. I figured you'd call after you had time to rest," blurted Jason full speed, happy to hear from his buddy.

"Yeah I was pretty tired. Being held hostage with a gun to my head was no fun, no matter how much they say it is," Aaron joked. He expelled a small laugh to lighten the mood, but mostly for his own amusement. "I'm so glad it's over. You and I worked well together bringing that jerk down. I know we come from different political perspectives. I'm more libertarian you're more liberal, and you don't believe nearly as much in the tea party stuff as I do."

"That's an understatement," related Jason, laughing very authentically.

"I'm just glad we overcame by proving common ground does exist once we allow all the bullshit to fade away."

"I fully agree man, that's part of the reason I came to New York. I knew it would be tough out here, but it's raw. There's so much going on, and so many people that need help I'll never be short of work. Considering how easily sneaky politicians clone themselves, I'll always have job security."

Jason and Aaron laughed like they hadn't in a long time. Their connection held immense philosophical purpose for both of them, at this particular point in their lives. Jason felt they were brought together after all these years because a certain purpose needed to be fulfilled.

"I've been wrapped up in the game for so long chasing what I thought was the right thing, that I haven't taken much time to live," remarked Aaron. He was exasperated about the ordeal, but his mind was fresh and thinking of all the possibilities in front of him. "I think I'll take some time off to travel. I've never seen South America, so I might go down there and just trip around. I heard Chile is nice. Since I'm trying to find myself, I figured 2000 miles of coastline is a good place to start."

Jason knew if he'd been held hostage, he would need to get away for a while too. Still, he felt trepidation that his partner was leaving, and now the old friend he just reconnected with was leaving also. "That does sound nice I heard Chilean food is really good." Jason was trying to make small talk, with sadness that was ratcheting up in his heart. "How long do you think you'll be gone?"

"I'll probably travel until I find an area I like, or if my heart tells me I have to stop and come back, I will. I'm open to all of the world's possibilities, whatever they may bring."

"I know that tune all too well man, all too well. Keep in touch, send me a postcard from some cool places, and make sure you find yourself some beautiful senoritas okay?"

"Of course man, South American chicks are smoking hot," chided Aaron with a chuckle. "Take care of yourself man, I wish you all the best. Don't forget to keep chasing those degenerate charlatans. If they ever feel like nobody is after them, well, you know what a kid does around cookies and candy if their parents aren't watching them?"

"They stuff their faces till they get sick."

"It's the same in the political world. If you pay close enough attention to what these crooks do, they'll divulge their entire plan just like that Congressman so artfully did. Their egos make them think they'll never get caught. Ridell is just one of many, many people out there trying to game the system and screw everybody if it makes them money. Whether it's business, politics, or any other profession in the world, everybody from time to time is un-accountable because we're all human. Some of us just have more power and influence than others."

"I missed our conversations, but you're right, there's plenty more work for me with this crazy world."

"That's for sure man. Just remember, we can all agree on the root of most major problems, because we're all human. Continue bringing people together because there's way more of us than there are of them. Once you help everyone realize that, there's nothing the top dogs can do, they'll run for the hills."

Jason felt like this was the last time he would talk to Aaron for a while, just like the conversation he had with Bryan. Seemed like he was getting plenty of practice, made him wonder what the future held.

"I'll make the politicians run away from me, and you make the pretty girls run toward you," added Jason from the bottom of his heart, while a tear rolled down his rosy cheek.

"Sounds good to me, take good care of yourself. I know it was a long time since we saw each other last, and it's strange to be parting ways again. Something tells me though, we will meet up in the future," explained Aaron because the feelings in his heart were controlling the words coming out of his mouth.

"Maybe. Take care of yourself man, and never forget to have fun."

"You too man, now go take down those con artists."

"You know I will, and this isn't goodbye, it's see you later."

"Sounds good, see you later."

"Later."

Jason hung up the phone not knowing what direction to take. The new partner he thought would be helping him to solve cases was gone. Likewise his old friend that sprung up to help immensely with the case he just finished, was leaving as well.

Jason knew that in life you have to expect the unexpected, and be ready for everything. He might have thought Bryan and Aaron would always be by his side, but it didn't mean he couldn't move forward.

Marty brought Jason to New York for a reason, since the people who helped him were leaving, he thought he should get back to work, and identify his next target.

He started thinking about what the Congressman said about the Six Entities controlling the world. Who were they, and what did they want? Since he couldn't answer those questions, he knew it wouldn't be impossible to bring them down, yet. Jason knew he had a lot of hard work ahead, but he was okay with it. He knew it was part of his earthly mission. Jason wanted to contribute to the betterment of humanity and help the human race consciously evolve. He might not be able to take down the entitled right away, but there were many other things he could put his efforts toward until they blipped on his radar.

Jason poured himself a scotch and walked out on his balcony to take in the view. When all the lights of the city reflected back into his soul, he knew there was plenty for him to do, and plenty of people to help him do it. He also remembered what Ridell the Congressman said about the string pullers who never show their faces in public, the ones who really control things.

There was a possibility the Congressman was taking orders from the Entities, it was worth checking out Jason thought. He wouldn't rest until he was satisfied he made a dent in the problem.

Jason knew there would be a lot of sleepless nights, but his soul could breathe easy in the fact he was doing right for the world.

Jason returned to the couch and took a sip from his scotch, which immediately caused a big yawn. Jason knew it was up to him to feel content. Nobody could do it for him, no matter how much he wanted them to.

Jason knew quite literally after having said it many times before, tomorrow was the next day of the rest of his life.

CHAPTER THIRTY FOUR

The sun beamed through the windows of Jason's apartment attempting to uplift his soul, not just to wake him from sound sleep. Jason slowly rolled over and barely opened his eyes before he felt an immense good energy pouring in. After yesterday's events and his friends deciding to take some "me" time, he was truly alone to figure out his next move. Where should he go and what should he accomplish? Motivation to drive him forward was coming in whether he wanted it to or not. He knew whatever happened, he needed to be relaxed and ease into the day.

Jason threw off the covers and stuck his feet in his slippers when the phone rang. "Hello."

"Hey Jason, it's Marty, how you doing this morning?"

"I'm good, barely coming to life. Probably take it easy after everything that happened and just get some breakfast for now," Jason replied still half asleep, and not able to get his thoughts to flow smoothly yet.

"I wanted to call and see how you were, that was crazy yesterday. You took down some very influential people. You did a great thing for the evolution of man, good job," Marty proudly expressed with an authenticity meant to portray how thankful he was for of Jason's work. "You accomplished exactly what I brought you here for, exposing heavy duty corruption and taking down the people responsible."

"Believe me it was my pleasure, those guys definitely had it coming," relayed Jason with a big smile because he felt he was carrying out his true purpose. "I would do it again in a heartbeat."

"That's actually why I called you."

Jason moved to the couch in the living room, "What's up Marty, what's on your mind?"

"I've been plugged into the system for many years now, and can get inside information nobody else can. Anyway, because of what you guys pulled off yesterday, a lot of politicians are having second thoughts about being untouchable."

A smile etched itself across Jason's face. "That's one of my goals, to make them think twice about their actions and who they truly affect. I feel good I was able to do that. It will help bring on the next step of evolution, or part of the next step," explained Jason as he felt his soul glow.

"That's all true, and like I said before, that's one of the reasons I brought you here. Now it's time to make sure you aren't a one hit wonder," remarked Marty. He took a deep breath because he wanted to convey the truth as plainly as possible. "They're running scared, and you're right, that's a good thing. However, since they feel like they could actually get caught, they scrutinize all potential threats much more intensely."

Jason knew he should have been scared shitless, but he wasn't, he was excited. He knew that if the string pullers were actually quaking in their boots, the change he was bringing into existence was taking shape. "One of the things they feel threatened by is me, right? You think they'll come after me?"

"They definitely know the phone number. Since they also know the address, I thought it would be a good idea if you worked from home for a while. I made sure your place was buried under so many layers of bureaucratic and legal crap, that it would take massive armies of data miners to dig through it all. I made sure you're off the grid, but still in the game." Marty hoped his statements didn't cause Jason to lose his head.

"That's cool, I didn't know this place was protected like that, but I'm very thankful," answered Jason, glad Marty took the extra precautions. He was sustained by the vibe he experienced when he first strolled into Marty's office. "So what's the next step?"

"I'll make sure your pay gets to you so you can get by. I'll wire the money to your account, under an alias with the full paperwork to back it up in-case you have to prove it. Even if it's for five or ten years, I want you to keep going after these people. Keep the Lincoln it will bring you good luck."

Jason was unable to form a sentence. Aliases, false bank accounts, he was really in the thick of it now. In the dark recesses of Jason's mind he knew he would have to go underground if he had a chance to make real change. He just didn't think it would actually happen. "I can handle that. Bryan said you didn't care about me turning in material. What would you like from me on that end?"

"Don't worry about writing right now. I want Ridell's financiers to be your main focus. I'll check in from time to time, but I want you to take the lead. If you continue hunting more political big game, the money will keep flowing to you. That part of the mission hasn't changed,"

~ 278 ~

Marty divulged using a kill to survive analogy. He felt like this ideological war was the beginning of something great if they succeeded, but if not.....

"That sounds good man, thank you again for everything. Thank you for believing in me. I wouldn't be fulfilling my dreams if it wasn't for you. Thank you for giving a crazy hippie from California a chance."

"Of course man, I want to do some good while I'm here too. You might be a hippie, but you're my kind of hippie, somebody that actually gets things done instead of endlessly talking about it. Go find the person pulling Ridell's strings, something tells me it will expose what's really going on. I'll fund you as long as you need until that happens."

"I won't rest till I do."

"You'll have more energy to find him if you do get some rest. Anyway, take care of yourself and we'll talk soon."

"You too, and thanks again for the opportunity, I won't let you down."

Jason hung up the phone and leaned back on the couch because there was a lot on his plate. He just took down some very powerful people which pissed off other powerful people who now feel threatened for the first time in their lives. Jason knew he was on the right track, but he also knew that if string pullers authentically felt threatened, they would hold onto their power by whatever means necessary.

Blinding slits of sun pinpointed through Jason's unopened blinds. Once he opened them the light cascaded in, making

Jason realize what it truly meant to be recharged. He knew he had major obstacles ahead of him, that they would pile up the deeper he went. Taking down a powerful Congressman and his fixer was a challenge. Taking down their boss would be more challenging. However, it would bring the changes Jason yearned for ever since he began questioning why things were the way they were.

Not wanting to answer the phone because he had to stay hidden in his own little world, Jason unplugged it. He knew the voice mail would pick up any messages. Jason walked over to the fridge for something to eat. Even though it was filled with delicious food that he would normally have no problem eating, for some reason none of it seemed appetizing. A special mission required special food, so he decided to call for something that always put a smile on his face, pork sandwiches.

After Jason finished shoveling, he buried himself in work so he wouldn't feel like he was wasting his time, but spending it on something worthwhile. How was Christina? How was her work going? Was she able to bring down some string pullers? Or at least get some disgraceful human beings off the street? Jason was still in love with her, with all the work and craziness in New York, he didn't have much time to work through the issues that remained.

He and Christina hadn't officially broken up they mutually separated, more of a mutual understanding if you asked them. They were at a crossroads that tested their love, because they let the other pursue their dreams. It seemed like an eternity since Jason had talked to her. He picked up the phone a million times, but didn't dial the numbers. He knew that if they were really meant to be, they would come back together, and wonder how they ever parted.

It might happen, it might not. Jason knew all he could do was move forward in a positive way, be good to himself, the earth, his fellow human beings and even politicians. Jason knew that even though politicians were stereotypically evil as far as everyone was concerned, they were still just people. If he was able to unite his fellow humans to unseat the powerful, the powerful would see that the way they're going might not be the best course of action, and would unite with them.

He couldn't get Christina out of his mind, even though he buried himself in work up to his eyeballs. He tried to find comfort in the fact that he was in a plush Manhattan apartment, thinking of ways to help the human race evolve; which might lead him back to Christina.

With all the predicaments that presented themselves since he stepped off the plane at JFK, Jason knew if he was honest about who he was, what he wanted to accomplish, and what kind of mark he wanted to make on the world, what was meant to happen, would.

Jason poured a nice scotch since it all of a sudden was afternoon, and he realized he'd been sitting on the couch thinking for several hours. Jeez, how lost in one's head you get if you really try he thought.

He grabbed his scotch and moved to the desk his laptop was on. It was adorned with a million sticky notes of clues to form cases, websites to visit, videos and movies to watch. Along with pictures of Christina, there were some random items from happy memories throughout Jason's life. It was a very inviting space for him to let his creativity flow.

Jason sat in the chair that he personally picked out because Marty knew he'd be spending many hours utilizing it. He planted himself, set his glass on the desk, and explored the next item on his agenda.

Deciding he could never let himself be afraid of the unexpected, Jason was ready for change. He had to adapt to anything that came before him. With dominant forces aimed his way, it was important to stay sharp so they didn't get the drop on him. He needed to get the drop on them.

The last thing Ridell uttered before they took him away was the Six Entities, who supposedly controlled everything. Even if the leadership was mixed from all different countries, Jason knew power hungry nature always has been and always will be color blind. Power and influence don't change as it corrupts every race and ethnicity. Jason knew if he had any hope of defeating it, he would have to stay vigilant.

You can't believe everything a politician says, even if they're being led away in handcuffs, especially if they're led away in handcuffs. It seemed like once Jason turned over one rock, he found three more. It was a chess match that never ended.

It would take immense energy, but these entities wouldn't stand a chance with Jason fully involved. Once they saw his pure need for the uplift of people was authentic, they would crumble before him. Jason knew it was improbable, but not impossible. He also knew that the bigger goals you set, the more you realize anything is possible.

Jason didn't find anything right away, but he didn't give up, because his enemies didn't give up. He would find them. It was only a matter of time.

CHAPTER THIRTY FIVE

One day ran into the next, as they not only blended together, they never seemed to change. Jason would wake up, get something to eat, turn on his computer and try to locate information regarding the Congressman's boss. Then he would get fed up that results didn't come immediately.

Jason knew the fight wasn't going to be easy, that it would test his strength and stamina. He just didn't realize the huge amounts of monotony it would produce. Everyday ended with the same results. Maybe the other side was using monotony against him. Maybe the entities plans were to make people think they can take politicians down, but instead lead them on a wild goose chase.

Jason knew what goose chases were all about, he had been on them before. Had it had been six months, a year, maybe two since his conversation about going underground. Marty checked on him, and made sure Jason had everything he needed like he said he would, which made Jason feel positive. The life he was forced to lead was fulfilling for his soul, but was very lonely. Jason worried about not having any real friends. Aaron and Bryan had been out of the picture for some time, and he yearned for positive human contact.

Every so often Jason would wake up to energy re-charging sunlight flooding through the window, but those days were few and far between. He took occasional walks in the park, ate sandwiches from the Cubano, and the Ethiopian place that wasn't too far away. He was becoming a big fan of theirs, especially their Injera. The lack of fulfillment started to affect Jason's emotional state. When he slowed down to think where he was, what he was up against, why he was doing it, and where he came from, good energy trickled back in, no matter how dark it seemed.

Those in Washington still wanted money and influence and always more, with regular people wanting the same thing. The irony is that people bitched about politicians, but emulated them in every way. They wondered why the person they voted for, somebody who told them whatever they wanted to hear, turned around and did whatever they wanted.

Jason was still in a good position to bring major change, but taking down Ridell seemed like forever ago. He was starting to feel old, like all the years were melting together. He needed to look at a calendar. Apparently it had been five years, had it really been five whole years? Had things grown so monotonous that he thought six months passed and it really had been five years?

He never pondered why the checks kept coming in, Marty never asked him about deadlines when they talked. Had this been a normal arrangement he would have been put in if they hired him off the street? Jason knew Marty wasn't all that he said he was, but when somebody is your corruption finding patron, you don't ask questions.

The bathroom mirror reflected back sparse gray hairs when Jason looked into it. His thirtieth birthday passed him by and he didn't recognize it, let alone celebrate with the crazy fun a major life milestone deserved. For five years he'd been paid for research to find Ridell's financier, he found some coffin nails, but not the final ones. Should he sit back down at his computer? Should he keep doing the things he's been doing? Would it always have the same ending? Should he try research in a different way, maybe he would get different results?

Jason was in a quandary. Marty collected his results every Friday and sent him a check, what was the point of it? Why keep getting paid to take somebody down, if he had been on the case five years with no results? He decided to continue searching for the string pullers. That was his mission. Jason knew he had to be on his toes to catch them, but also confident enough in his character to adapt to whatever came along.

Marty could cut him off at any time. He needed to find a backup plan. The road was in front of him, and Jason knew it was time to finally head toward his destination. He had been building a case for five years. He had to make sure it was for a reason.

It was almost as if Jason could make it by himself, but he couldn't think that far ahead. Hell if it wasn't for Marty's money he wouldn't have made it these last five years.

He was in the middle of a fight and wondered about its purpose, was it simply to take down evil? He had done that with Ridell, why should he continue? Could he even trust Marty who had been supporting him for five years? Jason knew what it was like to have loving parents, was that what was going on? Was Marty treating him like the son he never had?

Sure, Jason wondered what Aaron and Bryan were up to and what they were doing, if they were still searching for truth was unknown to him.

It was as if Marty set him on a course. Yes he checked in once a week for material, but never gave Jason much feedback. He gave Marty names of known associates, locations, dates, histories even sexual preferences, which Marty thanked him for. Then he would say "I'll be back in a week for more. If you don't have any information, no hard feelings but we will have to part ways. If you continue to produce, then the sky is the limit and my purse strings are limitless." Was Marty using the information to take out his enemies, ones that would actually harm Jason?

One thing was for sure, Jason was on a journey that was his and his alone. He would continue to travel as far as it took him, even if it led him toward Marty. Right now, his path was leading him to the beautiful, black 61 Lincoln convertible with suicide doors that Marty set him and Bryan up with. Jason kept it in pristine condition parked in the building's garage. He rarely took it out for fear it would be seen by the faceless entities Marty warned him about. Jason grew into a hermit, only emerging for the occasional walk, when he needed supplies, to eat at the Cubano or the Ethiopian place, and to let Marty know the leads he discovered. Why was Marty doing all this? Was it his elaborate plan to make Jason his scapegoat?

Jason unlocked the Lincoln and climbed in. The sunny day made Jason smile, especially the Lincoln because it was a convertible, he loved convertibles. The entire car was numbers matching, except for the stereo Jason installed for long road trips, and the push button convertible top; it definitely made life a whole a lot easier. Jason put the top down and turned the key, which brought the roaring V8 to life. Where would Jason go, he wasn't sure. He did know however, that he needed a nice long drive to clear his head. A drive always brought clarity to him in the past, a form of open eyed meditation.

Jason pointed the Lincoln north, New England would provide the beautiful scenery his heart needed, and the positive energy his soul needed.

He stopped at a small gas station two hours into the trip. When Jason exited the car, he noticed a few random people milling around. Some were pumping gas, some trying to figure out why they packed so much crap in their cars; all pretty normal he thought. He'd been searching for Ridell's patron for so long he forgot the simple pleasures regular people have. Whatever was out there wasn't going away, but Jason knew he was doing what he needed to do for himself. He knew a trip was just what he needed to clear his mind, and get the investigation moving again.

He fueled the tank with forty bucks, and continued roaring down the road toward the unknown. Jason realized the people he knew as a kid might recognize him, and they might not. He had changed, but he evolved without changing his inherent character.

A million different thoughts flooded Jason's cerebral cortex as he passed yet another red leafed tree, trying to remember what beauty was all about. Were political heavyweights still trailing him? Did he still need to be underground? Did they lull him into a false sense of security? Did they make Jason think he could pull their rug out at the last minute?

Whatever happened next, Jason knew the only way he could move forward was to let go of all his misconceptions, and just put one foot in front of the other. After scarfing down the most delicious roadside burger he ever tasted, tiredness washed over Jason because he had been driving most of the day. He needed to find a room.

After producing the documentation to the false identity Marty provided him, getting a room was no problem. "Here you go, Mr. Johnson. Enjoy your stay," relayed the clerk. He handed Jason back the credit card and ID that bore his picture, but were phonies Marty said were untraceable. Jason had to remember though that the government always had a funny way of surprising folks, causing nothing in life to be set in stone.

Jason thanked the clerk who gave him keys and a smile, before returning to his sports illustrated that appeared way more important than whatever Jason had to say.

This Red Leaf motel was like any other rundown "I don't want anybody to know I'm here" motel. When he opened his room door and walked in, Jason immediately felt that something was different, not necessarily bad; just different.

Jason put his bag on the ground, stretched out on the bed and flipped on the TV. He needed something to make him laugh. The first channel he arrived at was the news, talking about Ridell's case from years before, and how it reformed the political scene. Jason never received credit from the world community, let alone Ridell's constituency. Jason wasn't sure he would accept it even if they offered.

Several people were interviewed for the story, followed by a round table discussion about combating political corruption, and what can be done in the future. Jason agreed with half and disagreed with the other half, just like normal. What struck Jason this time was regardless of what political side the talking heads were on, they seemed more conscious and focused, and pondered all they could accomplish in their own personal evolution if they were truthful.

Was this conscious evolution in dialogue directly linked to the Congressman's case, Jason didn't know. He made a point to not get frustrated, like he did in his youth when results didn't come fast enough. He would keep pushing.

After twenty minutes Jason turned off the TV, he couldn't hang anymore and was exhausted. He knew if he ended his day on the right spiritual and mental footing, it would provide him motivation to accomplish anything he wanted.

The next day Jason felt a sunbeam penetrate through the window at seven am. It was the same energy he felt when he left Manhattan, it was time to get rolling. After eating a mountain of biscuits, gravy, potatoes, bacon, ham and sausage all piled on top of each other, not only was he full, but the food was so comforting he felt like nothing could stop him.

Jason paid the bill at the desk, hopped back in the Lincoln and continued tooling down the highway. Where would he end up? The world was a complex place, but Jason knew he would find answers sooner or later. When that happened, he knew he better be ready. His fights were far from over. Jason found a good classic rock station, and once Def-Leppard was turned up as high as it would go, a special news bulletin sounded.

Not wanting talking heads to blow his ears out, Jason turned it down so he could hear what was being said. There was a continuation of the Congressman's case. In exchange for a lighter sentence, Ridell agreed to testify about who funded him. Every time Jason thought it was over, corruption would scream back into his consciousness to say howdy, remember me, I'm still here.

F.B.I. investigations revealed shell corporations paid the Congressman for his services. Some records were found during what can only be described as extremely deep data collection. The Congressman was paid through an interwoven conglomerate of forty different subsidiaries set up by a herd of lawyers. The name of an individual didn't pop up. There was no super villain, at least not yet. What did get revealed was the name Moon Systems, the company at the heart of it all.

It had to be a coincidence. The same company Jason investigated years earlier had continued sending Ridell dividend checks, because he still owned stock. It turned out exactly how Jason thought it would when he started. How odd that the facts he discovered, were being discussed once again on all the morning news shows.

Was it a trap? Did the string pullers beam a signal exclusively into Jason's car just to needle him, slapping him in the face with the company he never got close to? Or was it a sign he should dig deeper, and help end the fight once and for all?

Jason recollected that Moon Systems headquarters was in California close to where he was born. It would be a long trip from New England, but if he found the final coffin nail, it would be more than worth it. Jason decided to make the journey. He would head to the City of Angels to see if Moon Systems led him to the big fish.

Jason slept only as long as he had to, and stopped only for gas, to pee and for food. Even though the yellow lines were burning through Jason's corneas it was important to keep going, they were leading him to the truth.

Jason arrived in Los Angeles, three days after hearing the Ridell story. He was happy to see the heavy traffic his former stomping grounds were so accustomed to. Jason never lived directly in L.A., but was there for countless concerts, conventions, and to see friends. Jason knew people in Pasadena and several little cities scattered throughout LA County, but debated whether he should call them before he found Moon Systems.

Jason decided it better to lay low until he knew what he was up against. He checked into a small hotel in Riverside, California. It was a ways away from LA with traffic, but it was important to Jason he not be in the thick of it when he made his move.

Sitting down at the desk of his temporary home, Jason threw his bag on the bed. He grabbed a cold beer from the sixer he brought up with him, and booted up his laptop to see what he could find. After looking at random internet distractions, he found a blog for people fed up with the status quo. The headline read that if a person wanted to better the government they should log on, join the community, and change the world.

Knowing it couldn't hurt because his computer was untraceable, Jason logged on. His alias was only known to a few people who were in Jason's life way before any of the conspiracy stuff. He figured nobody would recognize it, or know what he was up to.

Jason checked the haystack for that magic needle, and saw the usual back and forth about everything from government control, to how citizens have too much freedom and the government needs to tie up loose ends.

Halfway down the first page was a post by seercat69. "These jerks have taken advantage of us for the last time. It's time to fight back. I know people who worked for Moon Systems, they make you think you don't have a chance to stop them, but take it from me, you do. If your heart and mind are in a conscious place, you'll connect with other people who do too. They'll connect with other people and so on. Our group will be so large there's nothing Moon Systems could even attempt to do. Their power is an illusion, and they know it. If we band together, we can show them we know it too."

Jason thought wow, that's so true. They make us think they'll always beat us, when they really can't. This sounded familiar, like Jason heard it before, but where? Either way, he knew he wanted to respond.

Jason scribbled a short message about how he agreed with the points Seercat69 made, and a summary of his history with Moon Systems. He also mentioned he was in the Los Angeles area looking into them, and if they could help he should be contacted. He signed the message Jay Sherman, hoping any of the people currently after him wouldn't recognize the nickname from his early years.

Two minutes later he received a response.

"I've been looking into Moon Systems for some time and always fall short. I'd love your help to bring them down. Your post mentioned you were in LA. I'd like to discuss this in person, less of a chance we'll be tracked. There is a coffee shop on the corner of Los Feliz and Barlow st. in

Hollywood called the Trashy Rose. Meet me there at 8am tomorrow."

Jason responded that he would be there. This was too good a lead to pass up, and he knew it.

Jason made sure he arrived at the coffee shop fifteen minutes early, so he didn't miss whoever was meeting him. He didn't even ask if it was a man, a woman or what they looked like, but something told him that if they helped take down Mon Systems, it wouldn't matter.

Twenty minutes and two cups of coffee later, he began to wonder if this mystery person stood him up. When Jason was about to give up and leave, somebody tapped him on the shoulder.

"Hey Jason, it's been a while."

"Christina………………"

CHAPTER THIRTY SIX

Language was the lifesaving elixir that would save Jason from a hot and dry walk across the desert, but he couldn't find it.

"Are you just going to sit there with your mouth open? You going to say anything?" Christina wondered with a big smile on her face. She was just as excited to see Jason as he was to see her, but she could find language. "It's really good to see you."

This was the moment Jason dreamed ever since he left California. He could barely remember how long ago he left, the years blended together as he was told they eventually would. "I just can't believe you're really sitting in front of me right now. What are the chances you'd randomly have a blog that I randomly replied to because I was randomly in L.A. investigating a case?"

"We must have been destined to meet back up."

"I was hoping we were. I'm ecstatic to see you. I've thought about you a lot, and wondered how you've been. So, how have you been?"

Christina experienced a lot herself in the past five years. She didn't want to divulge too much right away because she didn't want to scare Jason off. Of course it wasn't like he was going to run for the hills if she was honest, that's what he loved about her.

"I've been good, worked my way up at Shane Corp," Christina proudly stated. She was happy, but sad when she thought about Jason leaving. "I'm not quite the boss yet, but I'm a supervisor and can make decisions."

"That's great, I'm so proud of you," exclaimed Jason. He was elated that Christina appeared happy, but knew it could be a ruse. "What brings you to L.A.? Did you ever move from Arcata? I can't expect you'd live in the same place. I'm sure you've moved on and found all the happiness and success in the world. I'm still chasing my tail trying to figure things out."

Jason blurted out his thoughts because the coffee he gulped down destroyed his filter. The fact that the love of his life randomly showed up was adding to the adrenaline coursing through his veins. "It's okay its okay, you don't have to blurt out all your thoughts at once," Christina replied. She sensed Jason's caffeine level, mixed with his anxiety about seeing her created a slop that could only be translated through conversation. "I've been good, just been working a lot. My company assigned me some major cases. I'm honored to have been given the opportunity."

Jason sensed Christina's vagueness like there was something she didn't want him to know. "Come on, give me some details. You can talk to me about anything."

Many things changed for Christina after Jason's departure. She got promoted at Shane Corp., that bit was true. What she didn't add was that she dated a few different guys, and wasn't sure Jason was the right person for her anymore. That of course was before they randomly met back up. "I've worked on a few murders committed by high up officials in the California government. Why do they always play it like it was simply the disappearance of some cute young intern? Anyway, bones were discovered buried in some thick woods, so they called me in to identify them. The science part was easy. I then realized the victim could have been any Joe Shmoe walking down the street."

"That's true, and in this business everybody can be a suspect," remarked Jason as he winked at Christina.

"So you think I'm a suspect?" Christina sniped as she gave Jason a smart ass look. "Am I the one you're investigating when you signed on to that blog?"

It was paramount Jason remember he came to the Trashy Rose to find incriminating evidence. "What do you know about Moon Systems?"

"They handle a lot of government contracts investigating crimes, supplying agents in the field, driving, basically any function the government used to do, they're there to make a buck." Christina knew if she described privatization, Jason's antennae would go up. "There was an interesting case a few years back. A young woman fresh out of college went missing. Most people thought her rapid rise with Moon Systems, was because she caused a rapid rise in the pants of the boss. I met her, she was a good kid. She had the critically thinking brain to get anything she wanted. She knew something funny was going on with a bill being debated."

"Was she a whistleblower? Did she work directly for Moon Systems? Was she contracted by them?"

"She worked directly for them and spotted financial inaccuracies that didn't seem right, so she checked them out. Three weeks later we find her body in the woods. She was a sweet person with the passion to create major positive change. You know, like we always talked about."

Jason remembered all the conversations he and Christina had about saving the world. They hoped one day they'd have the influence to go after those in society that deserved to be in jail, and recognize them for the societal downfall they were causing. Was this the time and place Jason and Christina would come together to fight the powers that be, and bring into existence a world they both dreamed was possible?

"You never found the culprit?" pondered Jason, trying to bring his thoughts back the situation in front of him. He was beginning to feel like he and Christina were coming together for something big.

"No, we found employee records proving she worked for Moon Systems, and reports she wrote while she was there, but nobody linked to who did this," Christina fired back to see if Jason could point her in a fresh direction. "We're kind of lost. We're pretty sure this is a straight forward silence the whistleblower murder. If I've learned anything though, it's that nothing is as it seems."

Jason was living proof of that, hell he didn't expect to do half the things he did while he was in New York. It's amazing what a person can pull off when they have the resources, the drive and the talent to not only outsmart their opponent, but be two steps ahead.

Jason remembered Ridell and his fixer Bill thought they couldn't get caught, but they did. "Sounds like this woman was sticking her nose where powerful people didn't want her to. She probably did investigate the reports you found, and the paperwork with her entire history and information could very well be authentic. However, if somebody wanted to conceal an identity, that's exactly how they'd do it."

Christina started remembering why she was drawn to Jason. His mind and inquisitiveness were extremely sexy. "We tested the body for DNA, dental records everything, and it was a 100% match. How can something like that can be faked?"

"I'm not saying that's for sure what happened, but if we're searching for the truth, we have to look at all avenues," Jason anticipated, realizing he sounded like a cop on one of those predictable shows that all end the same. A murder happens, cops investigate, find evidence, it leads them one way, then a twist and the person they least suspect, usually the person helping them the whole time ends up being the perpetrator. Jason knew this formula had extreme power and influence, especially if the highest-levels of the real-life government were using it, not just some fake government on a TV show.

"Sounds like one of those cop shows," teased Christina with a smirk because she knew what Jason was thinking. "We always had an uncanny ability to read each other's minds. That's what made us fall in love, and sustained us for so long."

"I think so too," echoed Jason, happier than he had been in a long time. "Let me get this straight, you're investigating a lady who worked for Moon Systems, and I'm investigating Moon Systems because they paid the Congressman I took down."

"Great job on that by the way, the 24 hour news channels took all the glory, but they always do. Sounds like you've been on these peoples trail for some time," theorized Christina, extremely turned on. No wonder her relationships didn't work, they didn't have the connection she and Jason had. "Crazy how you guys pulled it off, all those listening devices. How ingenious it was to make a politician's ego bring him down. It must be nice to have the backing of somebody with money who wants to do some good."

"I wasn't sure what to think of Marty when he called me in our kitchen that day. Once I got to New York, I realized he was as relentless as they come for doing good. He put me up and paid for everything I needed. I kept a few things, but I got rid of a lot of old stuff. I had a big office, a big apartment, basically everything I ever dreamed of. I didn't even have to write material. I would find evidence and bring it to him, Marty would give me direction on whom to go after, and then I would use it to take them down. Congressman Ridell hurt so many people, and at least will be in federal prison for a bit longer. Hopefully he is being forcibly married to a 300 pound guy named bubba who insists on being the man."

Jason and Christina laughed while peering into each other's eyes, remembering what drew them together. They always had an uncanny ability to make each other laugh. They also had the same passion for humanism and accountability of public officials.

"You going to order something?" snapped the waitress as she strolled up to their table, giving them a dirty look. Christina and Jason had been catching up at top speed for almost an hour, and didn't realize the whole world was turning all around them.

"Hold your horses," Christina requested who was hungry, and from the look on Jason's face, so was he. "I want two pancakes with a couple of over easy eggs, sausage, bacon and a side of hash browns. For him, let's see, I think biscuits and gravy, but could you put some hash browns, sausage and scrambled eggs on the biscuits before you dump the gravy on?"

"That sounds like our special, the mess. Great for a hangover," related the waitress with a small smile, proving to Jason and Christina she wasn't a total witch.

Since the waitress started to lighten up, Jason spoke, "that would be great. I'm sorry for us sitting here so long without ordering."

"That's okay, I just haven't had the best of start to my day. Which tends to happen when you find your husband in bed with your sister," retorted the waitress, catching Jason and Christina off guard by proving she was human. "Anything else I could get the happy couple?"

The happy couple, it felt good to hear, Jason and Christina didn't exactly stop the waitress from saying it.

"I think that will do, thank you," relayed Jason who was smiling from ear to ear.

"I'm so glad you responded to that blog, it's only been up for three months. I've gotten some hits, but nobody serious. Just the usual half-cocked diatribes with no real direction," explained Christina as she grabbed Jason's hand and looked into his eyes. "I don't think it's a coincidence we met here today."

"I don't think it is either," repeated Jason. He looked into Christina's soul and remembered the beauty he fell in love with all those years ago beneath that Japanese maple. "We're investigating the same company from different angles due to our expertise. We should start our own team, do this stuff privately."

Christina and Jason both laughed at the thought of a man and woman investigative team, it sounded like a bad TV show. "This is turning out to be a great day," realized Jason as their food arrived. "I have some good food, the most beautiful woman in the world, and I'm investigating Moon Systems with the one person I know always has my back, no matter how long we've been apart."

"I'll always be there for you, and this. Your passion is strong, and so is mine, that is why we mesh. Not only can we inspire and turn each other on with our passions, but we can also be inspirations for others, and that will save the world. What do you say partner, want to go out there and save the world?"

"I don't think I want anything more."

A great partnership was rekindled that day. Even though Christina and Jason never worked together in a professional capacity, they had an unstoppable ability to read each other, which made them both good at locating the truth. Moon systems had no chance once Christina and Jason were after them. Or was that what they were banking on?

CHAPTER THIRTY SEVEN

The end of the 20th century saw Moon systems established as a subsidiary of Sun Inc. It wasn't unusual for the government to use vague sounding names to keep people from deciphering who they were or what they did. It's not like somebody whose favorite pastime is buying Congressmen would have something up their sleeves.

Christina and Jason scarfed down breakfast in record time, eating like rabid dogs dying of starvation. "I remember the last time you shoved something in your mouth that fast. It had nothing to do with pancakes," Jason sniped with a devilish wink.

"Yeah, I did gobble that down. Just like when we were playing around in the bedroom and I asked you if you'd be embarrassed if I just……..," Christina fired back, trying to make Jason blush, but he cut her off mid-sentence.

"I'm so glad we met up today, it can't be a coincidence," Jason emphasized as he looked into Christina's eyes and experienced the beautiful spirit he fell in love with.

"Me too." Christina grabbed Jason and kissed him long and deep, schooling him in no uncertain terms that she didn't want to let him go, any more than he wanted to let her go.

After an eternity because neither one of them wanted the moment to end, Christina took a breath. Always the sound of reason she started analyzing. "So now we're pulled back together, for this case or whatever. This wasn't an accident. We have each other, and we have the case of the century leading us to who knows where. I feel like for the first time we control our destiny and the chessboard is set, we just have to make our move."

Jason grabbed Christina's hand and gave her one of those looks he was famous for that said he agreed. "I think we needed to grow before we were ready for each other. We thought we were ready before, but we needed to feel like we weren't holding the other back. We had to prove to ourselves that we could each help raise collective consciousness. People are starting to realize they don't have to put up with an endless stream of false promises, they can do something about it."

"I couldn't have said it better myself," reiterated Christina as she grabbed Jason's hand and sauntered out to the parking lot. "What are you driving these days?"

There stood the shiny black 61 Lincoln Jason washed right before they met up. "You drive that thing? Pretty cool, and I must say I like the convertible."

"I received it in New York. Marty got it for me because it was one of my dream cars."

"Besides the corvette?"

"Of course besides that," snickered Jason. He smiled because Christina knew him better than he knew himself. "I drove around with this guy named Bryan, who turned out to be my partner. He showed me the ropes and around town. Marty partnered us together because he'd been investigating Ridell for years, and thought me and Bryan would make a great team. He had a huge knowledge base. We ended up really good friends."

"Did you date at all in New York?" Christina put out there curiously as she and Bryan loaded into the Lincoln and pulled away.

"I was always so busy chasing down leads, that once Bryan and I were on the government's radar, I had to keep things hush hush. Marty thought it would be a good idea if I went underground. That's part of the reason I'm out here, not only to investigate Moon Systems, but also to be away from the lion's den for a little bit."

"Sounds like this Marty guy really had your back?"

"He did."

Jason and Christina listened to the radio as they cruised up the road with no particular direction. They simultaneously felt over the moon to be back in each other's company. Holding each other was the one thing they both thought about most while they were apart. There was also the little problem of Moon Systems trying to privatize all government functions. Anybody who found out or tried to stop them, were disappeared along with everybody they ever knew.

Jason continued driving up the coast because it seemed like the synchronistic thing to do. After yawning on an off for five minutes, Christina closed her eyes and leaned against Jason's shoulder for a quick nap.

He was on cloud nine being next to her, but Jason couldn't help but wonder what the next hour, day or week would bring. Would they end up married? Would they take down Ridell's financier? Would they end up living out the remainder of their days in a deep dark prison located in some country nobody could pronounce?

It was impossible to know what the future held, but with the most passionate people in the world working together, the road ahead was extremely bright. They were prepared to give it everything they had, and fight to the very end.

Jason realized they had been driving on PCH and were approaching Santa Barbara. "Want to stop at the beach and catch some rays?" Jason queried.

"Sure, it is nice out," Christina responded in a very relaxed and safe feeling mood. "Where should we start looking for Moon Systems?"

Jason always loved Christina's tenacity and insatiable ability to stay focused on the task at hand. "Not sure, but we'll find them together. If there's one thing I've learned from being apart from you in New York, is that if we're open, we'll pick up signals and be drawn to what we really want."

"I've always loved your unique ability to put things into perspective."

The Lincoln parked at the beach, while the windblown hair of Jason and Christina looked like they just rolled in the hay. "I like when I mess up your hair like that, it's sexy," expressed Jason who smiled a truly happy smile.

"You're always sexy to me," Christina shot back as she grabbed Jason's hand. "Promise me that whatever happens from this point forward, it will happen to us together. We reunited for a reason. Let's be together, love each other, and bring our relationship to its full potential like we didn't have the chance to before. We are finally ready. Oh yeah, and let's take down this exponentially greedy company. The world depends on it, and us."

Jason and Christina strolled down a practically deserted beach, which was highly unusual for Southern California when the weather was great, especially in Santa Barbara near the university.

"Is it just me, or is it weird we don't have to search for our square foot of sand?" Jason began to wonder if something was up. "This reminds me of back home when there were only a few scattered people. This is Humboldt crowded."

"For sure, I wonder where all the people are. Maybe they had other things to do," hypothesized Christina who knew that wasn't true.

"When did anything stop somebody from coming to the beach?"

"I just don't want to jump to conclusions before we have an answer. Let's see if that guy walking his dog over there knows something."

Jason and Christina approached the six foot tall gentleman who was walking a five year old Australian shepherd. "Excuse me, I don't mean to bother you, but do you know why the beach is empty today? Not that I mind, it just seems odd," questioned Jason. The man was surprised Jason walked right up to him.

"You're not bothering me at all in fact I miss the days when people would walk up to each other and have a conversation. We're so locked in with email, texting and Facebook that people have lost the ability to simply say hello to each other while they're walking down the street," remarked the nice gentleman who was almost seventy. "It's very strange that nobody is out here when it's always loaded with people. There are so many, that my wife wants me to stay away because of all the skimpy bikinis."

"I know what you mean," Jason agreed as he and the old man shared a laugh, while Christina gave him the death look, but in a light hearted "don't worry about it" way.

"Anyway, I heard on the radio that the ocean is contaminated. They think something is washing in from the ocean, some radiation, chemical spill or oil. I don't know, they said nobody should go in the water or even be on the beach," warned the old man who appeared just as curious as Jason and Christina.

"So if that's the case, why are you here? Aren't you afraid of being poisoned by whatever is out here?" investigated Christina who started getting a strange feeling.

"I've been around long enough and heard enough lies to know a tall tale when I hear one. I had to check it out."

"How do you know it's a tall tale?" Jason followed up, trying to ascertain the facts before they jumped to conclusions. Was this Moon Systems, they seemed to be involved in everything?

"I've been investigating the ever increasing Texas size floating crap pile in the Pacific. I was looking into materials that were found, when I came across something very strange. Somehow, a new organism was created because it's so polluted."

"A new species?"

"Yes, some new bacteria that could only survive surrounded by all the crap in that patch. When the news said it was washing up on the beach, I became concerned because that piles' remnants are the cause of so many different cancers and umpteenth rare diseases. Half of which don't even have names yet."

"Ok, so what else did you find?" theorized Jason whose eyes and ears were wide open.

"The bacteria is in a much higher concentrations than they let on. So I started thinking, if I was trying to fudge the numbers and make people think they're safe, why tell them to evacuate the beach at all? I got curious and started digging into who was reporting all the false information.

It turns out they've been on different radars for years and have had all sorts of charges brought against them. They beat them every time by laying the blame on low level expendable workers. When the patsy goes down for the crime, they PR the crap out of it, saying they're a good, wholesome company that people need in their lives. Once the company is up and running again, they continue with what they've planned since the beginning."

"What are they planning?"

"I don't know yet. I do know this company is privatizing everything it can, which is causing its stock value to go through the roof. Its top executives and investors are making so much money they could buy and sell anything."

Jason knew this sounded familiar, and he knew why. His life was leading him in a certain direction, and like he told Christina, the answers would come if they were ready for them. Almost positive of what the guy was going to say next, Jason decided to ask the question anyway. "What was the name of the company?"

"Moon Systems."

CHAPTER THIRTY EIGHT

Was life really as easy as finding out what you're looking for, making sure your heart and mind are in the right place, and being open, willing and ready to receive? Jason knew everything that happened was more than coincidental, it was synchronistic. First he reunited with Christina after five years because they were investigating the same company, then they take a walk on the beach to get re-acquainted, when they meet a guy who is well informed about Moon Systems, because he was also investigating them.

"What do you know about Moon Systems?" Jason politely demanded, hoping this was the break they were looking for, or at least a clue to find the person in charge.

"I know they're working on privatizing every governmental function, with the goal of building a fully functioning oligarchy. Instead of different companies running different functions, they want to be the one company doing it all, a one-stop shop," divulged the old man. He was delighted the young people he happened to meet were actually interested in what their government was up to.

"They pay off politicians that help them, and get rid of the ones that don't."

"I'll bet there aren't many that refuse," Christina interjected. She wanted to join in because she was thoroughly enthralled by how random yet meaningful this meeting was. Whoever the old man turned out to be, he was sure to be a clue pointing them in the right direction.

"There aren't many left, at least not many still breathing to tell the story. They want to own the government so they can make as much money as physically possible, or at least until natural resources run out. Money equals power, and power equals longevity."

For Jason and Christina it was inspiring. Was this random man on the beach the only other person investigating Moon Systems? Were others using their talents to bring down this menace that would ruin humanity? Would people stand up to stop it?

"Any idea where they might be operating? We're looking for a way to get to them, and at least throw a monkey wrench in their operations?" Jason inquired.

The old man thought these kids were crazy if they thought they could bring them down. Then again, didn't Moon Systems want people to have the illusion they could fight back. Maybe these young people were the answers. Maybe they were the ones with hearts pure enough to bring peace and healing to the world. He might as well give them a chance. If the company caught wind they would kill them anyway. What could it hurt? "Well there is something."

"What, anything would help," Christina chimed in, thinking that after years of failure, the old man still might have a glimmer of hope that something was possible. "Any idea where to look?"

"Moon Systems is ruthless, but I'm sure you already know that." The old man thought very carefully about forming his next sentence. "My brother used to say, the best place to hide something is in plain sight. Moon systems is a top down organization, if you cut off the head of the snake, the rest will wither and die. None of their underlings would dare take the reins, especially once all their crimes come to light. We're talking millions of people could be affected. For the healing of the world and especially the country, that bastard deserves to pay."

"Who does?" Jason tiptoed with a curiosity that would kill ten cats.

"The current boss of Moon Systems is one Charles Bowman. You may know him as the President of the United States."

Jason and Christina were floored. The President was the head of Moon Systems? How could they ever prove it? How could they ever get to the President? Even if they could, who would believe them? If they learned anything during the hunt, is that above all else Moon Systems believed in control, control of everything and everyone. If getting to the President was the way to achieve infinite influence, they wouldn't hesitate.

"So how do you know the President is the decision maker?" Christina wanted some proof of what this old man was saying before they boarded a flight to DC.

"I know he's the head of the snake, because my brother and I were buddies with him back in college."

"And who is your brother?"

"Marty Jackson."

The whole thing was starting to hit home. Was there even a possibility this was the truth? Was the guy who brought Jason to New York and told him to look into the spider web actually helping Moon Systems? Was that why he was told to go underground? Was he was getting too close? Was Marty a silent partner to his friend the President? Or was he actually fighting them from the inside? Marty never did explain his background. "I was writing for a magazine in New York when I started investigating Moon Systems. I was working for a guy named Marty," Jason carefully uttered because his ears were standing on end.

"I know. He talked about you all the time. He said he had this young prodigy, the first person who might have a real shot to bring Bowman down," the old man vaguely stated, not wanting to divulge too many details.

Jason and Christina wondered if this meeting on the beach was a coincidence, or a synchronicity. The only thing they could do now was to move forward and see what happened.

The sun climbed into the furthest reaches of the sky, and the heat was starting to affect their patience. "Why don't we go talk some more in the shade, any additional information you have would be immensely helpful." Jason pointed to a shadier part of the beautiful sand that stretched for miles with barely anybody on it.

"The President is the CEO, and you and your brother Marty investigated him, and?" Jason kept on, wondering why the old man and Marty weren't close.

"We parted ways because of difference of opinion. I wanted to go in one direction, Marty another. We just couldn't agree how to proceed. Since both of our end goals were the same, we wished each other luck before we parted. That was a long time ago, I guess he recruited some help in his quest," inferred the old man who wore his best fake smile.

"We met you randomly on this beach because we randomly decided to stop as we drove up the coast," inserted Christina. She knew the fight wasn't over. "We can catch this guy, but we need your help."

The old man wasn't sure if he should trust them, he met others along the way that talked a big game. They either disappeared, or became the President's ambassador to somewhere that made Moon Systems money. "Okay, let's say we do work together, how do I know you aren't going to screw me over?"

"You don't, and we don't know if you are going to take us down, that's the adventure. When you're looking for consciousness that will save the world, you're required to leave no stone unturned."

The three just stared, sizing each other up. They were deciding if the other should be trusted. When push came to shove, would the other push back or just lie down and give up?

"What the hell, what do you have to lose? An evil company is secretly being led by the most powerful man in the world, what's the worst that could happen?" pondered the old man, who knew exactly what could happen. These young kids could end up dead, instead of enjoying a nice sunny day at the beach.

"So how do we get to him," Jason demanded. He knew they might not have another shot and wanted to take it. He and Christina came back together because they were investigating the same company, and it was all coming down to this. The President of the United States needed to be held accountable. "There have been a few Presidents in the past that have committed crimes, hell most of them have. The few they could prove something about were reprimanded, but never punished. Hell, Andrew Johnson was the only one actually thrown out of office. And that was for completely screwing up reconstruction."

"Getting to Bowman won't be easy. He's covered in layers upon layers of security and duplicity. I've even seen him ride with stunt doubles, so even if we think we see him, it might not really be him," described the old man who knew what he had to do. "He is doing an immigration town tonight, not far from here in fact. That's what I'm really doing on this beach, spending some time in the sun before I go. I wanted to ask him a few questions, and hopefully get some answers because we used to know each other." The old man spoke like he'd been planning this for a while. "I'll do something similar to when you caught that Congressman. I'll make small talk, and then I'll get him to admit what he did. With all the circumstantial evidence I've built up over the years, this will make it more real. The information he conveys, will be beamed to Marty. He will in turn beam it to some friends at the UN, who will bring this guy down."

"That sounds good to me, but how do we know we can trust you or Marty, or anybody else involved?" Jason cynically wondered. He was trying to make sure this guy wasn't talking out of his ass. "Trust me is something I've heard many times, right before I was screwed over."

"I can tell you I'm truthful till I'm blue in the face, so all I'm going to say is that I want to end corruption just as much as you. I want to bring this guy down just as bad."

"So who does Marty know at the U.N.? After he divulges the information, who will arrest him? What jail would hold the President?" bellowed Christina in the most serious voice she had. It was something she rarely showed, even to Jason. She was trying to prove she shouldn't be messed with.

"The UN will contact the secret service, who will arrest him and bring him to a black site prison where he'd await trial."

Jason knew it could work, but would it really be as easy as it was to get Ridell? Could they just get the President to admit what he did, and then wait for cavalry to bust in and save the day? This was the President, not somebody who serves for two years and then disappears.

"Ok, even though I'm very skeptical, I think I can be okay with the plan," Jason deduced very hesitantly as he looked at Christina to see what she thought.

"What if you got Bowman to admit what he did, but instead of sending the information to Marty, we just broadcasted it for the world to see. You could secretly record the conversation, and then afterwards, when the town hall is scheduled to air, I'll have my hacker friend pirate in the feed. That way the American people who tune in to watch the President answer the same old stump speech questions, will see him answer some very different ones. Questions that will prove the government does illegal things, and should be held accountable. Then once it airs, the UN guy that Marty knows will see it, so will the secret service and they'll all know they've been duped. When the President boards Air Force One to go back to the White House, it will actually be the jailhouse. The people around him will see how untrustworthy he is and will want to bring him down just as much as we do," emphasized Christina like her mind was on fire.

"You have somebody that could hack like that?" queried Jason. He was impressed Christina was coming up with a solution that would help all Americans. Even though Jason was sure that taking down a President would make the public think twice about who is giving the orders, to change things permanently, it needed to be sustainable. The public had heard promises endless times, and lose interest quickly if they don't believe something is real.

"Yes, I do. Somebody I met on a case in the past. I saved his life, he owes me one," remembered Christina with an assuredness that Jason knew not to question.

"That sounds good," added the old man who thought the plan wasn't half bad. "I'm glad I bumped into you today, everything in life happens for a reason. Tonight, we help the world become a more conscious place by giving the American people a big peek under the covers."

"Tonight we take down the President by winning the hearts and minds of the people around him."

CHAPTER THIRTY NINE

The American people have always been ignorant to a certain extent about things around them, but have an amazing resiliency. They bounce back when they're down, and are quick to respond when they're shown irrefutable truth that corruption is right in front of their faces.

The University of Santa Barbara held many political town halls before, but never featuring a Head of State, let alone of the United States. The mission ahead had to be executed perfectly. If it worked and the President told the people all his crimes, Jason and Christina would know they served one of their major purposes in life.

People were starting to pour into the auditorium. It was an hour and a half before the President was slated to speak, but everyone wanted a good seat.

"I'd be interested in listening to this guy if I didn't know he kills to get his way, and is so focused on gaining more power and influence, that he's about to get crushed by the weight of his own ego. If Ridell thought he was above it all, I'm sure the President's attitude is ten times stronger," Jason illustrated. It was almost time to celebrate in the glory of knowing that they pulled off the unthinkable, take down an American President for crimes they committed. "I'm ready, let's do this."

"I need to find my guy that will get me close to Bowman. He is a secret service agent I met a ways back, he lived in the same dorm as me, Marty and the President," revealed the old man who was scanning the room for the familiar face of his old college buddy.

"Is there anybody you know from the past that's not linked to international corruption somehow?" Christina quipped trying to lighten the mood. "Next thing you're going to tell me your biology teacher started the Vietnam War."

"Oh you don't want me to tell that story," the old man bantered with a laugh. "I like you, you have spunk and aren't afraid to speak your mind. Hang on to this one man, she's a keeper."

Jason knew the old man finally uttered something he completely believed. He smiled at the love of his life because they were about to help each other find their destiny.

"There he is. I'm going to go talk to him. He'll lead me to the President so I can get him to spell out what we talked about. I'll get him to admit that he's secretly the head of Moon Systems, and has been filtering billions of dollars to further his business ventures, and his dreams of world domination. Once that's broadcast over the air instead of the town hall, the secret service will whisk in and grab him. Wish me luck, with great people like you by my side, how could I lose?" cajoled the old man who was laying it on pretty thick.

"Good luck, something tells me we'll meet again, but if we don't, thanks for everything," expressed Jason. He and Christina waved to the old man as he headed for the line of secret service agents standing in front of the Presidential podium.

"Hey Jason," whispered a concerned Christina.

"Yeah babe, what is it? We should keep this all business, we're about to do something really big. We can catch up on all of that "us" stuff later.

"Do you trust this guy? He's making some pretty big claims."

"I trust that he'll take down the President. Any more than that, I have no clue. Hell, I didn't think I was ever going to see you again, and here we are about to take down the most powerful man on earth. I would have the biggest boner right now if I wasn't scared shitless," blurted Jason half joking and half not.

Knowing he was prone to saying inappropriate things when he was nervous, Christina wasn't fazed. "This needs to happen. We're being drawn to it by forces bigger than us. Whatever transpires in the aftermath, we'll deal with it together."

Jason and Christina gave each other a look that said they would never again leave each other's side.

By the time they finished their gab session and Christina called her hacker friend, the old man finished talking to his secret service friend. He had gone back to talk to his former classmate, President Charles Bowman. "Is he back there already, he works fast," exclaimed Jason surprised somebody could scoot by the secret service so quick.

"He must be, I don't see that ugly suit of his. Somebody should really tell him polyester isn't in fashion anymore," Christina ridiculed in her best fake valley girl voice which made her and Jason crack up. Their laughing apparently became so loud, that the people next to them wondered what was so funny.

"Sorry, she just told me about a comic strip she read this morning," admitted Jason. He didn't really care if the old couple next to them were glaring, they were about to take down the President.

"How long do you think it will take the old man to get the President to spill the beans?" Christina muttered, still wondering if the old man could be trusted. "If he does, will the town hall still happen? Will the audience in this room be the only ones to see the President make his admission?"

"I don't know. I just hope the secret service has quickness and resolve once the message is received."

"Me too, you know how fast the government is when it comes to doing anything?"

Surrounded by various security personnel, the old man and the President sat for a fruitful conversation. "You know what you have to do right? If these stupid kids are this close, just imagine when real investigators catch wind. You have to resign, it will defame Moon Systems, but at least it will keep everything else intact," commanded the old man, trying to force the President to heed his words.

"I am the leader of the free world. I can handle two little nothings?" Bowman fired back like his manhood depended on it.

"I don't think you can. I don't think our bottom line can either. Once the press gets ahold of this, public opinion will take over and then there's nothing we can do. We must control it from the beginning."

"I spent a long time building my political career, just to have it go down in flames. I didn't think I'd ever be in this position. What would happen if I said no?"

"You could, but then you better be suspicious about everybody around you at all times. Don't mess with us. The Six Entities put you in office, and we can take you out. You can still be helpful, just not from the bully pulpit anymore. If you resign and confess everything, we will take care of you. The American people can never lose faith in the government we're trying to build. The peasants are so caught up in their bread and circuses that we could tell them everything, and they won't do a damn thing about it."

Just as Christina was preparing another witty retort to Jason's quip about the stupid government, the President walked out. "Finally, here we go. Let's see if the old guy made him crack," Jason declared eagerly, waiting for the words that would ring round the world.

After receiving applause for what seemed like an hour, but only five minutes in real time, the President walked up to the podium,

"My fellow Americans, I came here tonight for a town hall meeting about immigration reform. I know many of you have concerns, and it's my responsibility as your Commander in Chief to ease those concerns. It's also my responsibility to do whatever I can to protect you from harm, while abiding by our nations laws and respecting, upholding and defending the constitution.

In that vein I must come clean about a few things. Before I became President, I was elected senator through a successful campaign of authentic promises. You may or may not know that I was a CEO cam to Washington, a pretty successful one at that. You might recognize them as the top earner on many lists of extremely profitable companies. Moon Systems was my way to make everything in life run a little better than it was being run, and to treat people better than they were currently being treated.

My goal was realized, but I had no idea about the amount of money I would make. I wanted it to continue, because who doesn't want to continuously make an exponentially increasing amount of money. That was my first mistake. I let the greed get the best of me. I began to privatize everything I could get my hands on. This included many functions of the government, military and various spy agencies. The more money and profit that was cranked out, the better off I thought I would be. Of course I forgot the reason I ran the company in the first place was to help people. Entering politics was supposed to give me purpose and meaning because I could help people more easily.

I never resigned as CEO when I was elected President, all the opportunities that flowed my way were too hard to ignore. I began selling anything to anybody. Moon System's tentacles are woven into everything we see, TV, movies, pretty much all media has to go through our apparatus in some way. We own so much property and infrastructure around the world, that the military and C.I.A. has to ask our permission before they conduct a mission. I felt like emperor of the world.

That is why I come to you with a heavy heart to say I can no longer faithfully execute the office of President of the

United States, and hereby resign immediately. I want the American people to know that no matter how powerful somebody is or what influence they hold, they will eventually get caught. The guilt eats at them until they realize they have no other choice but owning up to what they did, or get swallowed alive by the monster they built. Again, I am sorry.

President Bowman then motioned to the secret service who was always all around when he did anything, and they led him away.

"I definitely didn't see that coming," uttered Jason. He was stunned and trying to make sense of what happened and what might come next. "What do you think the old man said to make the most powerful man in the world confess everything, and be led away like some unruly kid who got caught shoplifting? What were the actual words? It must have been some wild stuff."

As the crowds shared their anger about what just occurred, Christina spoke. "Doesn't this seem too neat and tidy? Like it's just one more scam. I mean they're the ones that invented scams in the first place."

"Maybe, but all we can do is see how it plays out. Let's go back to the beach, smoke a doobie and just relax. We aren't going to learn anything more here. If anything, we might be questioned because we were investigating Moon Systems. Certain people might want to hold us for a while. So before that happens, let's get the hell out of here."

"Plus a doobie in the sun sounds heavenly right about now," Christina admitted, always feeling at ease with Jason around.

The two of them walked out of the building as everybody milled around in shock. Jason turned the key to his trusty black Lincoln, and he and Christina made a bee line for the same beach where they met the old man.

"Hey, what about a different beach? We should go somewhere we haven't been for a while, maybe Big Sur. I know it's a bit of a drive, but it's beautiful and what else do we have to do? We were after the head of the Moon Systems snake who just happened to be the President, he just resigned, so I'd say our schedule is pretty wide open," proclaimed Christina. She smiled a beautiful smile because she was falling in love with Jason all over again.

"That's a great idea, I knew I kept you around for some reason," Jason ribbed. He smiled at Christina, which conveyed that he loved her more and more every day. He knew there was nothing that could tear them apart. The future looked bright for both of them.

After cruising down the road for about an hour, a special report came on the classic rock station Jason and Christina were listening to. "As if the President resigning wasn't bad enough, we regret to inform you Air Force One has disappeared from radar. NORAD has been deployed, along with numerous agencies on sea, land and air. We'll let you know more as soon we can."

With a here we go again look on her face, Christina spoke. "Something tells me there's a lot more where that came from."

EPILOGUE

"Is this really necessary?" requested a man from under the sheets in a very discreet doctor's office.

"You need plastic surgery to change your face so nobody recognizes you. The former President of the United States kind of sticks out," boomed an authoritative voice over a loud speaker. "Do you want to get caught? Do you want to go on being dead?"

It was a brave new world, the President resigned and Air Force One went off radar, leaving no evidence of what transpired. Lots of opinions abounded, everything from the plane crashed in the ocean and exploding, to a hijacking, to the Chinese or Russians hacking the plane, and making it look like the President was dead so they could kidnap him, and collect a hefty ransom.

After an exhaustive three year search and not finding the plane or any clue of what happened, the American public declared the President dead. Even though he resigned for massive corruption, he died so quickly after, that the public didn't hear details from a judge, jury, or a lawyer.

Statues were erected in many towns to revere him because nothing was ever proven. People were using the information they had before the President made his admission.

Christina knew it was too perfect. All of a sudden the President resigns, and then goes missing in the most recognizable plane in the world.

"I know it's been a while, but what do you think happened to the President's plane?" wondered Jason as he poured himself some cereal. He offered Christina some which she respectfully declined. "What about that old man? What do you think he said? What do you think happened to him?"

Christina wanted nothing more than to forget, but that wasn't an option. "I think the old man gave the President things to think about, but it didn't go down how everyone thinks. I'll bet something else was going on entirely. I feel it deep down in my gut, call it a hunch."

"Well I always trust your hunches. Anyway, until we figure it out, I'm glad we're sitting here at this breakfast table, eating together and loving each other," replied Jason. He became happier every day because he was able to look at the beautiful woman across from him. "Whatever happens from this point forward to us and to the world, I hope it's peaceful and filled with love and white light."

"Me too, but we should keep investigating these things; the President can't be the only corrupt politician out there. I mean don't corruption and politics go together like peanut butter and jelly?"

Jason and Christina shared a big laugh and kissed each other like they were the last people on earth, while everything else melted away.

"I agree, I think we should investigate these things, but privately. We wouldn't be an organization, nonprofit, or group that could be categorized in any way. We would just be people who get rid of corruption, while making sure humanity and accountability are the hallmarks of the world. The more consciousness we put out there, the more consciousness will spread. Then it will engulf everything, cause that's the goal, right?" expounded

Christina whose soul was so filled with energy, that if she didn't share it, she felt like she'd crack up.

"That's the best idea I've heard all day," Jason quipped. He was so happy with his life and how it turned out because it got better the more he learned about himself, and the people around him. "We need to uncover as many rug sweepings as we can while we're still vertical."

Just as Jason and Christina were leaning into kiss each other like the interconnected souls they were, the phone rang. "Maybe it's a guy from New York to make you an offer you can't refuse," teased Christina, giving Jason crap. "Maybe it is another Marty, or hell maybe it is Marty?"

"This time I promise I won't move away and become rich and famous and sleep with all sorts of women," volleyed Jason as he laughed heartily.

"You are such a man," relayed Christina as she shook her head. "Why do I love you again?"

Jason picked up the phone with a huge smile because his complete equal was sitting across from him.

"Hello."

"Don't think we disappear that easily," emphasized the voice that sounded very familiar to Jason. It was on the tip of his tongue. "You thought you helped end the President, Moon Systems and all they stood for. You aren't so stupid that you believe this whole thing gets squelched because one head of state goes down, are you?

Moon Systems might not be in the same form, but the Six Entities have irons in the fire that are above and beyond anything you've seen before. We are bigger than any State or Country. We control the entire world and everything in it. Our strength comes from people who fall in line and take orders. You did that magnificently by the way.

I'm not usually one to rub someone's nose in it, but we're very much alive and kicking. I hope it drives you nuts and proves all your years of searching for truth were for nothing. The ultimate torture in life is to know a problem exists, and not be able to do anything about it. I want you to internalize that you can never succeed. Try and stop us, and we'll end you so quick it'll make your head spin. Literally, we'll saw your head off and leave it on your mother's doorstep. Don't come after us again."

Just as quickly as the phone rang, the line went dead. Jason couldn't figure out who was speaking at first, but then it came to him. "Who was it sweetheart?" queried Christina very innocently.

"It was the old man from the beach, and I think he just threatened us."

www.ingramcontent.com/pod-product-compliance
Lightning Source LLC
Chambersburg PA
CBHW060422030726
47495CB00003B/694